QUICK D[...]

Hawkes decided then and there that he was going to go for the ponies these Northern Cheyenne were riding. He had to get to Laramie, and quickly. But he couldn't do that on foot with Laura slowing him down, and he certainly couldn't abandon her. So those Indian ponies looked like his best hope.

Motioning for Laura to stay put, Hawkes drew the pistol from under his coat and waited until the two warriors were as close as they ever would be, passing within thirty feet of his position. One of the Cheyenne scanned the trees that concealed the mountain man, then looked away, only to look back again—and Hawkes wondered briefly if the brave had seen something, or if it was just something instinctive, a premonition of danger. Hawkes didn't wait to find out. He rose to his feet, stepped out from behind the tree, and drawing a quick bead on the nearest warrior, fired the pistol.

MOUNTAIN RENEGADE

Jason Manning

A SIGNET BOOK

SIGNET
Published by New American Library, a division of
Penguin Putnam Inc., 375 Hudson Street,
New York, New York 10014, U.S.A.
Penguin Books Ltd, 80 Strand,
London WC2R 0RL, England
Penguin Books Australia Ltd, Ringwood,
Victoria, Australia
Penguin Books Canada Ltd, 10 Alcorn Avenue,
Toronto, Ontario, Canada M4V 3B2
Penguin Books (N.Z.) Ltd, 182–190 Wairau Road,
Auckland 10, New Zealand

Penguin Books Ltd, Registered Offices:
Harmondsworth, Middlesex, England

First published by Signet, an imprint of New American Library,
a division of Penguin Putnam Inc.

First Printing, May 2002
10 9 8 7 6 5 4 3 2 1

Copyright © Jason Manning, 2002

All rights reserved

 REGISTERED TRADEMARK—MARCA REGISTRADA

Printed in the United States of America

PUBLISHER'S NOTE
This is a work of fiction. Names, characters, places, and incidents
either are the product of the author's imagination or are used ficti-
tiously, and any resemblance to actual persons, living or dead, business establishments, events, or locales is entirely coincidental.

BOOKS ARE AVAILABLE AT QUANTITY DISCOUNTS WHEN USED TO PROMOTE
PRODUCTS OR SERVICES. FOR INFORMATION PLEASE WRITE TO PREMIUM MAR-
KETING DIVISION, PENGUIN PUTNAM INC., 375 HUDSON STREET, NEW YORK,
NEW YORK 10014.

Prologue: The Saga of Gordon Hawkes

In 1832, at the age of sixteen, Gordon Hawkes accompanies his parents on a voyage to America aboard the barque *Penelope*, sailing from Dublin harbor (*Mountain Passage*). Gordon's father, Thomas, was of stout Scottish stock, and had been lured to Ireland many years earlier by the promise of abundant land—a promise made by an English government hoping to undermine the hold of the Catholic Church on Ireland by importing a host of good Protestants. Unfortunately, Thomas had found the promise unfulfilled. All he received for his pains was a parcel of poor land where he could scarcely raise a decent crop of potatoes. For that reason, he determined to venture to America. It was either that or risk losing his land for failing to pay taxes. If that happened he would become a tenant farmer—as would his son after him.

But Tom Hawkes does not live to see America and a new beginning. During the crossing, ship fever takes his life. Gordon's mother was already a fragile soul both physically and mentally; the tragedies of several miscarriages had led to an addiction to laudanum. Completely lost without her husband, Mary Hawkes makes an arrangement with the *Penelope*'s skipper, the sadistic Captain Warren. He will take Gordon as his cabin boy, and in return make sure Mary gets passage back to England. Upon arrival in America, Gordon escapes Warren, aided by a fellow traveler, the Scottish adventurer William Drummond Stewart. Together they journey to New Orleans. Stewart's ultimate goal is to see the western frontier by joining a fur-trapping outfit upriver at St. Louis. In order to fund this endeavor, he bets heavily on a bare-knuckle boxing match held in Slave Town—and loses everything. When he discovers that the fight was fixed, Stewart confronts the man responsible, a Creole planter by the name of Remairie. Stewart and Gordon get their money back and return to New Orleans, leaving the planter none the worse for the experience, only to learn that Remairie has been murdered and that they are the prime suspects.

They flee north to St. Louis. Barely escaping the clutches of bounty hunters, the pair join up with the Rocky Mountain Fur Company expedition to the Yellowstone River for the purpose of erecting an outpost there. During the long trek across the plains, Gordon kills an Arapaho youth who is part of a hunting party that tries to steal the company's horses. He also meets the Reverend Marcus Hancock, who is bound for Oregon with his wife and daughter to open a Methodist mission and convert the Indians there. Hancock's daughter, Eliza, is a willowy, golden-haired girl of fifteen, and Gordon isn't the least bit attracted to her.

The Yellowstone outpost is built, and their first visitors are the Absaroke Crow, who erect a village adjacent to the post. When a blizzard sweeps through, the wife and youngest son of the Crow chief, Little Raven, are trapped on an ice floe in the river, and Gordon risks his life to rescue them. The ties between the Rocky Mountain Fur Company and the Absaroke are further cemented when Gordon is presented with an Indian bride, Mokamea. He lives that winter among the Absaroke, and all seems right with the world, even though his friend Stewart moves on— and even though his "marriage" breaks Eliza's heart. He joins the Absaroke in a raid against their enemies, the Blackfoot Indians, and upon his return learns that the Blackfeet have answered in kind by raiding the Crow village and taking Mokamea captive. Rescuing her and nursing her back to health after the ordeal, he is repaid with infidelity; Mokamea takes up with a warrior, and an embittered Gordon Hawkes strikes out alone into the wilderness.

His solitude is interrupted by the arrival of a mountain man named Talley—a man who has learned that there is a price on Gordon's head, and intends to collect. Gordon prevails in the fight that follows, but is gravely wounded. He is found by a Flathead Indian named Joseph, who takes him to his village where, as it happens, the Hancocks have established a mission. Hancock's criticism of Flathead ways leads to resentment among some of the Indians, and when they attack the mission, Gordon manages to escape with Eliza. They flee together into the mountains. By this time he has fallen in love with the missionary's daughter. She has become everything to him—friend, lover, heart, soul, world. Their blissful isolation is interrupted by a trio of bounty hunters, but with Eliza's help Gordon survives.

For eight years Hawkes and Eliza prosper in their mountain sanctuary (*Mountain Massacre*). She bears him a son, Cameron. Hawkes is perfectly content to remain in the wild country with his family for the remainder of his life. Rarely does he venture down from the mountains. But when he visits Fort Bridger he discovers that an emigrant train has brought a letter for him, a letter from a Missouri lawyer who informs him that his mother has died. Mary Hawkes has left a package for her son in the lawyer's keeping. Hawkes decides to go to Independence, Missouri, to learn what the package contains. He travels with a trader named Dane Gilmartin. Along the way they run afoul of Charley Ring's buffalo-hunting outfit. Ring wants to make off with the plews Gilmartin is hauling back to St. Louis, and Hawkes is forced to kill Ring to prevent that from happening.

When they reach Missouri, Gilmartin convinces Hawkes to let him go into Independence and represent himself as Mary's son in order to pick up the package, just in case it's a trap. Hawkes reluctantly agrees. Gilmartin's suspicions are well-founded. The attorney has hired a trio of toughs—Geller, Cooley and Dolan—to help him collect the bounty on Hawkes's head. Worried about Gilmartin, Hawkes shows up just in time to get his friend out of a bad spot, though he has to kill Dolan in the process. As they flee Independence, Geller kills the lawyer. He doesn't want to share the bounty, and figures that Hawkes will get the blame. Not far from Independence, Hawkes and Gilmartin run into John Bonham, a Mormon assassin, one of the men chosen to protect the church against its enemies. As Hawkes discovers, the Mormons have plenty of enemies. Seeking refuge with Hawkes at the Mormon town of Nauvoo, Gilmartin falls in love with Bonham's wife, Patience. The latter is unhappy in her marriage and returns Gilmartin's affections. It's a dangerous situation and Hawkes doesn't approve, but there is no way to dissuade his friend.

Hawkes agrees to act as scout for the great westward migration of Mormons led by Brigham Young. Then Geller shows up, and though Hawkes kills the bounty hunter, he is wounded in the process. Found by an eccentric Omaha Indian named Loud Talker, he is returned to the Mormon caravan. When at long last they reach Fort Laramie, Hawkes is confronted by Charley Ring's vengeance-seeking brother. In a duel behind the walls of the outpost, Hawkes wounds Billy Ring, crippling him for life, but decides to let him live. It is a decision he will one day regret. The Mormon pioneers press on. Once they reach the "promised land"—the desert around the Great Salt Lake—Hawkes decides to go home. He has been gone from his wife and son for more than a year. In the meantime, Gilmartin and Patience run away together.

Ten years pass. In 1857, Hawkes is once again visiting Fort Bridger when he learns that a war between the Mormons of Deseret and other settlers has broken out. His friend Bridger is involved; Old Gabe has agreed to scout for the United States Army marching against Brigham Young and the Mormon Battalion. John Bonham is in the middle of the action, and Dane Gilmartin returns from California, where he has lived all these years with Patience, in order to have a final

reckoning with the Mormon assassin. His relationship with Patience has soured—the burden of guilt
has been too great for either one of them to bear—
and she has decided to go back to the Saints, though
she doubts Bonham will welcome her with open
arms. The group of volunteers they travel with are
an undisciplined bunch of hard cases, and when they
stage a mutiny against their officers, Gilmartin and
Patience leave the party. They are pursued by three
men. An injured Gilmartin takes a stand in a rock
outcropping and sends Patience on alone. She prom-
ises to bring back help.

Joined by Loud Talker, Hawkes tries to mediate
between the warring camps—a task made more difficult by the Mountain Meadow Massacre, in which
Mormons have slain a party of settlers. Brigham
Young charges Bonham with finding the Mormon
leaders who are responsible for this outrage and
bringing them to justice. Joined by Hawkes and Loud
Talker, the holy killer does just that. The trio then
accompany Patience to rescue Gilmartin. But they arrive too late. Gilmartin has bled to death. Much to
her surprise, Patience finds that John Bonham is willing to take her back.

Some time later, Hawkes is asked by his friends,
the Absaroke Crow, to go with them to meet repre-
sentatives of the White Father, who wishes them to
sign a treaty (*Mountain Courage*). Hawkes reluctantly
agrees, and travels with the Absaroke delegation to
Fort Laramie. In return for the government's promise
of annuities, the Absaroke agree to stay on their land
and live in peace with their neighbors. Hawkes
warns the government's commissioners that while

the Absaroke will keep their word, the Dakota Sioux are the ones that will surely cause the trouble. This turns out to be all too true, for the next year, 1858, when Hawkes and his friend Plenty Coups go to Fort Union to escort the shipment of annuity goods to the Absaroke, they are captured by Dakota Sioux led by Long Horse, who attack the shipment and kill all the other men. Long Horse executes Plenty Coups right before the mountain man's very eyes.

Hawkes is taken to the Sioux village, where he suffers torture and humiliation before his fate is decided by a council that includes Jumping Bear, father of a young woman named Pretty Shield, who takes a liking to Hawkes. The Sioux are impressed by Hawkes's courage, and decide that he will live. Jumping Bear advises Hawkes to forget ever returning to his old way of life, and urges him to accept the Sioux way. Meanwhile, Gordon's son, Cameron, rides to the Absaroke and asks for their help in finding his father. Two hundred warriors set out to ride against the Sioux, but the United States Army intervenes. The last thing the government wants is an Indian war, and besides, as they tell Cameron, the consensus is that Gordon Hawkes is not still among the living. Cameron refuses to believe this. He enlists the aid of a few Absaroke braves, including Hawkes's old friend He Smiles Twice, as well as several mountain men, to join him in a daring mission deep into Sioux country to find and retrieve his father. Another member of the party is Billy Ring—and Cameron has no idea that Billy is his father's enemy. The only reason Ring is along is because he doesn't want the Sioux to kill Hawkes, as he

would like to do that himself. The Army dispatches
Lieutenant Thayer to keep an eye on Cameron.

After a failed escape attempt, Hawkes faces certain
death at the hands of the Sioux—until Pretty Shield
saves him with the fiction that she is pregnant with
his child. This leaves Hawkes with two choices—either marry the Sioux maiden or be killed. Hawkes
still longs for his family, still loves Eliza, keeps gazing westward at the mountains he once called home.
Pretty Shield loves him, but knows in her heart that
she can never have him completely. Once closely
watched by the Sioux, Hawkes gradually earns more
freedom. He is allowed to go hunting alone. On one
such excursion he is found by Cameron's outfit.
Though his son urges him to leave with them now,
Hawkes instead returns to the village. He will not
abandon Pretty Shield. She has risked so much for
him, and when it is discovered that she is not with
child it goes badly for her. Together they execute a
daring scheme to escape the village and join Cameron's bunch. Long Horse leads the pursuit. Hawkes
and the others decide to make a stand on an island.
In the battle that follows, the Sioux doggedly persist
in their attacks until Hawkes kills Long Horse—
wreaking vengeance for the death of his friend Plenty
Coups. He believes he has also dealt with Billy Ring.
When he reaches Fort Union, Hawkes finds Eliza
waiting for him. Though she finds out about Pretty
Shield, Eliza forgives her husband. Meanwhile, Cameron falls in love with Pretty Shield. And Billy Ring
turns up again for a final reckoning with Hawkes.
This time no doubt remains that Hawkes has killed
his nemesis.

In 1860, a prospector named George Jackson is trapped in the high country by a blizzard, and is rescued by Gordon Hawkes (*Mountain Vengeance*). Jackson goes on to discover gold in Clear Creek. When word spreads of his find, a gold rush begins, and soon the mountains where Hawkes has found sanctuary are being inundated with gold seekers. They establish a camp called Gilder Gulch, a lawless boomtown where anything goes and life is cheap. To this camp come a gambler named Devanor, a mysterious woman named Alice Diamond, a newspaperman by the name of Luther Harley and three no-account brothers—Chandler, Mitchell and Harvey Doone. Cameron Hawkes also goes to Gilder Gulch, against the wishes of his father. They have had a falling out because Cameron has come to realize that no matter what he does, Pretty Shield will always love Gordon more than him. Pretty Shield reluctantly accompanies Cameron, hoping she can keep him out of trouble.

Afflicted by gold fever, Cameron stakes a claim and begins to work it. The Doone brothers want not only his gold but also Pretty Shield. In the conflict that arises between them, Cameron kills Mitchell Doone in self-defense. Realizing that he is unlikely to get a fair trial in Gilder Gulch, Cameron makes a run for it. Chandler Doone leads the posse that sets out in pursuit. Wounded in a clash with his pursuers, Cameron convinces Pretty Shield to leave him behind, urging her to go tell his father what has happened. When he is captured, Cameron is summarily executed by Chandler Doone, seeking vengeance for the death of his brother. And when Gordon Hawkes

learns that his son has been murdered, he vows to
wreak a terrible vengeance on all of Gilder Gulch,
even though Eliza tries to talk him out of it. Pretty
Shield feels responsible for everything that has happened; it was her fault, after all, that Cameron argued
with his father and went to the gold camp in the first
place. She joins Hawkes in his quest for revenge.

Harvey Doone is the mountain man's first victim,
and his death causes an uproar in the gold camp.
Men take up arms and set out to locate Hawkes. The
Army is called in to establish some measure of law
and order in the camp. Commanding the troops who
arrive in Gilder Gulch is Lieutenant Brand Gunnison,
a young and talented officer for whom duty and
honor are as precious as life itself. Aware that all hell
is in the process of breaking loose, Devanor tries to
persuade Alice Diamond to leave the camp with him,
but she refuses. Against his better judgment, Devanor
also stays. Luther Harley wages a futile battle to re-
store calm and sanity to the situation. But Chandler
Doone effectively plays on the fears of the prospec-
tors, encouraging them to find and kill Hawkes.
Chandler knows that he is the mountain man's principal target. But in clash after clash Hawkes gets the
better of the gold seekers, and eventually many of
them choose discretion over valor and leave the
mountains.

Aware that Hawkes and Doone are the sources of
all the trouble, Lieutenant Gunnison captures both,
slaps them in irons, and proceeds to take them to the
nearest Army outpost. Devanor and Alice Diamond
leave with the soldiers, and it is then that the gambler learns the reason why Alice has been reluctant

to depart earlier; she has carried to fruition a plot to steal a carpetbag full of money from the owner of a Gilder Gulch gambling den. When Chandler manages to get away from the soldiers, Hawkes does likewise, pursuing him back to Gilder Gulch, where the mountain man triumphs in a fight to the death. He discovers that spilling blood for the sake of revenge cannot expunge his grief at the passing of his son. No matter how many men he kills, he cannot bring Cameron back. And Pretty Shield realizes that she isn't helping matters any. Her presence just causes the man she loves more pain. As they leave Gilder Gulch, she says farewell to him, and strikes out alone. Hawkes returns home to Eliza and his young daughter, Grace, vowing that he will never take another life. It is a vow Hawkes will find very difficult to uphold in the years to come.

In the summer of 1864 the Cheyenne Indians are trying to avoid conflict with the whites, and to that end sign a treaty (*Mountain Honor*). In return, Cheyenne chief Black Kettle is given a United States Army garrison flag. He is assured that as long as he flies that flag above his village, signifying his intention to keep the peace, no harm will come to his people. Unfortunately for the Cheyenne, Colorado Governor John Evans has other ideas. Along with Colonel John Chivington, commander of the Colorado Volunteers, Evans is determined to start an Indian war so that he may enhance his political fortunes by appearing to be the savior of the territory or, failing that, as the man who rid Colorado of Indians once and for all. Indian trader William Bent, who is married to a Cheyenne woman and has two sons by her, inter-

cedes on Black Kettle's behalf, pleading with Evans
to call off the Volunteers. At the same time, Eliza
and Grace Hawkes are in Denver with their own plea
to Evans; they are asking him to grant amnesty to
Gordon Hawkes, who now faces several murder
charges for what transpired several years earlier at
Gilder Gulch. Evans agrees to do so in exchange for
the mountain man's help in persuading the Indians
to attend yet another treaty-signing at Fort Lyon. The
treaty will effectively force the Cheyenne to give up
their lands. While in Denver, Grace meets Lieutenant
Brand Gunnison. It doesn't escape Eliza's notice that
her daughter and the dashing cavalry officer are
smitten with one another.

Colorado's "Indian problem" swiftly gets out of
hand. Sioux and Arapaho depredations against emigrant
trains are blamed on the Cheyenne, and Cheyenne
Wolf Soldiers clash with the Colorado Volunteers.
Several Cheyenne braves are captured and hauled off
to Denver. At Eliza's behest, Gordon Hawkes gets
involved and tries to free the captured Cheyenne, as
it seems abundantly clear that they will be executed.
He manages to get only one away from the soldiers
and takes him back to Black Kettle's village. As several Volunteers lost their lives during the rescue attempt, Hawkes is blamed for their deaths, though he
had no hand in them. Since the mountain man has
eluded capture, Evans orders that Eliza and Grace be
placed into custody, hoping this will lure Hawkes
into his clutches. Instead, William Bent persuades
Lieutenant Gunnison to assist him in freeing Gordon's family. They take Eliza and Grace back to Black
Kettle's village, where they are reunited with Hawkes.

A detachment of Volunteers who are in pursuit find themselves confronted by a superior force of Cheyenne Wolf Soldiers. Evans considers this an act of war by the Indians and orders Colonel Chivington to march in force against Black Kettle. Meanwhile, Hawkes takes his family back to their mountain sanctuary, knowing that a full-scale war is imminent, and he wants to ensure that Eliza and Grace are out of harm's way.

Upon arrival at Sand Creek, where the Southern Cheyenne are encamped, Chivington ignores the garrison flag that flies above the village, a symbol of the chief's steadfast commitment to peace. When the Volunteers attack, hundreds of Cheyenne are killed, including many women and children. Many of the Wolf Soldiers, disenchanted with Black Kettle's decision not to fight, had previously left to join Roman Nose and the Northern Cheyenne. Still in Denver, William Bent is arrested by order of the governor. Hearing of the massacre and Bent's arrest, Hawkes realizes that he must do two things—free his friend Bent and make sure, somehow, that Lieutenant Gunnison survives the conflagration that is bound to follow the Sand Creek incident. He must do the latter because he has discovered that his daughter is in love with the cavalry officer, and her happiness depends on Gunnison's survival. As for Gunnison, he is dismayed to find that through the governor's influence, his regiment's command has been given to a glory-seeking major named Nathan Blalock. Blalock thinks he can achieve everlasting fame as an Indian fighter at the expense of the Cheyenne. His orders are to make sure that the remnants of Black Kettle's band do not join forces with the Northern Cheyenne. Black Kettle's people, however, have embarked on a desperate migration southward in the dead of winter, fleeing the Volunteers. Once he has freed Bent, Hawkes joins them and resolves to do what he can to see them safely out of Colorado.

Having learned of the massacre at Sand Creek, the Wolf Soldiers return in time to ambush the reckless Major Blalock and wipe out his command—all but a small detachment commanded by Lieutenant Gunnison. Hawkes convinces Gunnison to help him protect the Southern Cheyenne from the Colorado Volunteers and escort them to safety.

As we proceed to the events described in this book, Grace has become the bride of Brand Gunnison while Hawkes has returned to his mountain home, hoping to live out the rest of his years in peace with his beloved Eliza. The Sioux nation is preparing for war against the white men. They have noted the fate that befell other tribes who tried to live in peace with the whites, and they are not going to make the same mistake.

Chapter One

As was his custom, Brand Gunnison awoke a little before the crack of dawn. It was something he had been doing almost all of his life, first as a boy on a farm, then as a cadet in the military academy, and now as an officer in the Second Cavalry Regiment, United States Army. But it had not been until fairly recently—the last couple of years, in fact—that he had awakened with Grace, the love of his life, beside him. And so, as happened every morning since that happy day when Grace Hawkes had consented to be his bride, Gunnison paused for a moment to gaze in wonder at the sleeping woman who shared the narrow field bed with him. She lay more or less on top of him, an arm and a leg draped over him, her head resting on his shoulder, her tousled cornsilk-yellow hair tickling his nose, and her sweet breath warm against his skin. Though she had spent her entire life in the mountains, her skin was soft in spite of long exposure to the sun and wind. Willowy and graceful, she was the most beautiful woman Brand Gunnison had ever seen. He knew this was the case, that it wasn't just because he was somewhat biased toward her that he thought this way. She was a vision. Her beauty made all else pale by comparison—even the big sky of the high plains, and the majestic snow-capped peaks of the distant Rockies. There was simply nothing in the world that could surpass her beauty. Best of all, this beauty was not solely external. Grace Gunnison was a beautiful person on the inside. Everyone thought so. All of Gunnison's fellow officers were envious of him—even those who were married. For himself, Gunnison just wondered how he could have been so lucky. Why he was so blessed. And every morning, without fail, he thanked God for her.

Reluctantly he slipped out of bed, moving slowly, carefully, so as not to wake her. She stirred, moaned softly, and rolled over. He pulled the covers up over her. Though it was the end of July, the nights could still be on the cool side. Pulling trousers on over his long johns, Gunnison sat down on a folding camp chair and tugged some socks on his feet, then stepped into his boots. Sliding the trousers' suspenders over his broad shoulders, he paused to gaze at her again. He couldn't imagine being without Grace, and was happy that she was with him. Yet he was worried, too, because they were deep in hostile country at the very beginning of an Indian war, one that promised to be worse than any that had come before. Naturally, he was concerned for her safety, even though they were camped among seven hundred men who had with them four pieces of artillery. A large force, by frontier standards. The problem was that no one knew for sure just how many Indians were amassing against them. There were the Oglala Sioux, and the Brulé Sioux, as well, along with a great many Northern Cheyenne and some Arapaho Dog Soldiers. Their leader was Red Cloud, and best estimates placed at several thousand the number of warriors he could put into the field.

When Gunnison's company had been assigned to Brigadier General Henry B. Carrington's Twenty-seventh Infantry and departed Fort Laramie, Brand had tried to talk Grace into staying behind. Their assignment was to build a fort on the Bozeman Trail between the Powder River and the Bighorn Mountains, and this was country that everyone knew the Indian alliance would contest. But Grace had insisted on accompanying him. And, considering the fact that she was the daughter of the legendary mountain man Gordon Hawkes, there could be no question that she was a very determined and resourceful young lady. That meant she usually got her way. Other officers were taking their wives and children, and Grace saw no reason why she should not be among that number. Peril meant little to her. Having spent her entire life on the frontier, being in danger was nothing new for Grace Gunnison.

"It isn't that I don't want you with me, darling," he had told her. "God knows, I can hardly bear to think of our being apart. But there is certain to be trouble and I don't care to put you in harm's way."

"If something were to happen to you," she countered, "I would not be able to go on living anyway. So if you are going off to your death, Captain, then you might as well get used to the fact that I'm going with you. You are my life." And with a saucy grin she added, "So just get that through your thick head and help me start packing."

"Your father would probably kill me if he knew I · was even thinking about letting you come along."

"My father is a thousand miles away. That means I'm the only Hawkes you have to worry about."

"That's just it, Grace. I would worry about you constantly."

"If you left me here you would have cause to worry."

"Why do you say that?"

She had laughed—a laugh full of mischief. "Because I'm the prettiest lady in the fort. You've said so yourself. And you've also said that any number of the men here have said the same. You would have to worry about all of them if you left me here alone."

He had pretended to scowl at her. "Are you telling me that you might be susceptible to the entreaties of other men in my absence?"

She had shrugged. "You will be gone a very long time, won't you? I'll be terribly lonely."

"Why you little devil!"

He had reached for her then, and she spun away, only to leap back into his embrace and wrap her arms around his neck and kiss his lips with such passion and promise that it robbed him of breath.

"Now," she had said, when at last the kiss was over, "you look me in the eye and tell me that you can live without that for a very long time."

He had sighed. "I don't think I could survive even a day without you, Grace."

"Then why are we having this discussion?"

In hindsight Gunnison realized that he was bound to lose—he was utterly incapable of denying her anything. And so here they were, together. It was meant to be that way. He had known that much from the moment he'd laid eyes on her in Denver. Grace had been there with her mother on a mission to save the lives of captured Cheyenne braves by making an entreaty to the governor of Colorado. But Governor Evans had not been inclined to show mercy. In fact, his ultimate goal had been to start an Indian war and appear to the nation as the savior of the West by vanquishing the Cheyenne and their Arapaho brothers. The governor's henchman, Colonel Chivington, had marched against the Cheyenne with his Colorado Volunteers and committed what in Gunnison's opinion was a heinous crime by attacking a village of peaceful Southern Cheyenne led by Black Kettle. The Sand Creek Massacre was one of the principal reasons that there was going to be a full-scale Indian war soon. The Southern Cheyenne had fled southward, aided in their escape by Gordon Hawkes and Gunnison himself. There were some in the Army who now called Gunnison an Indian lover. Brand had a feeling even his new commanding officer, Carrington, had some doubts about him on that score. Meanwhile, the Northern Cheyenne had moved north, to join forces with the perennially troublesome Sioux. They wanted revenge for what had happened at Sand Creek, and privately Gunnison didn't blame them. He just hoped they wouldn't get it at his—and his wife's—expense.

Bending over to softly kiss his wife's cheek, he finished getting dressed and stepped out of the tent. The pink banners of an approaching dawn streaked the sky above the eastern horizon. Throughout the encampment cook fires were crackling, and a pall of woodsmoke hung over the site selected for the fort. They were going to name it after Phil Kearney, one

of the heroes of the war against Mexico twenty years
earlier. There was a Fort Kearney in Nebraska. In
fact, that had been the previous post for Carrington's
regiment. The Twenty-seventh had departed from
there two months ago on what had come to be called
the Powder River Expedition.

A wiry, grizzled sergeant was hunkered down beside the nearest cook fire, tending to a pot of coffee.
Gunnison could smell the brew from where he stood.
The sergeant, upon seeing him emerge from the tent,
poured some of the java into a tin cup and brought
it to him.

"Morning, Captain. This ought to make the hair
grow."

"Thanks, Sarge. Did Denning get back last night?"

The sergeant grimaced. "No, sir. No sign of the
patrol."

Gunnison cursed under his breath, then sipped the
coffee. It was strong and hot, just the way he liked
it. With the sergeant watching him like a hawk, he
tried not to appear as worried as he felt. In keeping
with orders from Carrington, Gunnison had dispatched a patrol of twelve men under the command
of a young but dependable lieutenant, John Denning.
Denning's orders had been simple enough—to make
a complete circuit around the location of the future
fort, keeping an eye out for sign of the hostiles, and
to return by dark. He was overdue, and that was not
a good sign. Gunnison knew the sergeant was itching
to order the entire company to horse and set out in
search of Denning's detachment. It was exactly what
Gunnison wanted to do. But he would have to get
permission from Carrington first.

"I'm going to take a walk," he told the sergeant, checking his timepiece as he gulped down the coffee. "The general has scheduled a staff meeting for an hour from now. If my wife gets up before I come back—"

"Don't worry, Captain. I'll fetch her breakfast."

Gunnison nodded, handed the cup back to the sergeant and walked away. He had gotten into the routine of walking around the site of the new fort every morning. Carrington had picked a good location, on a plateau alongside Big Piney Creek, which ran into the Powder River. Just a few miles in the distance was the Big Horn Range, dominated by Cloud Peak—an aptly named mountain that soared nine thousand feet, and was usually wreathed in clouds. This morning, though, there didn't seem to be a cloud in the sky, and the snow-covered heights of the mountains gleamed with the rosy hue of daybreak. The plateau itself was treeless and lay between two branches of the creek. To the east, beyond one branch, rose a knoll that they had called Pilot Hill, while to the west, beyond the other branch, was Long Trail Ridge. The Bozeman Trail—the protection of which was the reason for the new Fort Kearney—came along past Pilot Hill, crossed the Big Piney below the plateau, and circled around the ridge westward. From there it turned north, crossing Goose Creek, which was a tributary of the Tongue River.

It was beautiful country, thought Gunnison. Rolling, grassy plains, fertile valleys rich with game, thick pine forests down along the creeks and up on the hills and ridges. Carrington had set up a sawmill on Piney Island, about seven miles away, right in the middle of a large expanse of timber. Every day at least one and often two wood trains would depart from the encampment, travel to the sawmill, and return loaded down with lumber. The wood trains were heavily guarded, and sentry posts had been established on Pilot Hill as well as Long Trail Ridge, each with an excellent view of the country for ten miles in every direction. Almost immediately the Indians had begun to test Carrington's defenses. In the past few weeks, raiding parties had harassed the sentry posts as well as the wood trains. In each case the Indians had been driven back. Lives had been lost on both sides. Some of the officers on Carrington's staff were of the opinion that Red Cloud would decide not to launch a full-scale attack on the encampment. He would sustain heavy losses, and that was just not the way Indians waged war. Instead, they would lurk in the distance, waiting and watching, attacking patrols and wagon trains.

But Gunnison wasn't too sure about that. For that reason he was keenly interested in the daily progress of the fort-building. The way Carrington had staked it out, the post was a rectangle, six hundred feet by eight hundred, its exterior wall a palisade of stout pine logs eight feet high with blockhouses on the corners, and loopholes for rifles in every fourth log and portholes for the four mountain howitzers in the blockhouses. The logs of the stockade wall were eleven feet in length altogether, buried to a depth of three feet in gravel-filled trenches. A continuous banquette alongside the inside of the perimeter stockade provided the soldiers with access to the numerous flared loopholes. Within this rectangle the headquarters' building—a two-story structure with a watchtower on top—was being constructed, along with barracks for the enlisted men, quarters for the officers and four large warehouses, all arranged around what would one day be a dusty parade ground. There would be a hospital, a chapel, a sutler's store, a guardhouse. East of this compound was a slightly smaller corral encompassed by a palisade of cottonwood logs. Located in this adjacent cantonment was a hay yard, a blacksmith shop, the quarters for the teamsters and stables for the horses belonging to Carrington and his officers as well as Brand's company of cavalry. Within a few yards of this area's eastern gates was one of the branches of Big Piney Creek, called Little Piney by the soldiers.

This particular morning, Gunnison was happy to see that the palisade around the encampment had finally been completed. Work was advancing apace on the officers' quarters, and he was glad of that as well—not for his own sake, but out of care for his wife's comfort. In a day or two she would have a roof over her head. Of course, that was of absolutely no consequence where Grace was concerned. In her opinion, the tent she shared with her husband was very "cozy." But a tent's canvas sides would not deter a bullet or an arrow. Gunnison wanted to get her behind stout walls. Still, in his estimation it would take several months to complete the construction of Fort Kearney. The logging operation would have to continue well into the winter months. Until that time, he felt, there was a very good chance that Red Cloud would attack in force. He wouldn't wait until the fort was completed.

As Gunnison made his circuit he observed the encampment come awake and spring to life. Men gathered around cook fires and had their coffee and breakfast. Then they took up their tools or weapons—depending on whether they were on guard duty or work detail—and began the day's labors. Before he had made it back to his tent, Gunnison's ears were filled with the ringing of broad axes and cross saws and mallets against chisels. The sun made its grand entrance, a blazing ball of orange, and the last of the stars blinked out in the brightening sky. Approaching his company's camp, located at the southwestern corner of the plateau, Gunnison saw his wife standing among a dozen men at the cook fire in front of their tent. He marveled at the way the sunlight was captured in her yellow hair, and at how radiant she looked in the early light. She wore a plain brown gingham dress and was barefoot. Gunnison had bought her some men's work boots in the smallest size available at Fort Laramie. Very serviceable footwear, in his opinion. But Grace preferred moccasins of Mountain Crow design, or going without anything at all on her feet. She was just that way—a wild, free spirit, and not the least bit concerned with convention.

"Sorry, boys," said Gunnison as he reached the fire, "but I'm going to have to take you away from her. Sergeant, I want the entire company ready to ride in an hour."

"Yes, sir!" said the sergeant with enthusiasm, and began barking orders at the men gathered around the fire as Gunnison escorted Grace back inside their tent.

"They tell me Lieutenant Denning is overdue," she said quietly, watching him buckle on his belt, with holstered Remington Army pistol on one hip and saber on the other.

Gunnison nodded. "He might be in some kind of trouble. If so, we'll get him out of it."

"I had better pay a visit to his wife."

Gunnison looked at her. Denning had brought his young wife and two small daughters along on the expedition, and he remembered that Grace and Laura Denning had become friends during the journey. "That would be a good idea."

"But I would rather go with you."

He thought she must be joking, but quickly realized that she was in deadly earnest. "Now you know that's not possible, darling."

"And *you* know that I can ride and shoot as well as any of your men," she replied.

"Yes, I know, but . . ." He took her by the shoulders. "Please, Grace, stay here. It will be one less thing I have to worry about."

She sighed. "Oh, all right, but only on one condition. That you promise me you'll come back safe and sound."

Gunnison grinned. "Of course. Haven't I always?"

"So far," she said, and looked away, but not in time to prevent him from seeing the anxiety, the fear, in her eyes. Not for the first time Gunnison considered the terrible price he was asking Grace to pay by being the wife of an Army officer. Until recently he had never even considered the possibility of finding another profession. The Army had been his life. But these days he wasn't so sure about that. Grace had supplanted the military as the focus of his future, the reason for his existence. The only problem was that he had no idea what else he was qualified to do. But at this moment, feeling the agony she was experiencing and trying so hard to conceal from him, Gunnison wondered if that was reason enough not to make a change. He could resign his commission first and then worry about what to do afterwards. Of course, he could not resign until Fort Kearney was established and the Indian threat subsided. That would smack of cowardice, and worse, it would betray the trust of the men in his command, men who depended on him for leadership. Grace knew all this—they had talked about it before. She had never pressured him to resign. She wasn't the kind of person who would do that. But he didn't doubt for a moment that such a decision on his part would make her very, very happy. And making her happy *was* the most important thing, after all.

"I promise I will come back to you, Grace," he said softly.

She brushed at a smudge of dirt on the shoulder of his tunic, and her fingers lingered there. "I had better go see Laura," she said, and with a brave smile for his sake, turned away.

Chapter Two

The staff meeting took place under a canvas tarpaulin that shaded several camp tables put end to end and then laden with a breakfast served on silver platters, most of them covered to ward off the dust and insects. There were eggs, ham, bread, flapjacks and milk, as well as marmalade and honey. It was all quite stylish, thought Gunnison—and, considering the setting, pretty incongruous. But not all that unusual. There were many officers in the Army who went to great lengths to transplant their Eastern culture to the Western plains. Especially among regimental and post commanders there seemed to be quite a few "ballroom soldiers" or "carpet knights"—men that the ranks spoke of as "Dandy Jacks" with some disdain. Gunnison wasn't quite sure yet whether General Carrington fit into that category.

A graduate of Yale College, Carrington hailed from Ohio, and before the Civil War he had been a man of affairs in that state—a lawyer, a scientist, a teacher and an engineer. A student of military history, he had acted swiftly in his role as Ohio's adjutant general when war broke out, taking it upon himself to launch the state's militia into battle at Phillipi. Subsequently he was appointed a colonel in the

Eighteenth United States Infantry in 1861 and pro-
moted to brigadier general in 1862. The Eighteenth
had been designated the Twenty-seventh Infantry
after the war, and transferred to the frontier. Carrington was a citizen-soldier in every sense of the word.
Without the benefit of an education at the military
academy he had acquitted himself well during the
conflict between the states, and Brand was willing
to acknowledge that the man had acted competently
enough during the expedition into the Powder River
country, as well as in the layout of the fort now
being constructed.

Carrington had been present some months earlier
when commissioners from Washington had sought
to negotiate a treaty with the Sioux and the Northern
Cheyenne at Fort Laramie. The purpose of the treaty
had been to secure the right of way for emigrants
traveling along the Bozeman Trail. The Oglala Sioux
chief, Red Cloud, had been the most prominent of
the Indian leaders who objected to the treaty, and it
was Red Cloud who had named Carrington "White
Eagle"—and then proceeded to predict that Carrington had come for the express purpose of securing
the road through Sioux country whether the Indians
approved of it or not. Spotted Tail, chief of the Brulé
Sioux, had argued that it was futile to make war
against the white men, and favored the concession.
But Red Cloud refused to be lulled by the commissioners' assurances that all the United States wanted
was right of passage. He was convinced that this was
just the first stage of the white man's plot to steal
the land away from the Sioux. In the end he rode
away, vowing to take to the warpath if the soldiers

came into the Powder River country. He was supported by Roman Nose and the Northern Cheyenne, who had already learned that an Indian could not trust the white man's treaty paper.

Also present at the staff meeting was Captain W. J. Fetterman, senior captain in the Twenty-seventh and a man Carrington heavily relied upon. Captains Frederick Brown and James Powell—a man Gunnison thought bore an uncanny resemblance to Ulysses S. Grant—were also accounted for. Among the other aides and commissioned officers under the tarp stood a grizzled man in buckskins. This was Jim Bridger—who, along with Kit Carson and Gordon Hawkes and Tom Fitzpatrick, was one of the mountain men who had become legends in their own lifetimes. Brand was aware that "Old Gabe," as friends called Bridger, was an acquaintance of his father-in-law. Bridger had been called upon by the government to act as scout and advisor to Carrington on this expedition, and Gunnison was glad of his participation.

Gunnison arrived just as Carrington emerged from his nearby tent, accompanied by several adjutants. Most of the other officers were in the process of eating breakfast, and the general bade them to continue as he accepted a cup of coffee from one of the two white-coated stewards charged with making sure that the gentlemen present were served in a timely and proficient manner.

"As you gentlemen are aware," said Carrington, "our purpose for being here is simple. We are charged with the responsibility of establishing and maintaining a series of outposts along the Bozeman Trail, for the protection of the emigrant trains that

will pass this way. The government has encouraged
the emigrants to proceed with their travels, and has
given assurances that the United States Army will
protect them from hostile Indians. In pursuit of that
goal, I am ordering Captain Kinney to march with
two companies ninety miles northward to the Big
Horn River, where he will build another fort. Once
that is underway, a third detachment will be dispatched even further along the trail for the purpose
of establishing yet another outpost. Your comments
and observations are welcome."

"My concern is that we don't have enough men to
adequately garrison three posts," said Captain Powell.

Captain Fetterman put down his fork and spoke up.
"We have traveled six hundred miles and been here for
nearly three weeks—and by now it seems safe to say
that the threat posed by Red Cloud is not of a magnitude to prevent us from carrying out our orders."

"I think we are more than a match for any number
of warriors that Red Cloud might put in the field
against us," said Captain Brown. "Though it would
help if more of our men were armed with the new
Spencer breech-loading carbines, rather than those
old Springfield muzzle-loaders."

"Regardless of that, we've proven how handily we
can deal with the raiding parties Red Cloud has dispatched against us," said Fetterman. "I'm confident
we've convinced him that we are here to stay, and
that if he is foolish enough to attack us, we will make
him pay dearly."

Carrington glanced at Bridger. "And what do you
say, Mr. Bridger?"

Chewing phlegmatically on a wad of tobacco, Old

Gabe contemplated his answer for a moment. "I say it's when you don't see many Injuns that they're out there, thick as fleas."

Carrington and some of the other officers stared at the mountain man for a moment, deciphering this somewhat cryptic remark.

"What are you saying, then?" asked Captain Fetterman.

"Just sayin' you can't go by what you see—or don't see. You got to follow your instincts."

"And what do your instincts tell you, Mr. Bridger?" asked Gunnison.

Bridger's eyes were squinty and sunwashed, but they were still quite intense as they fastened on the cavalry officer. "I think Red Cloud is going to draw a line in the sand and say that beyond this line the white man must not go. And I think that we're gonna find that line right around here, somewhere. And when we cross it, all hell is going to break loose."

Carrington grimaced, sipped his coffee, and then cleared his throat. "Be that as it may, we have our orders—and those are to establish a line of outposts along the Bozeman Trail and protect the emigrant trains."

"My patrol is overdue, sir," said Gunnison. "I would like permission to take my company out in search of it."

Carrington gazed at him, stern disapproval apparent on his features, as though he held Gunnison personally responsible for this bad news. "You realize that your company are our eyes and ears, Captain. Surely you don't expect Captain Kinney to march to the Bighorn without benefit of a cavalry screen."

"Perhaps Captain Kinney's departure could be delayed a day or two—until I find out what happened to my patrol, General," said Gunnison.

Carrington nodded. "I suppose that will have to be the case," he said without enthusiasm.

"I'd like to go along with the captain," said Bridger.

"I was hoping you would say that," admitted Gunnison.

"No," said Carrington. "I need you here, Mr. Bridger. Send one of the other scouts. Send Bob North."

Bridger was inscrutable. "Bob North is under arrest, General. He drank a little too much snakehead whiskey and struck an officer."

Carrington sighed and turned to one of his aides. "See to it that North is released from custody so that he may accompany Captain Gunnison."

Gunnison almost felt sorry for the general. Things just weren't going Carrington's way, and since they weren't he was having to face reality. Like his superior, General William Tecumseh Sherman, commanding officer of all the military forces in the West, Carrington had high hopes that the Powder River Expedition would be a successful—and peaceful—enterprise. Sherman himself had been in Nebraska's Fort Kearney to see the Twenty-seventh regiment off, and from what Gunnison had heard, he had actually encouraged the wives of regimental officers to accompany their husbands. This, Gunnison supposed, was designed to give the impression that all would be well in the Powder River country, that the Army was in control of the Indian problem, that Americans could feel confident as they moved westward along the Bozeman Trail. Carrington wanted everything to go as planned, a neat and orderly progression of establishing the three posts—this one as well as two others on the Bighorn and Yellowstone rivers. As far as Gunnison was concerned, this was just wishful thinking on the general's part. Things would not go in a neat and orderly fashion because the Sioux knew what the future held for them and they were not the type to go quietly into oblivion.

Carrington asked the officers assembled if there was anything else that needed to be addressed, and seemed quite relieved when no further problems were brought to his attention. As Gunnison turned away, Old Gabe caught up with him.

"I'll make sure Bob North is sober, and knows what's going on here," Bridger told him.

Gunnison nodded. "Thanks. But I'd rather have you along."

Bridger grinned, shaking his head. "I honestly don't know why I got myself into this. Guess I was hoping I might be able to save a few lives. But I can't do that stuck here in this encampment."

"General Carrington depends on your advice. And for that I'm grateful."

"I haven't made up my mind about Carrington yet. But some of his officers—Fetterman especially—well, Captain, they just look like trouble to me. They come away from that big war back east thinking that since they whipped the Confederates they won't have any problem with the Indians. And they're absolutely convinced that they are superior in every way to the red man."

"I know," said Gunnison. "And a few of them find out otherwise—the hard way."

"You're different. You've been up against the Arapaho and the Cheyenne more than a few times, and you have respect for what they can do. I admire what you did after Sand Creek. You made it possible for Black Kettle's people to get out of Colorado."

"I had some help."

Bridger nodded. "I wonder how old Hawkes is faring these days. Heard tell his wife was very sick."

"The last letter Grace got was from Taos. That's where Hawkes took her, to see if any of the doctors there could find out what was wrong with her."

"Well, good luck to you, Captain."

Bridger watched Gunnison for a moment as the cavalryman headed back to his company, then made his way to the tent where he knew Bob North was being held, accompanied by one of Carrington's aides, who informed the sergeant of the guard that the general had authorized the release of their prisoner. While this business was being conducted, Bridger went on into the tent. He found North sprawled on a narrow cot, his hands and feet shackled.

"Mornin', Bob," said Old Gabe. "You're going to get a chance to die today."

Bob North sat up. He was a big man, thick through the chest and shoulders, with a profuse, sandy beard and tangled hair down to his shoulders. His eyes were a muddy brown beneath a scowling brow. His hands were the biggest Bridger could ever remember seeing, with long, thick, blunt fingers and deeply scarred knuckles. It was rumored that Bob North had been a prizefighter back East, before trying his luck as an Indian trader. Others said he had been in a traveling show, wrestling bears and panthers and killing them with his bare hands. He stretched now, like a big cat—for all his bulk Bob North possessed an animal grace, lithe and agile. His stretching done, he just sat there on the cot and glowered at Bridger.

"Sounds good to me," he said, and his voice was like the rumbling of not-too-distant thunder. "Beats laying around in here all to hell."

"Captain Gunnison is taking his company out to find a lost patrol. You're going with them."

"Am I now. Why aren't you going?"

"I wish I could. But you get the honor today, Bob."

"What about the charges against me?"

"I reckon they'll be waiting on you when and if you get back."

North chuckled. "If they're going to lock me up in Fort Leavenworth for hitting an officer, why the hell should I help the Army?"

"So you can get out of those irons, for one thing. Tell me, why *did* you hit that officer, anyhow?"

"He called me a squaw man. You know how some folks are. They think you're filth if you ever lay with an Injun woman."

Bridger nodded. "She was Brulé Sioux, as I recall."

"Aye, that she was," said North wistfully. "But I didn't hold it against her. She was a real wildcat. Meaner than hell with the hide off. Always talking back to me. But she kept my blankets plenty warm."

"You know the Sioux as well as anyone. You used to trade with them."

Bob North's grin was sardonic. "I did more than that, Gabe. Hell, I used to live with them. They never done wrong by me. Which is more than I can say for my own kind. I know what you're thinking. You're wondering why I signed on to scout for this expedition."

Bridger shrugged. "I'd be lying if I said the question hadn't come to me."

"Because I need the money. I had good business going with the Sioux—until the damned government muddied up my water. They been messing with the Sioux so much that even I wasn't welcome around their lodge fires anymore."

Carrington's aide entered the tent, accompanied by the sergeant of the guard, who proceeded to unlock the shackles North was wearing. Rubbing his wrists, North stood up. He towered over the other men. His form seemed to fill the confines of the tent. Bridger figured the man stood at least six feet six. The aide and the sergeant watched him warily, expecting trouble. But North just flashed a wolfish grin at them and stepped out into the morning sunshine. He paused just outside the tent and filled his lungs with air. "What a damned fine day this is!" he exclaimed in a voice that Bridger thought could probably be heard on the other side of the cantonment.

"Better go fetch your horse and weapons," advised Bridger. "And take along plenty of cartridges. I have a feeling you might be needing them."

" 'Course I will. Like you said, I know the Sioux. Now Red Cloud, he's Oglala, so I don't know him personally. But I've heard tell plenty. About him and a young war chief by the name of Crazy Horse. When and if they decide to, them Oglalas will make short work of General Carrington and his boys in blue. You see this, Gabe?" With the sweep of an arm he indicated the fort. "All this is going to go up in flames one day. You mark my words, and mark them well."

"You sound like you think the Sioux actually have a chance of winning this war."

"Maybe not the war," conceded North. "But the United States Army will know it's been in one hell of a fight before the Sioux are done. Be seeing you, Gabe."

Bridger watched Bob North head for the corral at the east end of the encampment. He had no doubt that when it came to knowing the ways of the Sioux there were few who could top North. But he had to wonder if the man could be relied upon. The general consensus was that North was loyal only to his own interests. The Sioux would kill him as quickly as any other white man, and since the Army was paying him well for his services, Carrington believed he would do his job. Bridger hoped that was true— mostly for Grace Gunnison's sake. Old Gabe counted her father as one of his dearest friends. He had known Gordon Hawkes for a very long time, more than twenty years, in fact.

All in all, Hawkes had not had much of a fair shake in life, mused Bridger. He'd lost his only son, and he'd lived most of his life as a fugitive from the law. Now it looked like he would even lose his beloved wife, Eliza. Bridger didn't think there was much he could do to make life any easier for his friend, apart from making every effort to see that Gordon's daughter didn't lose her life, or her husband. For that reason more than any other, Old Gabe had wanted to go along with Gunnison on this foray. Since that wasn't possible, all he could do was hope that Bob North would do right by Gunnison.

Like all men who had survived the wild country for any length of time, Jim Bridger had learned to trust his instincts. And, unfortunately, he had a gut hunch that North was not a man to be trusted.

Chapter Three

Nearly all of the men in Gunnison's company were veterans who had clashed with Indians before, and a good many of them had seen action on the bloody battlegrounds back East during the Civil War. Gunnison knew they could be relied upon. And the men reciprocated with a great deal of trust for their commanding officer. They knew he was no "Dandy Jack," no martinet. He had marched with them, suffered all the hardships of the campaign with them and had fought side by side with them.

The troopers had wasted no time preparing for the foray to find Denning's patrol, and by the time Gunnison returned from the staff meeting, they were ready to ride. The sergeant came up to report that this was so, and Gunnison went through the motions of inspecting his command. Even though he knew everything would be satisfactory, the cavalrymen expected this ritual to take place, and he would not disappoint them. As he walked along the ranks of men who stood at attention and held the reins of their horses in one hand and their new Spencer breech-loading carbines in the other, Gunnison reflected that officers like Carrington probably did not approve of his company's appearance. These were not spit-and-polish soldiers, and he did not expect

them to be. Nary a one of them wore what a by-the-
book commander would consider the appropriate full
uniform. Some of the troopers had discarded regula-
tion tunics for flannel shirts of varying hues. Others
had dispensed with cavalry trousers and replaced
them with civilian breeches of deerskin or stroud.
Still more had exchanged cavalry-issue forage caps
and felt campaign hats for broad-brimmed sombre-
ros. More than half of them had grown beards to
protect their faces from the elements. Gunnison knew
that many of the officers in the Twenty-seventh Infantry were of the opinion that his company didn't
look very soldierly. He didn't care in the slightest
what they looked like, as long as they fought well.
And these men did just that.

Nor did Gunnison have to pay particular attention
to the preparations his men had made. They had all
been through this before, and they knew what they
needed for the task ahead. Blankets and sidelines
were strapped behind the saddle cantles. Lariats and
picket pins and canteens were also strapped down.
Their saddlebags contained ammunition, extra horse-
shoes and nails, socks and underwear. Even so, this
was much less than regulations called for. Gunnison
was willing to overlook the discrepancies. The regulations, for the most part, had been written by arm-
chair soldiers back East. He trusted his men to bring
everything they thought was required for their survival and the successful completion of the mission.
Anything else was superfluous, such as knapsacks,
metallic cartridge boxes and shelter tents. Provisions
were carried on several pack mules—coffee, flour,
hardtack and some sidemeat. Gunnison didn't doubt

that some of the individual saddlebags contained tobacco and jerky and perhaps even flasks of whiskey.
He didn't object to men having a drink now and
then, so long as they remained sober and able to
carry out their duties. If they didn't, they could expect him to be quite harsh in his punishment.

Satisfied with the men and their preparations,
Gunnison returned briefly to his tent to gather up
his scouting book, in which he would keep a log of
the foray. When he reemerged he found a huge,
bearded man in buckskins talking to the sergeant.
Seeing Gunnison, the man sauntered over and stuck
out a hand. Gunnison would have preferred a salute
and considered refusing the proffer, but figured there
was nothing to be gained by getting off on the wrong
foot with a fellow who was obviously the scout assigned to his company. So he took the hand and
shook it, and was impressed by the iron grip the
buckskin-clad hombre possessed.

"The name's North," said the scout. "Jim Bridger
sent me."

"I assume he told you what we're doing."

North nodded. "Something about a lost patrol.
How long you figure we'll be out?"

"As long as it takes to find my men," replied Gunnison briskly. "Surely that was a rhetorical question."

North frowned. "What kind of question?"

"Never mind. Let's get going."

At a nod from Gunnison, the sergeant utilized his
bullhorn voice to order the company to mount up.
Nearly sixty men climbed aboard their mounts. Most
of them slid their carbines into a ring attached to
their saddlehorns. Accompanied by North, the ser-

geant and a corporal who carried the company's regimental guidon, Gunnison advanced to the front of
the column. He noticed that some of the men from
the Twenty-seventh Infantry had paused in their labors to watch the departure of the cavalrymen. And
as they rode out of the uncompleted fort, Gunnison
also noticed that Grace was standing arm in arm with
Laura Denning outside the latter's tent. Even at a
distance he could tell just how distraught Mrs. Denning was, and he was inclined to stop the column
and ride over to her in order to give his assurances
that he would bring her husband back alive. But that
would be a guarantee he could not make—and Laura
Denning, being a cavalry wife, would know as much.
Instead, he nodded as Grace waved a hand in farewell, and led his men away.

It didn't take them long to find Denning's trail. As
per instructions from Gunnison, the lieutenant had
taken his patrol due west. At some point between
four and seven miles from the encampment, he was
to turn north and complete a clockwise circuit of the
new Fort Kearney's location. Exactly how far west he
chose to go before making that change in direction
was up to his discretion.

There had been eighteen men in Denning's patrol.
Considering the proximity of several thousand hostiles, to send any less would have placed the troopers
at the mercy of any fair-sized hunting or raiding
party. So it wasn't hard for Bob North to find the
sign left by eighteen shod cavalry mounts and a
pack mule.

By early afternoon Gunnison calculated that they

were about eight miles north-northeast of the encampment, and he called a halt so that the men and their horses could rest. He forbade any campfires, so the men had to settle for water and hardtack. He told North to continue his scout eastward for a couple of miles and then wait for the rest of the company to catch up. North rode off alone, without complaint. Gunnison had the distinct impression that riding alone was something the man much preferred. He didn't seem at all concerned by the prospect that he might run into a bunch of Sioux warriors who would want nothing less than to skin him alive and take his scalp. Such men were accustomed to living every day with the knowledge that they could die at a moment's notice. After a while it became old hat.

Gunnison kept an eye on his timepiece, as he intended to have his men back in the saddle after a half hour of rest. Just as he was about to tell the sergeant to get the company mounted, Bob North came boiling over a distant rise, pushing his lathered cayuse into a stretched-out gallop. Every man in the company knew instantly that something was amiss and leapt to their feet with weapons in hand. North checked his horse and made a running dismount; Gunnison saw that for such a big man, he was amazingly agile.

"I found your patrol, Captain," said North.

Gunnison braced himself for the worst. "And?"

"What's left of it is boxed in by what looks like the entire Sioux nation."

Gunnison pointedly ignored the excited murmuring that passed through the men who had gathered around.

"How far?" he asked.

"About two miles east of here. They're on an island in the Tongue River. You'd hear the shooting from here except the wind's all wrong."

"How many Indians?"

North shrugged. "Plenty more than you can handle with this force, Captain."

"Thanks for your opinion, but I asked you how many."

North tugged on his beard. "I'd say three, four hundred at least."

Gunnison had to wonder if the man was still exaggerating. There was only one sure way to find out if that was the case, and he turned to the sergeant.

"Let's mount up," he said.

The sergeant barked the order, and the men sprang into their saddles.

"We going back to the camp, right?" asked North.

"No," said Gunnison curtly.

"Damn it, Captain, you're going to need a lot of help—and the only help available is back at the camp."

Gunnison ignored him, climbed aboard his horse and led the hastily assembled column eastward at a fast pace. North was slow in remounting. He stood there, reins in hand, watching the troopers gallop by squinting against the drift of dust kicked up by the horses' hooves. He couldn't understand these damned bluebellies. Put a uniform on a man and he thought he could whip the world. He was of half a mind to take off in the other direction, but decided he'd better not. The Army would not take too kindly to his quitting at this particular moment, and the Army could make a man's life a living hell if it wanted to. Muttering under his breath, North fit a moccasined foot into the stirrup and swung into the saddle, turning his horse to follow the cavalrymen.

When they had gone a mile Gunnison could hear the distant gunfire. Three quarters of a mile farther he called a halt behind a crescent-shaped rise. Dismounting, he motioned for North and the sergeant to join him, and then walked up the long slope of the rise. At the top they hunkered down and took a look over the crest.

The valley below was crawling with Indians.

Gunnison could clearly see the island North had mentioned—a wooded spit of land located right in the middle of a broad river that curled like a serpent through the valley. There were mounted Indians on both sides of the river, and even as he wondered where a ford might be he saw a continent of warriors crossing the river from north to south several hundred yards below the island. Watching for a moment in grim silence, he could not discern what the Indian strategy might be. There seemed to be no rhyme or reason to what they were doing. Puffs of gunsmoke from the trees on the island assured him that the patrol was still putting up a good fight. But how long had they been fighting? How much ammunition did they have left? And how many of them had been killed? It was impossible to tell. One thing was clear—North hadn't been too far off in his estimate of the Indian numbers. Gunnison calculated that at least three hundred warriors were milling around in the valley.

"What are we going to do, Captain?" asked the sergeant.

Gunnison hesitated. It cut against the grain to turn tail and leave the patrol to its fate. Could he get to the encampment and back again before the island was overrun by the Indians? He doubted that Carrington would order a night march, and there wasn't enough daylight left to get there and back. That meant the patrol would have to hold out on its own for almost twenty-four hours. There was no way of knowing if they could do that. On the other hand, Gunnison was well aware that he held the lives of the rest of the company in his hands. He had asked them to risk their lives before. He had given them difficult and dangerous tasks on numerous occasions. But he had no right to lead them to certain death. His troopers did not ask for much. But they did expect at least a fighting chance.

He turned to North. "Carrington is about ten miles southwest of us. You can be there well before sundown. Convey to him my suggestion that he march here immediately with all the men he can spare—that is, unless he wants to lose his eyes and ears."

"What?" North was incredulous. "You sayin' you aim to stay here and fight them Injuns? You've been chewing on locoweed, Captain, if you think you have a prayer of winning this fight."

"I don't have to win it. I just have to hold the Indians off until the general gets here."

North glanced at the sergeant, expecting to see by the noncom's expression that he wasn't the only one who thought Gunnison was crazy. But the sergeant's look of approval as he gazed at Gunnison indicated otherwise.

"You damned heroes," said North, shaking his head. "You're all gonna be dead. Your hair will be decorating Sioux lodgepoles before tomorrow breaks."

Gunnison grabbed him by the arm. "Listen to me, North," he said, his voice very calm but his gaze intense. "I'm depending on you to get word to Carrington. Don't fail me."

North grimaced. "Sure. I'll go. I sure as hell don't want to hang around here and commit suicide."

Gunnison nodded. The three of them went back down the slope to their horses and rejoined the rest of the column. North checked his horse at the head of the column, but the captain continued to ride down the line, talking to his men.

"Lieutenant Denning's patrol is under attack by a superior force of Sioux warriors. Those men need our help. So what do you say?"

The cavalrymen let out a shout filled with belligerent enthusiasm. They unlimbered their Spencers, dug in their saddlebags for extra cartridges. Gunnison returned to the head of the column and glanced at the sergeant. "We will ride straight through the Indians," he told the noncom. "And straight into the river. We will try to swim our horses across the island. But the main thing is that we get there."

The sergeant nodded, and went down the line with specific orders for the men. Gunnison looked at North, who was watching these proceedings with a bemused expression on his face.

"I had hoped you would already be on your way, Mr. North," said Gunnison curtly.

North just shook his head. "You soldier boys are a pure wonderment," he said, and then wheeled his horse about and rode south at a good clip. He looked back once, in time to see the cavalry column galloping over a rise and disappearing down the far side. He glimpsed Gunnison in the lead, his saber down and the sun catching the blade, and the regimental guidon flapping in the wind, and then all those gallant fools were gone from his sight. He was sure he would never see them alive again.

He had gone but a few miles when suddenly a dozen Indians burst from a bosquet of timber to his right. Whooping, they goaded their war ponies forward and gave chase. Cursing under his breath, North veered away from them and urged his own horse to greater exertion. As he started up a long easy slope of grass, North was stunned as another group of Indians, seven or eight of them—he didn't have time to count—appeared at the crest of the rise above him. Again he turned his horse, but the animal made a funny noise and then stumbled. An instant later North heard the gunshot—just as he kicked his feet out of the stirrups and leaped clear of the dying horse. Falling, he rolled downslope a ways before he could stop himself. Then he started for the fallen horse—and his rifle—only to have his path blocked by several mounted Sioux. Instinctively, he reached for the pistol in his belt, but thought better of it. There were twenty of them. He had only one slim hope.

"Don't kill me!" he roared in the Dakota tongue. "I am a brother to the Sioux."

The mounted warriors were swirling around him,

taunting him, pointing their rifles at him, and for a moment North despaired, thinking they would surely kill him, until one of the warriors barked curtly at his companions.

"I know this white man," said the warrior. "He was my sister's husband."

"Spotted Calf!" exclaimed North. "Thank God! I'm saved!"

Spotted Calf turned a stern gaze upon him. "You live only because you were once a friend to the Sioux. But now you ride for the bluecoats. We will let the elders decide your fate."

"No, I have always been on the side of the Sioux, Spotted Calf. I would never raise a hand against your people. That is why I am riding away."

Spotted Calf looked skeptical. "You ride to bring the other bluecoats here."

North shook his head emphatically. "No, no, that's not so. Sure, that's what the captain of the horse soldiers thinks, but I wasn't going to do it. I led the horse soldiers here, and then left, knowing that my Sioux brothers would make short work of them."

Spotted Calf pondered this for a moment. Then he said, "Tell your story to our chiefs." He spoke to one of the other warriors, who slid off his war pony and advanced on North. The latter stood his ground, knowing that a show of fear might doom him. One thing Sioux warriors could not stand was even a glimmer of cowardice. They were like wolves; if you stood up to them you might live, but if you ran they would bring you down and end your life. The warrior relieved North of his pistol and knife. Then Spotted Calf brought his horse closer and extended a hand to North, who took it, and found himself swept up onto Spotted Calf's pony behind the warrior who had once been his brother-in-law. Then they were off, galloping across the plains, and North was amazed that he was still above snakes. He had to wonder if he would remain that way for much longer.

Chapter Four

Brand Gunnison couldn't be certain how the Sioux would react when he led his command over the rise and down into the valley, but he hoped that he would at least have the element of surprise on his side. It was even possible that the Sioux would think that his appearance meant that a much larger force was in the vicinity. But to even hope that they would break off the attack on the island where Denning and his men were making their stand was just wishful thinking. Gunnison just wanted to get to that island and join forces with Denning. If he could do that it was entirely likely that the entire company could hold off a few hundred Indians for twenty-four hours.

As they boiled over the rise and thundered down the long grassy slope into the valley below, Gunnison was initially pleased with the reaction of the Sioux. Caught off guard, those nearest to the cavalry scattered. As he reached the bottom of the slope—about a thousand yards from the river, by Gunnison's calculation—most of the Indians on this side of the stream were heading for timber on the far side of the valley. It looked like an all-out retreat. Gunnison shouted at the sergeant who galloped along behind him to commence firing, and the order was passed on down the line, and the troopers began shooting, most of them using their carbines—some using just one hand and others both hands, the latter steering their mounts with their knees. Gunnison didn't expect them to hit a lot of Indians, most of whom were out of rifle range, but he hoped that the shooting would add to the confusion of the enemy.

The column was nearly halfway to the river when Gunnison realized that things weren't going to be all that easy. Some of the Sioux war chiefs had managed to rally their braves, and suddenly small clusters of warriors were charging toward the cavalry and returning fire. One of these groups—about fifteen warriors in all—placed themselves directly in the path of the hard-charging column. In response the troopers fanned out and laid down a withering fire from horseback, emptying half the Indian saddles. The other braves faltered, and then Gunnison and his men were charging right through them, and the group seemed to simply disintegrate. When all was said and done only three of the Sioux were left alive, and the cavalry were still surging forward, ever closer to their destination.

When they reached the river, about a hundred warriors were closing in from all sides. Gunnison didn't hesitate. He urged his horse into the water. He caught a glimpse of troopers among the trees on the island, trying to position themselves so that they could lay down a covering fire while shouting at Gunnison and his men, exhorting them on. Not knowing how deep the river was at this point, or how swift the current, Gunnison made sure he entered about a hundred yards above the island, so that, with any luck, the current would not sweep him beyond the island. If that happened he would be virtually defenseless, with Indians on both banks. He was prepared to abandon his horse and swim for it if it looked as though this might happen. But his horse swam strongly, and reached the shallow at the downriver end of the island. Gunnison immediately leaped from the saddle and turned to see how the rest of his command was faring. Almost all of them were in the water now, though a handful had formed to fight in a rear-guard action on the far bank. Gunnison's heart swelled with pride as he watched these brave men, who confronted a charging horde of painted warriors with such calm professionalism.

More than two-thirds of the men reached the island with their horses. The others faced being swept downstream, and Gunnison shouted himself hoarse as he ordered them, above the din of the gunfire and the rush of the river, to leave their mounts and swim for it. All but a few heard him and obeyed. A few seemed reluctant to give up their horses, and were carried away. Gunnison helplessly watched them go. There was nothing he could do for them. There were Sioux warriors milling about on both banks now, and one by one the men who had stayed with their horses were killed.

Gunnison found the sergeant. "Pick ten men and have them round up the horses," he ordered. "Have them taken to the center of the island. Then deploy the rest. I'm going to find Lieutenant Denning."

"Yes, sir!"

Gunnison made his way through the trees, stop-

ping to ask several of the troopers who were part of
the patrol where the lieutenant was located. None
of them knew for sure. He pressed on, even though
a hail of bullets was searing the air, moving
through a blizzard of leaves and shattered pieces
of branches that had been clipped from the trees.
He noticed that Denning's men had done the best
they could to protect themselves from this onslaught. Some had used their knives and the stocks
of their rifles to excavate shallow pits in which they
lay, and others had piled dead wood into barri-
cades behind which they could crouch. Several
horses had been killed, and their bodies were used
for cover as well.

As he wandered through the melee, Gunnison was
approached by a trooper who told him that Lieutenant Denning had sent him to find the captain.

"The lieutenant, he's bad hurt," said the trooper.

"Take me to him."

A few minutes later Gunnison was kneeling beside
Denning. The lieutenant was propped up against the
trunk of a tree. Off to the right about fifteen yards,
several troopers were steadily firing their carbines
from behind a gravel bank. It seemed the Sioux warriors would occasionally launch an attack, of sorts,
riding along the bank and firing at the island's de-
fenders in groups that numbered between twenty
and a hundred braves. One such attack was underway at that moment, but Gunnison's attention was
focused on Denning's condition. The lieutenant's
right leg had been shattered by a bullet. It was bound
tightly with a makeshift dressing, but the dressing
was soaked with blood. Denning looked very pale,

and he was in a lot of pain. Gunnison could see as much in his eyes, buried deep in dark sockets.

"Glad to see you, Captain," said Denning. "Was beginning to wonder if I ever would again."

"What happened?"

"They hit us yesterday, middle of the afternoon. Seemed to come out of nowhere. Lucky for us this island was handy, or they would have wiped us out. As it is I've lost six men. And most of our horses have been killed. We're low on ammunition. But at least we've got plenty of fresh water and plenty of horse steaks."

"When were you wounded?"

"First thing this morning. Things were pretty quiet last night, though about a dozen Sioux did swim to the upstream end of the island and cause us a little trouble. We killed most of them. Then at daybreak they started up again. I think they were hoping we would run out of ammunition. When that happened they figured they could come in and finish us off. And that *would* have happened, by tomorrow morning for sure."

"By tomorrow morning Carrington will be here."

Denning nodded. "That would suit me."

Gunnison took a closer took at Denning's leg.

"Doesn't look good, does it?" asked Denning. "I reckon I'll lose it."

"Maybe not."

"Beg pardon, Captain, but you're not a very good liar. The bullet struck me right in the knee. It's completely shattered."

Gunnison figured Denning was right. And if he was, that would be the end of his career in the cavalry, which was a shame, because the lieutenant was a competent officer who, like Brand, felt that the Army was his entire life.

"This will go hard on Laura," murmured Denning. "I don't think she ever expected to have to deal with a one-legged man for a husband."

"What are you saying? Laura is a good woman and she loves you more than anything. Your losing a leg won't change that one bit."

"Yeah, right." Denning didn't sound convinced. "The truth is, I'd have been better off had the bullet killed me. And Laura would have been, too."

Gunnison thought it might be wise to change the subject and took a look around. "We're in a pretty strong position here. It's one I don't doubt we can hold until help arrives. I'm reminded that my wife's father and her brother, along with a mere handful of others, held off a large force of Sioux warriors on an island just like this one."

"Gordon Hawkes." Again Denning nodded. "Yeah, I've heard about that fight. Who hasn't? But you're wrong. They only had Indians on one bank. When it was certain that the island would be over-run, Hawkes and a buffalo runner by the name of Billy Ring stayed behind to hold the Sioux off as long as they could while the others slipped away by crossing to the other bank." The lieutenant gave Gunnison a long look. "What happens if for some reason Carrington doesn't get here tomorrow? What if the messenger you sent doesn't get through?"

"Even if he doesn't get through, Carrington will know something is wrong when we don't show up back at the fort today. He'll come. Don't worry."

At that instant the trooper who had escorted Gunnison to Denning's location, and who was sitting on his heels about ten feet away, suddenly sprawled backward. Gunnison leaped to his side. The man was dead, shot through the head.

"This may be insubordination," said Denning, "but you shouldn't have come charging in here, Captain."

"You would have done the same thing."

"I wouldn't bank on that."

"And you call me a bad liar," said Gunnison with a taut smile.

Spotted Calf and four other braves took Bob North to the Oglala village, while the rest of the warriors in the group that had captured the Army scout joined the fight against the horse soldiers trapped on the island. They unrelentingly traveled well into the night, stopping only at moonrise. Throughout the remainder of the night the warriors took turns keeping an eye on North, whose hands they bound with rawhide. Just east of the camp was a broad river, its waters looking like molten silver mixed with black ink in the moonlight. North thought it was the Powder River, and if it was, then the new Fort Kearney was directly downriver, no more than twenty-five miles away. If he could purloin a pony and get away, dawn would find him safely among the soldiers. But his Sioux captors were too alert to provide him with an opportunity, and the next morning they continued on their way, traveling north by northeast, with the river beside them, and before midday arrived at their destination.

The village was massive; North estimated that there were at least four hundred lodges, sprawled all along the western bank of the river. A horse herd numbering at least two hundred head grazed to the west and north, carefully watched over by mounted guards. As North entered the camp he realized that not all of the Indians who came out to look at him were Oglala Sioux. There were Northern Cheyenne here as well. It was easy enough for a man of his experience to make the distinction. Leaving their cook fires and skin lodges, the Indians—men, women and children—lined the route that Spotted Calf took to reach the center of the encampment. What struck North was how silent and somber the throng was. There was no cheering, no taunting of the prisoner. No insults were hurled in his direction. This was quite odd. As North well knew, Indians were generally a very expressive people, and it was troubling that these people were acting so out of character.

Spotted Calf called a halt in the middle of the encampment. He dismounted and bade North to do the same. North then found himself escorted to a skin lodge. Spotted Calf told him to go inside and wait. He was not to emerge without permission. Spotted Calf didn't have to tell him what would happen if he didn't follow these instructions. North went inside. The skin lodge was unoccupied. There were only a few skins on the ground, and a blackened ring of stones around a pile of ashes—all that remained of a long-ago cook fire. North sat cross-legged on the skins, facing the lodge entrance, and awaited word of his fate.

The wait was a long one. A few hours later an

old woman came in with a small bowl filled with pemmican. North greeted her in her own tongue, but she made no response, merely peering at him with rheumy eyes before setting the bowl down and departing. Starving, North wolfed down the food and then licked the bowl clean. He lay down and tried to sleep, but sleep eluded him. It was hard to relax when at any moment warriors could burst into the skin lodge and drag him out to meet his death.

Several more hours passed. Then, hearing voices outside, North sat up, holding his breath. Night had fallen, and it was very dark in the skin lodge. A boy came in with an armload of kindling and placed it in the ring of stones, casting apprehensive glances at North. As soon as the boy was gone a young warrior entered with a burning brand, and set the kindling alight. Once he had gone three men entered. One was Spotted Calf. A second was Red Cloud. North knew him by sight. The Oglala chief wore a headdress of eagle feathers, as befitted his station. North didn't recognize the third man. The three Sioux sat across the fire from him, with Red Cloud flanked by the other two. North tried to look calm and confident—yet all the while he was afraid his pounding heart would burst.

"Spotted Calf has told me what you said to him," began Red Cloud. "I have decided that he was right to spare your life. I am not sure yet that I will do the same thing."

North gulped, trying without success to dislodge the lump in his throat. "You remember me, Red Cloud. You know I am a friend of the Sioux. I have lived among your people and I respect their ways. I have supplied them with goods, as well as guns and ammunition. I have been married to a Sioux woman, a woman I cared for deeply, and whose loss struck like a knife in my heart."

Red Cloud nodded once, his old, lined face bearing a grave expression. "I know you were *once* a friend of the Sioux. But now you ride with our enemies, the bluecoats."

North realized that this would be his one and only chance to explain his presence among the soldiers. Red Cloud was giving him an opportunity because of his past history with the Sioux. If he failed to explain himself satisfactorily he would die. It was as simple as that. In essence, he was on trial for his life.

"If it had been my choice I would have remained with the Sioux forever. But the actions of other white men poisoned the minds of many against me. I did not leave of my own free will. I was driven away. To be exiled by my Sioux brethren saddened me deeply."

"My people have good reason to mistrust the white man."

"I have never done wrong by your people, Red Cloud, I swear on my mother's grave."

"Yet you scout for the Army."

North had always prided himself on being a good liar. This time, his life depended on it.

"As I told Spotted Calf," he said, looking Red Cloud straight in the eye, "I agreed to scout for the Army because I figured it was the best way for me to be able to help the Sioux."

The third man, the one North did not know, grunted skeptically.

"No, hear me out," insisted North. "The bluecoats depend on their scouts to tell them what their enemy is doing. I make sure I tell them what is in the best interests of the Sioux. Today I encouraged the bluecoat captain to join his men on the island, and promised him I would ride to the fort and bring the rest of the bluecoats. I had no intentions of doing that, though. I figured your warriors would kill all the horse soldiers."

"And what would you tell the bluecoat chief, Carrington?" asked Red Cloud.

"That I got separated from the column, and then pinned down by a bunch of warriors and that by the time I got free, well, it was too late for the horse soldiers."

Red Cloud stared at him with such impassivity that North could not even guess what the Oglala chief was thinking. He realized that his story was far-fetched. But under the circumstances he could not think of a more believable one. His only advantage was that Indians were generally a trustworthy—and trusting—lot. Some might even call them gullible. This had been a grave liability for them in their past associations with whites. It just wasn't all that hard, usually, to deceive them. Of course, Red Cloud was no ordinary chief, and the Sioux were no ordinary Indians.

"I do not know if I should believe you," said Red Cloud at last. "But there is a way to find out if you tell the truth."

"I'll do anything you ask. Just name it."

"Good. Then you will return to the bluecoat chief, Carrington. You will tell him that the horse soldiers are trapped on an island by my warriors. But you will say that there are only a hundred warriors, and that the island is on the Powder River, not the Tongue. Then you will lead the men he sends out to rescue the horse soldiers to the place where the Clear Creek joins the Powder."

North didn't like the sound of any of this, but he nodded. "And then what happens?"

"I will be waiting there with my warriors, and we will destroy the bluecoat army."

North was silent for a moment as the full dimensions of what Red Cloud was asking him to do sank in.

"What happens to me?" he asked.

"I will tell my people to let you live. And if you do, you will be free to go on your way."

"I'll have no place to go, Red Cloud. If I lead the Army into an ambush and walk out alive I'll be hunted down and killed by my own kind."

Red Cloud thought it over. North recognized that his own fate was not really of any concern to the chief. He could only appeal to the man's sense of fair play and hope for the best. Red Cloud was already offering him his life in exchange for a betrayal of Carrington's command. He couldn't expect anything more than that.

"If we defeat the bluecoat Army with your help," said Red Cloud, finally, "you will be allowed to live among the Oglala."

North swallowed hard. All his talk about how much he felt a kinship with the Sioux was just that— talk. They had been good customers for a long time, and they had treated him fairly while his wife lived.

But he'd never desired to live the rest of his days among them. Or to become a man reviled among his own kind as a traitor. But what choice did he have? Just one. To die.

"I will do what you ask," he said.

Chapter Five

When the sun finally dropped below the mountains to the west, Gunnison was hoping there would be a reprieve from the harassing attacks launched by the Sioux. This was unlike anything he had experienced in more than six years of fighting Indians. It ran counter to everything he had personally witnessed in Indian tactics. Customarily, they did not risk their lives unless the outcome was fairly certain. But this time was different. The Sioux were taking substantial losses in stride on the off chance that with every attack they made they would kill one or two horse soldiers. And they weren't far off the mark in that calculation. Denning had lost six men before Gunnison's arrival. Four more were killed and as many wounded the remainder of the avenue.

Indeed, when darkness fell, the attacks ceased—or so Gunnison thought. A couple of hours later the first few Sioux warriors entered the river upstream of the island and let the current carry them down. They all reached the island, and with the element of surprise managed to kill one soldier and wound another before they were shot down. A short while later, two more suddenly appeared. This pair, though, allowed the current to carry them past the upper end of the island; they came ashore near the downriver end, and once more surprised the soldiers. One of the Indians was killed, the other leaped into the river and disappeared from sight. Gunnison told his men to stay alert, and that they did, all night long, even though there were no more Sioux interlopers to deal with.

The attacks resumed on the following day. Between twenty and fifty warriors would suddenly charge forward, gallop along the bank and fire at the soldiers on the island before riding out of range—there to pause and throw jeering taunts at their enemy. Gunnison could do little more than to encourage his men to make every bullet count and assure them that help was on the way. By midday he was starting to worry. What if North had failed to get through? And even if he had, what if Carrington, for some reason, was slow to put the rescue in motion? Or, what if the general decided, for some reason, that it was too risky to even try to rescue his cavalry? Gunnison didn't think the latter was likely. But when midafternoon came and went and there was still no sign of the Twenty-seventh Infantry, he began to wonder.

By this time Lieutenant Denning was in bad shape. As he'd feared, the wound in his leg had become infected, and Denning became feverish, drifting in and out of consciousness. Now it was not a question of whether he would lose the leg, but whether he would lose his life. Gunnison did not have a surgeon with the company, but there was a trooper named Dayton whose father was a Philadelphia physician and Gunnison consulted with him about Denning's condition.

"I'd say that leg has to come off by morning," said Dayton, after inspecting Denning's wound. "Or he'll probably die. But I'm not sure, Captain. I'm no doctor, though my father always wanted me to be one. In fact, I tried medical school and just couldn't do it. That's why I joined the Army."

Gunnison nodded. "I think you're right. I've seen a few wounds like this one. Question is, can you take that leg off in order to save the lieutenant's life?"

"Me?" Dayton turned pale. "With what, Captain?"

Gunnison grimaced. "Never mind. I guess I'll have to do it. Have to cut the flesh away from the bone above the knee, and then cut the bone with a hatchet. Cauterize with hot iron."

Dayton shook his head. "I don't think he'll survive that."

"Well, he sure won't survive if we don't do something," snapped Gunnison. "That's certain."

"Yes, sir," said Dayton, mollified. "Captain—I'll help you."

"Thanks. We'll wait a while. Hopefully the Twenty-seventh will be here before morning. And the regimental surgeon is bound to come with it."

But as the day waned Gunnison was entertaining serious doubts that Carrington was ever going to come. And if he didn't, what could be done? Most of the horses were dead by now, and there was no chance of getting back to the encampment on foot. The Sioux would cut them down in no time at all. After sending the sergeant around to find out how much ammunition the men had left, he decided that they could hang on for maybe two more days. Then they would be out of ammunition and at the mercy of the Indians. Gunnison figured he had no choice but to send another message to the fort. That meant finding a volunteer who would try to slip past the Indians. The best hope was to slip into the river under cover of darkness and let it carry him downstream. He shared his thoughts with the sergeant, who agreed.

"Then find me a good man for the job," said Gunnison.

"No need for that, sir. I'll do it myself."

But then, just as the sun began to dip below the rugged western skyline, the Sioux disappeared. And they left in such a hurry that they abandoned their dead on the field of battle. That, too, was very uncharacteristic.

"Must mean Carrington is on his way," said the sergeant. "That's the only way this makes any sense at all."

Gunnison agreed. But an hour passed, and then another, and still no rescue force. A patrol of five mounted men was sent out; they rode their horses into the river and emerged a couple of hundred yards downstream to ride to the high ground south of the island. They returned without seeing any sign of the infantry—or the Sioux, either.

"I don't get it," said the sergeant. "Why would the Injuns just up and quit like that? They had us between a rock and a hard place, and we all knew it."

Gunnison shook his head. "I can think of only one reason. They're massing for an assault on Carrington now that he's out of the encampment."

"Or it could be a trick to get us off this island, sir."

Gunnison pondered his options for a moment. But

he was not an indecisive man, and made up his mind fairly quickly.

"Sergeant, burial details for the dead. Another detail to make travois for the wounded. We have about twenty horses left alive. They'll pull the travois. The able-bodied will walk. We're going to leave tonight. If we push it, by dawn we'll be nearly to the encampment."

"What if Carrington is riding into an ambush?"

"We wouldn't be of much help to him anyway— and my responsibility is to my command. I will not leave the wounded behind while I ride off to join the Twenty-seventh. Once we get to the encampment and get fresh horses, we can ride out and see what we can do."

"You mean *if* we get to the encampment."

"If it's a trap then we're done for," conceded Gunnison. "But we're done for anyway if we stay here."

By midnight, all the necessary preparations were made. It was touch and go getting the wounded across the river, but not a single man was lost, and before long what was left of Gunnison's company was heading south by southwest across the moonlit plains, bracing for an attack that never came.

When they reached the encampment, the first thing Gunnison wanted to do was spend some time with Grace. She was there, among the people who gathered to watch the bloodied column arrive, standing with Laura Denning, looking much as she had when he had left—what had it been, the day before yesterday? That was odd, as it seemed like weeks since he had seen her last. It was early in the morning and the sun had just risen, and its light was captured in her golden hair. Gazing at her as she ran to him, Gunnison had to wonder if he was dreaming. For the first time he allowed himself to confront the fact that there had been moments in the past twenty-four hours when he'd been pretty sure he would never see her again. Then she was there, flying into his open arms and embracing him, brushing her soft lips on the stubble of beard that darkened his gaunt cheek. He closed his eyes and gave a prayer of thanks to God Almighty.

The sound of Laura Denning's sobs brought him back to reality. She had found her husband, tied down to a travois and looking more dead than alive, and now stood there trembling, hands covering her face. Gunnison was about to suggest to Grace that she should go to her friend, but he didn't need to—in a glance Grace realized what had transpired and, with a final brush of her fingertips against Gunnison's lips, murmured, "Thank you for keeping your promise," and then went to Laura. He knew what she meant by that. He had promised to come back safe and sound. But it had been a close thing.

Snapping orders, Gunnison had the wounded carried to the hospital building. The latter wasn't quite completed; the roof had not gone up, but at least the walls were there to protect the wounded from the wind that seemed to constantly scour these plains, as well as from prying eyes. Dying, after all, was a very private thing. Gunnison also dispatched the spent horses to the stables, and he told the sergeant to prepare all the able-bodied men for another departure. That meant fresh mounts, cartridge boxes filled, more provisions. Looking at his men, most of whom had not slept a wink in forty-eight hours, men who had fought a desperate battle for survival against great odds, Gunnison wasn't too sure if they had the grit to make another foray without rest. But he could tell in a glance that most of the Twenty-seventh Infantry was no longer in camp. That meant they had marched to rescue him—which in turn meant that his worst fears might have been realized.

One of Carrington's adjutants appeared at his side, and informed him that the general wanted to see him immediately. Gunnison nodded and wearily trudged along in the wake of the aide. Arriving at Carrington's tent, he was escorted inside. Carrington was bent over a field table, studying a map.

Seeing Gunnison, he snapped, "Where are Captains Fetterman and Brown?"

"I have no idea, sir."

"What do you mean you have no idea. We received word that you were besieged by a vastly superior force of Sioux and needed immediate assistance. At dawn yesterday I dispatched Fetterman and Brown with two hundred men to march to your aid."

"They never showed up. Late yesterday the Sioux who had us boxed in just vanished. We marched through the night to get here."

Carrington stared at him. "This simply cannot be," he said, and Gunnison thought he heard an edge of panic in the general's voice. "Bob North brought word of your peril, and I sent him with Fetterman to lead the rescue column straight to the Powder River."

"The Powder River, sir?"

"Yes, damn it. He said he knew right where you were."

"But we were on the Tongue River, General."

"How could a man with North's expertise make such a mistake?"

They stared at one another, and even as Gunnison came to the only possible conclusion he saw by the expression on Carrington's face that the general was doing the very same thing at the very same time.

"God in heaven," breathed Carrington. "You must be mistaken, Captain. You must have been on the Powder."

Gunnison shook his head. "No mistake, sir. North told me himself that it was the Tongue. And I confirmed that later."

Right before Gunnison's eyes Carrington seemed instantly transformed from a ramrod-straight Army officer into a feeble old man. He reached out with a slightly shaking hand to find his camp chair and eased his frame down into it.

"North betrayed us? Is it possible?"

"Seems like the only explanation," said Jim Bridger.

Gunnison turned to see the mountain man coming through the flap of the tent's entrance.

"Damn it, Bridger," said Carrington hoarsely. "You're chief of scouts. North was your responsibility."

"No, sir. As you'll recall, I advised against his being hired in the first place. But he convinced Captain Fetterman that nobody knew the Sioux any better than he did. And that may be true. After all, he traded with them for many years, and lived among them, too. But I never trusted him."

"You mean you think he meant to betray us from the start?"

Bridger shook his head. "I dunno if that's so. But he never seemed to me to be all that convinced that the Sioux needed to lose this war."

"There's another possibility," said Gunnison. "He might have been captured by the Sioux after I sent him to bring word to you of our situation, General. He might have cut a deal to save his own life."

Carrington shook his head. "Nothing could justify turning against your own kind." He gave Gunnison an appraising look. There could be no mistake that the cavalry captain was bone-weary. And with one look you could tell he had been through hell. His uniform was torn and stained with grime and blood. Apparently the blood of his own men, mused Carrington, as Gunnison himself appeared unscathed. Many Army officers scorned their counterparts in the cavalry as rash glory seekers long on dash and daring but short on reliability. Carrington hadn't been sure of Gunnison until today. In fact, there were some who said Gunnison was an Indian lover—based, presumably, on his actions during the flight of the Southern Cheyenne following the Sand Creek Massacre. Gunnison had prevented the Colorado Volunteers from committing yet another atrocity. Carrington considered what Gunnison had done in that instance fully justified, under the circumstances. But the doubt had lingered. Now he was sure he could put that doubt to rest. Gunnison was a fighter, a good, solid officer.

"Captain, I commend you and your men for what you have done. I know you must be exhausted. Yet I have no recourse but to order you into the saddle again."

"I understand, General."

"Take every man in your command who is fit to ride and fight. And then mount as many men from the Twenty-seventh that we have horses for, and take them with you."

Gunnison didn't like the idea of trying to convert infantrymen into cavalry on such short notice, but he wasn't about to object.

"As soon as possible you will ride for the Powder River. Mr. Bridger will go with you. You will join Captain Fetterman and return here. I will send Captain Kinney with three companies of the Twenty-seventh to follow you."

Gunnison glanced at Bridger. What Carrington proposed would split the command into four small parts—Fetterman's, Kinney's, his and the contingent remaining at the encampment. He wasn't sure if that was wise. But he understood that Carrington wanted Fetterman to receive the reinforcements—and a warning about Bob North—as quickly as possible.

"I'll leave in an hour's time, sir," he said.

Carrington nodded. "Good, good. As for North, I want you to bring him back dead or alive."

While Bridger headed for the stables to supervise the mounting of the infantrymen, Gunnison returned to his tent. Aching from head to foot, he stretched out on his cot—but only for a moment. He felt guilty lying there while Fetterman's command was out there somewhere—possibly under attack by the

Sioux. Groaning, he got up and filled his cartridge box. The sergeant came in with a cup of hot, thick coffee. Gunnison sipped it gratefully. Java had never tasted so good. Then Grace came into the tent—and he forgot all about the coffee. Tears streaked her cheeks.

"Lieutenant Denning is dead," she whispered.

Gunnison glanced at the sergeant, who nodded and left him alone with his distraught wife.

"I'm sorry, darling," said Gunnison, putting his arms around her. "How is Laura taking it?"

"How do you think she's taking it?" asked Grace, angrily, pulling away. "Her whole world has been destroyed. She has to bury her husband. I can't think of anything worse."

"He was a good man. A fine soldier. He died bravely."

"Oh, save that nonsense for his eulogy!" she snapped.

Gunnison was startled by her vehemence. "What's gotten into you, Grace?"

Fists clenched, she turned her back on him. "I just hate this," she railed. "I hate it all!"

"I see now it was a mistake to bring you. This is no place for a woman."

"This is no place for anyone! This is all so . . . so unnecessary. Why can't we all just live together in peace? It's not like there isn't more than enough room for everyone, white and red alike."

"It just doesn't work that way," he replied, well aware of how lame that comment really was. But he couldn't think of anything else to say.

"It *could*. But you don't want it to. And now you have to ride out again, and maybe this time they'll bring you back all shot up and dying, or maybe already dead, and then I'll have to bury you. Another fine soldier who died bravely."

"You knew this was my life when we met, Grace."

"Yes, I knew! But I fell in love with you in spite of that."

"And now you regret having done so."

She turned, her expression softening. "No," she said, and sighed. "But I have a feeling I will live long enough to regret it."

Gunnison just looked at her. Words failed him. "I came back to you last time, and I will this time, too."

"You keep making that promise. But one day you won't be able to keep it."

"I always thought the job I did was important. That this uniform was something to be proud of. Something *you* could be proud of."

She launched herself at him then, catching him completely off guard, and tore at his tunic, popping some of the buttons. "I *hate* it!" she cried. He fended her off, holding onto her arms, and for an instant she struggled, fighting him like a wildcat, only to suddenly go limp, and he let her down gently onto the cot. She wrapped her arms around his neck and pulled his lips down to hers, kissing him with a hard passion, and he could taste the salt of her tears. He answered her passion with his own, and even though he knew how incongruous it would be to make love to her at this moment, he could not contain his desire for her. But she contained it for him, pushing him away.

"Go on," she said huskily. When he hesitated, she said, more forcefully, "Go *on*! Go do your duty."

Dazed, Gunnison could only obey, and left the tent.

"I love you," she said softly, although it was too late for him to hear.

Chapter Six

On the previous day, Fetterman and his command had left the unfinished Fort Kearney shortly after daybreak. There were one hundred and twenty-six bluecoats in the column—two companies of the Twenty-seventh Infantry, followed by two supply wagons and an ambulance. Led by Bob North, they traveled at a brisk pace along the western bank of Clear Creek, which Fetterman knew would soon make a confluence with the Powder River. According to North, a few miles above this confluence was an island, upon which the cavalry was making its stand against two or three hundred Sioux warriors.

North had arrived at the encampment a few hours prior to dawn, riding an Indian pony. His story was that shortly after Captain Gunnison dispatched him with a message for Carrington, he was set upon by a band of Sioux. His horse was killed out from under him, and he was captured. The warriors debated at length among themselves as to his fate, and it was decided that he would be taken to Red Cloud, who would make the final decision. Three of the warriors agreed to take him to Red Cloud's village. The rest continued on their way southward, as their mission was to scout in the vicinity of the encampment to see what Carrington was doing. According to North,

when the warriors camped for the night he got his
hands on a knife, cut his bounds, slit the throat of
the warrior who stood guard, and made his escape
on the Indian pony.

Fetterman believed that all of this was true. He
could see the marks on North's wrists, where rawhide had rubbed the skin raw. He also believed that
his force was sufficient to triumph over a few hundred savages. Like so many of his peers, Fetterman
had nothing but contempt for the prowess of the Indian warrior. The Indian, he thought, was cunning
and dangerous if he had the advantage. But in a fair
fight, with the odds even, the red man was no match
against the white soldier. So he was supremely confident of the outcome of his foray, and ached for the
chance to close with the enemy and prove, once and
for all, that this Sioux threat—the threat that had so
many people gnashing their teeth and pulling their
hair—was nothing to be concerned about.

Early that afternoon he got the chance he was hoping for. About twenty Indians on painted war ponies
appeared at the edge of some timber about a quarter
mile away. They seemed startled by the appearance
of Fetterman's column. There were fifteen infantrymen that Fetterman had mounted to serve as makeshift
cavalry, since Gunnison's troopers were otherwise oc-
cupied. These fifteen were under the command of
Lieutenant Bingham. Fetterman accepted the fact that
Bingham was not well-versed in cavalry tactics, but
there wasn't anything really complicated about the
orders Fetterman gave him at that moment. He was
to charge those Sioux warriors and engage them.
How difficult could that be?

It proved to be exceedingly difficult—indeed, impossible. Bingham obediently led his mounted soldiers forward. The Sioux warriors hurled a few taunts in their direction, then turned tail and vanished into the timber. Bingham gave chase. Fetterman pressed his foot soldiers onward in their wake. As they reached the woods, Fetterman was keenly disappointed that he heard no gunfire from up ahead. What was Bingham doing? He sent Bob North ahead to find out.

A few moments later, Bingham and his mounted men reappeared. The lieutenant excitedly reported that there was a large number of Indians on the other side of the woods.

"How many would you estimate, Lieutenant?" asked Fetterman.

"At least seven or eight hundred, sir. Maybe even more. We didn't linger long enough to count heads."

Fetterman was skeptical. "Where is North?"

Bingham shrugged. "I have no idea, sir. I thought he was with you."

"I want to see this Indian horde with my own eyes," he said, annoyed—and ordered the column to advance.

When they reached the edge of the timber Fetterman got his wish. There, arrayed before him, were the Sioux warriors. He realized that Lieutenant Bingham hadn't been exaggerating—there *were* at least seven or eight hundred of them. Much as he hated to admit it, Fetterman had to acknowledge that they made for quite a splendid and daunting spectacle, adorned in their war regalia. But what were they waiting for? They had spotted Bingham's contingent,

and yet hadn't given chase when Bingham withdrew.
It seemed as though they were daring the bluecoats
to come out of the woods and give battle. It wasn't
difficult for Fetterman to resist the temptation to ac-
commodate them. Regardless of his opinion about
the superior fighting prowess of white soldiers, he
wasn't about to take on such odds unless he had to.
He promptly ordered his command to withdraw to
the river, and told Bingham to deploy his fifteen
mounted troops as a rear-guard screen.

The infantry was halfway through the stretch of
timber when Fetterman heard an explosion of gunfire
from the rear. A moment later nine of Bingham's
men reappeared, with hundreds of Sioux warriors on
their heels. Fetterman noted that the lieutenant was
missing. But he couldn't worry about that now. He
shouted orders, trying to form the infantry into a
square. Before this maneuver could be successfully
completed, complicated as it was by the thick brush,
the Indians were upon them. Instantly the woods
were filled with the din of crashing volleys and thick
with drifting powdersmoke. Though a handful of
mounted warriors rode straight into the ranks, most
of them swept past on one side or the other. The
former were brought down, and the withering fire of
the soldiers killed many more as they thundered
past. Yet Fetterman was alarmed by the fact that over
a dozen of his men also fell.

As the balance of the Sioux force passed on
through the timber to reform on open ground near
the river, some remained behind on the flanks of Fetterman's command. Most of these dismounted and
used the abundant cover afforded by the under-

growth to continue a harassing, lethal fire. Fetterman's horse was killed, as were the mule teams that drew the supply wagons and ambulance. Reluctant to leave these behind, Fetterman gave up on his hopes of moving his command to the edge of the trees, where they would at least have a clear field of fire in one direction, and proceeded to form a square, using the wagons for cover on two sides. A second assault by the Sioux warriors commenced immediately. This time, though, the soldiers were ready for them. Volley after volley broke the assault before it reached the square, and the warriors dispersed into the trees.

Several more assaults occurred as the afternoon progressed, first against one side of the bluecoat square and then another, participated in by hundreds of warriors both mounted and afoot. Each time, withering fire from Fetterman's ranks blunted the attack and then turned it aside. The Sioux suffered terrible losses. But they were not deterred. That surprised Fetterman. It went against everything he had been told about the way Indians fought. In spite of himself Fetterman reluctantly admired their courage and resolve. If they persisted the outcome was inevitable. It was a matter of attrition—with each attack he lost more men. Before long the position would be overrun.

By nightfall nearly half of Fetterman's command was dead or wounded. Fortunately, the spirited resistance by those who were still able to fight kept the Sioux at bay. The attacks ceased as night descended. What followed was in some ways worse than full-scale assaults, as small groups of warriors would slip

close to the square and then open fire. A volley fired
in return would kill them or send them packing, but
more often than not another soldier was hit each time
such a foray was attempted. As the night progressed,
Fetterman's hopes dwindled. It would not be possible for his command to last another day. It was painfully evident that there was no escape. The only
recourse was to fight on gallantly, to the end, then
to die a soldier's death. Fetterman found his dispatch
book and by the moonlight—no one dared light a
fire, or even a match, for fear of making himself a
prime target—tried to write a last letter to his wife
back east. Once before, during the war against the
Confederacy, had he felt compelled to write such a
missive, and that had been before going into battle,
when the orders for his regiment made it abundantly
clear that losses would be extremely high. He
thought it a miracle that he had survived that battle,
and with great relief he had torn up the letter he'd
left behind in case he failed to return to bivouac.
Now he undertook that painful duty once more. It
was difficult because he knew how hard his death
would be on his poor wife, and it took him hours to
complete the task. He felt certain that other men in
his command were doing the same thing. He didn't
have to tell his men that the situation was bleak. A
soldier knew such things without having to be told.

Fetterman spent the rest of that sleepless night
dreading the arrival of dawn, and when the first gray
shreds of daylight began to lighten the eastern sky
he braced himself for another Sioux attack. But then,
much to his amazement, Captain Gunnison and
about forty mounted men came slashing through the

timber, catching the Indians by surprise, bugle blar-
ing, muzzle flash from dozens of carbines and pistols
fracturing the night-gloom that yet lingered beneath
the trees. Fetterman saw Gunnison himself, pistol in
one hand and saber in another, guiding the horse
beneath him with his knees, felling one warrior with
a sweeping blow from the saber and then another by
shooting him through the chest at nearly point-blank
range. Jim Bridger was riding with Gunnison, and
doing his fair share of the fighting. Caught between
the cavalry onslaught and Fetterman's square, the
Sioux scattered. Gunnison urged his men to press
their advantage and Fetterman, quick to seize the
moment, ordered his own men to leave the cover of
the wagons and pursue the fleeing Indians. Though
bone-tired, the men of the Twenty-seventh lit out
after the Sioux like hounds after a fox. Some of the
warriors stood their ground, and fierce hand-to-hand
fighting ensued. But before long the bluecoats had
driven most of the Indians from the timber. Fetterman called a halt at the edge of the forest. There
his men formed a ragged line and kept firing until
the Indians were out of range.

The fight over, Fetterman returned to the wagons,
and met Gunnison and Bridger there.

"I must admit," he said, "I wasn't expecting you,
Captain."

Gunnison smiled grimly. "I wasn't expecting to see
you, Captain. Not alive, anyway."

"Had you been much later, you might not have."

Gunnison told Fetterman how he had come to be
here, and then Bridger asked about Bob North.

Fetterman shook his head. "He disappeared when

the Sioux sprang their trap. I assumed he had been killed. I find it hard to believe that he would betray his own kind."

"Well, we'll worry about North later," said Gunnison. "We were damned lucky this morning. Caught the Sioux by surprise. They might come back, so we'd better get moving as soon as possible."

Fetterman nodded. "If you will be kind enough to provide me with a rear guard, Captain, I will have my men on the move in half an hour."

There were only enough horses to make a team for one wagon. Fetterman had the supplies removed from that conveyance so that the wounded could be transported back to Fort Kearney in it. He hated to leave the dead behind, fearing that the Indians would return to the scene and desecrate their corpses, but there was no other recourse. The burial details dug twenty-eight shallow graves—including one for Lieutenant Bingham. Then they were on their way, warily expecting the Sioux to show up again. It was a long and anxious march, but they arrived back at the encampment without seeing another Indian.

Once the Sioux had sprung their trap on Fetterman's command, Bob North departed the scene with all due haste. He found himself momentarily alone, the sounds of battle behind him, and he considered riding like hell until he was far removed from the Powder River country. He decided instead to return to Red Cloud's village. He had done what had been asked of him, and he felt confident that the Sioux would wipe out the bluecoat column. His part in it caused him a twinge of guilt—but only a twinge. It was every man for himself out here, and he'd simply done what was necessary to stay alive. Red Cloud had said he could live among the Oglala Sioux, and that seemed to be the best place for him. If both Fetterman's command and Gunnison's were wiped out, it was conceivable that the Army would not know of his treachery. They might assume he had perished with Fetterman. But if he was ever seen alive, and identified, questions would be asked— questions about how and why he had survived that he probably could not answer satisfactorily. So he would take his chances with Red Cloud, at least for the time being.

He approached the village cautiously, well aware that many Sioux warriors probably disagreed with Red Cloud's decision to let him live. And while they would not blatantly challenge the chief, North figured they would be looking for any opportunity to do away with him. Riding in with a strip of white cloth tied to the barrel of his rifle, he was met by several braves who belonged to the Strong Heart clan. This clan served the Oglala as a kind of tribal police, and were committed to carrying out Red Cloud's wishes. They escorted him to the skin lodge where he had first met the chief, and there he waited, not daring to venture out into the village, and knowing that the Strong Hearts would inform Red Cloud of his presence.

The night passed uneventfully for North. Around midmorning he was called upon by Spotted Calf. A glance at the warrior's expression warned North that something was wrong. And when he heard that the

Sioux had failed to destroy Fetterman's command, he uttered a curse under his breath.

"That settles it, then," he told Spotted Calf, feeling more than a little sorry for himself. "Now everyone will know I betrayed the soldiers. I have nowhere else to go—I have to stay here."

"Red Cloud said you would be allowed to if we were victorious," said Spotted Calf.

"I did everything that was asked of me. It's not my fault that you couldn't kill the bluecoats when you outnumbered them ten to one."

Spotted Calf's eyes narrowed. He clearly did not appreciate the aspersions North was casting upon his brothers.

"So what happens to me now?" asked North.

The warrior shrugged his indifference. "That has not yet been decided. It will be up to Red Cloud. He has many other more important matters to think about."

North grimaced. Of course he couldn't fathom that anything would be more important than whether he would live or die. It was bad enough that he had no say in that decision. Worse still was not knowing the outcome.

Chapter Seven

When Red Renshaw walked into the Taos cantina he was ready for a binge of drinking and whoring that would go on for at least a week—or until his money ran out, whichever came first. After which he would make a decision about his immediate future. He had just spent six months out on the lonesome plains with a bunch of buffalo hunters, and in his opinion a little fun was past due. He bellied up to the bar and ordered the barkeeper, a paunchy, mustachioed Mexican, to bring him a bottle of tequila. He slapped some hard money down—part of the proceeds he had received as his share of the profit made from the two wagonloads of buffalo hides he and his erstwhile partners had just brought into town. When he got the bottle he pulled the cork out with his teeth and took a long drink. The fiery liquor seared his throat and exploded in his belly, and Renshaw gasped with delight.

"You gonna share that with your pard, Red?"

Renshaw looked askance at the man who had appeared at his elbow. The man's name was Dooley, and he was one of the buffalo hunters Renshaw had teamed up with the previous winter. Renshaw had never done any buffalo running before, but he'd been looking for a way to make a peso or two and the

buffalo hunters had recently lost one of their shoot-
ers. Since Renshaw could shoot the eyes out of a bird
at fifty yards with one shot, they had agreed to sign
him on. So his job had been to kill as many buffs as
he could and leave the skinning to Dooley and the
other two. Dooley was a scrawny, smelly little man
with the face of a ferret—and in Renshaw's opinion,
he was about as trustworthy as one of those conniving critters.

"Buy your own, Dooley," growled Renshaw, a
menacing glint in his eyes.

Dooley scowled. "Now that ain't very friendly,
what with everything we've been through together
these past months."

Renshaw put the bottle down very carefully on the
counter, and half turned to face Dooley. "I never said
anything about this before, Dooley, but I had a hunch
from the very beginning of our business dealings that
you and your amigos planned to do me in when the
hunting was done and you no longer had a need for
my services."

Dooley looked shocked. "How can you say such a
thing, Red?"

"So you're telling me that ain't true."

"It sure as hell ain't," protested Dooley. "I would
never do a thing like that."

"You're a liar," said Renshaw flatly. "And you're
just damned lucky you and your boys didn't have
the nerve to try anything, because I would have kilt
the whole lot of you—and skinned you, too, just like
you do them shaggies."

Dooley stared at Red Renshaw—and did not
doubt for a moment that he was hearing the gospel.

In fact, he and his two partners *had* discussed cutting Renshaw's throat once the wagons were filled with hides. They had done that very thing to Red's predecessor. But then, the previous season's shooter hadn't been a mountain man like Renshaw. Red slept with one eye open and one hand on his rifle, and he had never given Dooley or his cronies an opportunity.

"You're just flat-out wrong, Red," he said.

"No I ain't. You boys just didn't have the gumption. If I was wrong you'd be mad as hell, and would challenge me right here and now. But you know I'm right—and you've got a yellow streak down your back. So why don't you just go away and let me drink in peace."

He picked up the bottle and took another long draw—and Dooley made a discreet exit.

Feeling much better with a belly full of tequila, Renshaw took a moment to look around the room. His attention was drawn to a man in buckskins who sat in a rear corner of the dimly lit room, his back to the fly-specked abode wall. The man sat with shoulders slumped, his head down, a hand wrapped around a bottle that stood on the table. Renshaw could tell that the man was an Anglo, and there was something vaguely familiar about him, though his features were concealed from view. And Renshaw wondered if he was even conscious—though he didn't have to wonder for long. A young Mexican woman who worked the cantina as a percentage girl, trying to get the male patrons to buy her—and themselves—more drinks, approached the man in buckskins. Even as the man slowly raised

his head, the woman moved so that she blocked
Renshaw's view. She didn't linger long, though, for
as she placed a hand on the man's arm he shook it
off and curtly ordered her away, speaking in Span-
ish, his voice a hoarse rasp. In Renshaw's experience,
such women were not usually put off so easily. In
fact, they could be downright pesty, at times, in their
determination to seduce men into spending their
money. But there was evidently something about the
man in buckskins that discouraged this woman from
pressing the issue.

The woman moved to another table, where two
Mexicans sat drinking mescal, and Renshaw noticed
that this pair was paying the man in buckskins an
inordinate amount of attention. For his part, the latter let his chin drop to his chest again, and seemed
not the least bit concerned that he was being observed. Renshaw didn't like the looks of the two
Mexicans. They were rough-looking characters, and
based on their attire he pegged them as Comancheros—men who plied the perilous trade of doing
business with the Comanches who ruled the Staked
Plains, selling the Indians guns and liquor in return
for the loot the Comanches stole during their raids
in Texas. You had to be tough as whang leather
and meaner than the devil himself to do that kind
of work.

Renshaw wasn't surprised when, after a few minutes consultation with the woman, one of the men
rose and sauntered over to the table of the man in
buckskins. He stood there a moment, expecting to be
noticed, his thumbs hooked under a belt that was
laden with a pistol on one side and a sheathed knife

on the other. But the man in buckskins seemed not to be aware of his proximity.

"Hey, gringo," said the Comanchero. "Are you dead?"

His partner, still at the table, and now with the woman in his lap, chuckled. But the man in buckskins didn't move.

"Hey, I am talking to you," said the first man, louder this time, more aggressively.

Fascinated, Renshaw watched as the man in buckskins slowly raised his head and looked up at the Comanchero. And at that moment Renshaw recognized him. Even though it had been nearly twenty years since he had last laid eyes on Gordon Hawkes, and even though Hawkes had changed substantially in his appearance during that time, there wasn't the slightest doubt. Those piercing blue eyes fastened now on the Comanchero belonged to the mountain man who was as legendary in his own right as Bridger and Smith and Fitzpatrick and Sublette.

"I heard you," said Hawkes in a hoarse whisper. "You do not like my friend? Why will you not buy her a drink?"

Hawkes leaned slightly to one side so that he could look past the Comanchero and see the woman sitting on the lap of the other man.

"Because I don't like the company she keeps."

Renshaw grinned. A quick glance around the cantina revealed to him that all the other patrons seemed to be frozen in place. They were all keenly aware of the fact that trouble was brewing in the back corner. A few were even making discreet exits. Turning his attention back to the table, Renshaw saw the Comanchero place one hand on the knife sheathed at his side.

"You had better buy her a drink now, gringo," said the Comanchero, "or I will take offense to what you said."

"I don't think so," replied Hawkes, sounding bored. "Now go away."

The Comanchero didn't go away. Instead, he drew the knife from his sheath and with the other hand overturned the table that stood between him and Hawkes. Only then did he realize something that Renshaw, being the very observant person that he was, had already noticed. While Hawkes had one hand around the bottle on the table, his other hand had been under the table, concealed from everyone's view. Now it was no longer concealed—and the Comanchero could plainly see that it held a Walker Colt. Renshaw was familiar with the weapon. A big, cumbersome revolver that was carried by many Texas Rangers, the Walker Colt was a long-barreled hand cannon of the .45-caliber variety. It was enough to give the belligerent Comanchero pause. But Renshaw didn't think such a man would back down. And he was right. The Comanchero let out a snarl of incoherent rage and grabbed for his own pistol. Hawkes didn't hesitate. He pulled the Walker Colt's trigger. The gunshot was deafening in the confines of the cantina, and the results were shocking; at such close range the bullet striking the Comanchero squarely in the chest lifted him clean off the floor and hurled him back against the wall. Renshaw figured he was dead before he hit that wall, and as his

body slid limply to the ground it left a smear of
blood on the cracked and peeling adobe.

Hawkes stood up, then, kicking his chair away—
and the other Comanchero was also on the move,
dumping the woman unceremoniously out of his lap
as he leapt to his feet and drew his own pistol. But
Renshaw knew he didn't have any more of a chance
than his deceased partner. Hawkes had already
thumbed the Walker Colt's hammer back, and a
heartbeat later the big-bore pistol thundered again.
The second Comanchero fell dead. Standing there
with revolver in one hand and bottle in the other,
gunsmoke drifting like a veil across his face, Hawkes
bleakly scanned the rest of the cantina to see if he
was going to have to kill anyone else that night. His
gaze lingered just a fraction on Renshaw. Then, without interest, it moved on. Apparently convinced that
he had no further need for the Walker Colt—at least
not for the moment—the mountain man put the pistol away, righted the table and his chair and sat back
down, totally oblivious to the fact that the woman
who had been the catalyst of all this mayhem was
sobbing hysterically, scrambling on hands and knees
across the floor to get away from the corpse of the
second Comanchero. Renshaw looked around. The
cantina was quickly emptying. Even the bartender
had vanished.

Carrying his own bottle, Renshaw walked over to
the woman and reached down to grab her by the
arm and lift her, none too gently, to her feet. "I think
you better vamoose, senorita," he drawled.

She took his advice, fleeing out of the cantina. Renshaw walked over to Hawkes's table, dragged a

nearby chair over, and positioned it across from the mountain man.

"I'm wondering if you remember me," he said.

Hawkes nodded. "You worked with Dane Gilmartin, hauling plews and trade goods between St. Louis and Fort Bridger. That was back in '46. Your name is Renshaw, as I recall."

Renshaw nodded. "You have a good memory. Mind if I sit down? Don't worry, I won't ask you to buy me a drink. As you can see, I brought my own."

Hawkes shrugged. "Suit yourself."

Settling into the chair, Renshaw said, "You know the local law will be here any minute. I reckon they'll place you under arrest. But I'll stand as a witness for you, if it comes to that. I saw the whole damn thing." He glanced at the slain Comancheros bleeding all over the floor a few feet away. "Those boys clearly intended to clean your plow. Might be they were in cahoots with the woman from the start. Hoping to get you so drunk you wouldn't feel a thing when they took you out back and slit your throat and took your poke."

"Would have been a lot of effort for nothing," remarked Hawkes. "I spent my last peso tonight."

"What I don't understand is, why are you still sitting here? I mean, while you were just acting in self-defense tonight, if the local law finds out who you are then your goose is cooked for certain."

Hawkes just stared at him.

"You *are* still wanted for a couple of murders back East, aren't you?" asked Renshaw. "Not saying that you're guilty of all charges, of course. Some folks say you were framed, in both cases. But that's just some folks, and I wouldn't count on the Taos sheriff being one of 'em."

"It doesn't matter," said Hawkes flatly.

Renshaw frowned, perplexed. "What doesn't matter?"

"Anything."

"I don't savvy," admitted Renshaw. "Seems strange to hear that from a man who's spent most of his life trying to stay free. Or maybe you're just tired of living."

"I'm tired," said Hawkes, "of talking to you."

Renshaw blinked. Hawkes had laid the Walker Colt on the table—within easy reach.

"Well, then I guess I'll go mind my own business," he said, and went back to the bar. As he did a man wearing a tin star on his frock coat appeared in the cantina doorway. He was a tall, wiry man with a thick mustache and the squinty look of someone who had spent a lot of years in the wild country. A pearl-handled Navy Colt was visible in a cross-draw holster under the coat. He paused at the threshold to warily survey the interior of the cantina. He glanced at Renshaw, then peered at Hawkes, and his gaze lingered there a moment. Renshaw immediately felt sorry for the man. He looked like a capable officer of the law, someone who was no stranger to trouble, and who knew how to handle it, but then Gordon Hawkes was not your ordinary kind of trouble. He had just killed two men without blinking an eye, and Renshaw wasn't sure that piece of tin on the lawman's coat was going to make a bit of difference to the mountain man.

The Taos lawman finally stepped inside. Instead of advancing on Hawkes, who was staring at the bottle

in front of him and who didn't seem aware of anything that was going on around him, the badgetoter
approached the bar.

"Who are you?" he asked Renshaw.

"Just an eyewitness. It was self-defense, Sheriff. I
can testify to that."

The lawman nodded, looking at the two corpses.
"Yeah, I'm sure it was. I know those two. The
world's a better place without the likes of them. I
figured Hawkes might end up doing something like
this. It was just that pair's bad luck that they tangled
with him today."

"You know Hawkes?"

The lawman nodded. "He showed up here about
a month ago. Brought his wife down from the mountains to see the doctors here. She was sick, real sick.
She died a week ago."

"Lord Almighty," breathed Renshaw, staring
across the cantina at Hawkes. "Now it makes sense."

"What does?"

"Why he doesn't care what happens to him."

The lawman nodded again. "It hit him hard. From
what I'm told, they'd been together for a long time."

"Probably thirty years, would be my guess. Maybe
longer." Renshaw shook his head. "I learned a long
time ago that it just doesn't pay to get too attached
to anybody. You just buy into a world of hurt if you
do. So I've spent my whole life alone, and all I can
honestly say is I have no regrets."

"You a friend of his?"

"Not exactly. I was partners with a man who was
his friend, though. That was a lot of years ago. You
going to arrest him?"

The lawman grimaced. "I guess I should have arrested him weeks ago, when I found out who he was. I know that he's wanted in Louisiana and Missouri on charges of murder. But to be honest, the idea of putting a man like that behind bars just didn't sit right with me."

"How come?"

"Well, for one thing, I have heard the story of how he lost his son. And it was plain that he was losing his wife, too. Besides, I have to admit I admire what Hawkes did for the Southern Cheyenne after that bloody mess at Sand Creek."

"I've never had a good thing to say about an officer of the law," said Renshaw, with a slow grin. "But damned if I might not have to make an exception in your case. I never was convinced that Hawkes committed those murders. He just don't strike me as the type to do that sort of thing. Sure, he's killed plenty of men in his time. But my guess is they all deserved it."

Still watching Hawkes, the lawman didn't seem to hear. "I just hope," he said, softly, as though thinking aloud, "that I don't have to kill him."

"I don't think he would care," said Renshaw.

The lawman headed across the cantina—and Renshaw watched with admiration. Cornering a wounded grizzly would be a safer proposition than what the Taos sheriff was doing. Stopping across the table from Hawkes, the lawman said a few words that Renshaw couldn't quite catch, they were so softly spoken. Hawkes merely glanced at the sheriff with that bleak, I-don't-give-a-damn look in his eyes—and then, much to Renshaw's astonishment—pushed the

Walker Colt across the table. The lawman picked up
the gun, stuck it under his belt and heaved a sigh of
relief. Hawkes took one last long pull on the bottle,
then got up and walked out of the cantina without
looking in Renshaw's direction. The lawman followed in his wake.

Chapter Eight

The longer the Taos sheriff kept Gordon Hawkes in jail, the more he felt sorry for the mountain man. Hawkes paced his cell like a tiger, and the sheriff figured it had to be tough for a man who was accustomed to living free in wild country to adjust to the confines of a strap-iron cage. He was amazed to learn that Hawkes had never been incarcerated before. It was quite an accomplishment, mused the lawman, for someone who had been wanted for about thirty years.

Taos was a bustling town, and the sheriff usually managed to keep his jail pretty full. There were trappers and traders and wolfers and buffalo hunters and even some Comancheros who used Taos as a base of operations, or at least as a place to come to let off some steam. But he always kept Hawkes in a cell by himself, even if it meant cramming a half-dozen reprobates in a single cell. He did so for two reasons—one was out of respect for Hawkes. The other was to keep the others alive. Ever since his wife's death, Hawkes had become a real menace. The Taos sheriff understood why. The mountain man had ceased to care about his own life. And anyone who didn't care about living was liable not to give a lot of consideration to the lives of others. Some men recovered, in time, from a personal loss. Some, however, never could. The sheriff wondered which category Hawkes would fall into. Clearly the man had dearly loved his wife, and felt lost without her. Having lost his own wife some years back when cholera had swept through the town, the lawman knew how tough it could be.

The secret, of course, was to find a reason to live. Like a lot of people, the sheriff knew the Hawkes legend. And he seemed to recall it being said that the mountain man had more than one child. His son had been murdered in a Colorado gold camp, but there had been at least one other. The Taos lawman decided to do a little checking. He asked everyone in Taos that he thought might be more familiar with the subject. He finally happened upon an Indian trader who had done a lot of business with the Absaroke Crow. This man mentioned that Hawkes, who was very highly regarded by the Absaroke, had often spent summers with the Crow tribe, bringing his family down from the mountains. And that family included a little girl. The trader did not recall ever having heard her name mentioned. The sheriff decided to consult the source, and one day asked Hawkes flat out if he had a daughter—hoping fervently as he broached the subject that the girl still lived.

"I do," said Hawkes. "Her name is Grace. She's nearly twenty years old now."

"Where does she live?"

Hawkes smiled faintly. "That's a good question. She married a cavalryman. An officer in the Second

Cavalry. Last I heard they were posted at Fort Laramie. Why do you want to know all this?"

The Taos lawman shrugged. "Just wondering if you had any family left."

"My daughter would be better off if I was gone."

"I'm sure she would not agree. Does she know that her mother has passed away?"

"No."

"Don't you reckon she deserves to know?"

Hawkes stared at the sheriff a moment, and the latter figured he was on the verge of being told to mind his own damned business. Instead, the mountain man nodded.

"I guess you're right."

"Want to write her a letter?"

Hawkes hesitated, and the sheriff knew precisely why. Penning such a letter would be an extremely difficult and painful task. But then, life was full of just those kinds of tasks. And Hawkes didn't strike him as a man who would shirk a responsibility just because it was a tough one.

The mountain man heaved a sigh. "I reckon," he muttered.

It took him two days to finish the letter, and when he handed it to the sheriff through the cell's iron straps his hand was shaking slightly.

"I'll see that it gets to Fort Laramie," said the lawman.

"I'd be obliged if you didn't include any news about me," said Hawkes. "It wouldn't do her much good to know I was in jail for killing those two men." He shook his head, a rueful expression on his face. "It's funny. After that business at Gilder Gulch, I swore I'd never take another life. Managed to stick to that vow, too, until the other day. I wish now it hadn't happened. It's not like it mattered much what those two did to me."

"The judge will hear your case in a couple of days," said the sheriff. "But I can tell you right now you won't be held to account for what you did in that cantina. The main reason you're my guest, Hawkes, is because those Comancheros had friends in these parts. They've been lurking around town, talking about vengeance. In fact, it's safe to say you're the topic of a great deal of conversation in Taos these days."

"How come?"

"Because you're famous, whether you like it or not. Some of the decent folk are wondering why I haven't contacted the U.S. Marshal in Denver about you, since you're wanted on so many other charges."

"And why haven't you?"

The sheriff shrugged. "Even though it's my job— and believe you me, I've been reminded of that fact plenty of late—it just doesn't sit right with me. Besides, sooner or later, one of those decent, upstanding men will send a wire to Denver on his own."

Hawkes looked utterly indifferent.

The Taos sheriff did not immediately send the letter off to Fort Laramie. He wanted to make sure, first, that Grace Hawkes was, in fact, residing there. Considering the state of the frontier's postal services, it would be a small miracle if the letter got to its destination in the first place. And if its intended recipient was not there, then it would require a miracle of much greater magnitude for it to find her. The lawman thought he owed it to Hawkes to do everything in his power to get the letter delivered. So he first sent a wire to the Western Military District's headquarters in Fort Leavenworth, Kansas.

When he received a reply a few days later, he wasted no time in sharing it with his prisoner.

"Seems your daughter's husband, a Captain Gunnison, was attached to the command of a General Carrington," said the sheriff. "Carrington's command was sent up into the Powder River country a few months back to establish a series of outposts along the Bozeman Trail, in order to protect the emigrant trains passing through Sioux country."

Hawkes could tell just by looking at the lawman that there was more—and that he probably wasn't going to like it.

"Apparently," continued the sheriff, "a good many of Carrington's officers took their wives and families along. The Army is pretty sure Captain Gunnison took your daughter with him."

"Into Sioux country," murmured Hawkes.

The sheriff nodded. "Word is there's been a lot of trouble up there. Carrington has his hands full with Red Cloud's Oglala Sioux, who have joined forces with the Northern Cheyenne. The Indians are putting up one hell of a fight, by all accounts. Hate to say it, but looks like your daughter is right in the thick of things."

He peered into Hawkes's eyes—and for the first time since he'd locked up the mountain man, he saw what he was looking for: a sense of purpose.

"When is my hearing?" asked Hawkes.

"You're not having one."

"I don't understand. A few days ago you said . . ."

"I've already talked it over with the judge. We agreed there's no reason to waste his time with this case."

"Then you need to let me out of here."

"And what are you planning to do?"

"What do you think?"

"I want to hear it from you. I don't want any more trouble from you, Hawkes. My job is to keep the peace in Taos, and that's going to be damned hard to do if you go out there and tangle with more of those Comancheros."

"I'm not staying in Taos. I'm going to the Powder River country."

The sheriff nodded. "Good. Glad to hear that. But how are you going to get there? You don't have any money. You sold your horse and even your rifle to pay the doctors who treated your wife."

"I'll walk if I have to."

"Let me see what I can do."

"I want out of this cell," rasped Hawkes.

"You'll just have to wait a bit," replied the sheriff, his voice steel around the edges.

In a week's time Red Renshaw had made a serious dent in the profits he'd made from hunting buffalo— and most of his hard-earned wages had been spent in the same cantina in which he'd witnessed Gordon Hawkes kill the two Comancheros. It seemed as good a place as any. In fact, he took up with the very woman who had been in league with the pair of dead men in their ill-advised attempt to victimize Hawkes.

Renshaw didn't hold that against her. She'd just been doing what they had paid her to do. And as long as he had pesos in his pocket, she would do likewise for him.

So when the buffalo skinner named Dooley started looking for Renshaw, the cantina was one of the first places he looked. And Renshaw was there, propping up the bar and drinking tequila like it was going out of style.

"Howdy, Red," said Dooley, approaching with caution.

Renshaw looked at him without any enthusiasm. "What are you doing here, Dooley? I thought I told you to leave me alone."

"Got a business proposition for you."

Renshaw shook his head. "I'm done hunting shaggies. I think I'll find me some other way to make a living."

"What do you have in mind?"

Renshaw frowned. That was the problem. He didn't know what he was going to do. Back in the old days he'd done a brisk business trading with Indians, hauling a wagonload of cheap trade goods west from St. Louis and making a tidy profit for his trouble. But these days, with the frontier opened up the way it was, the competition in that field had become fierce. There were some pretty big operations going now, and Renshaw couldn't compete with them. And he didn't cotton to the idea of working for somebody else as a mule skinner or translator.

As for buffalo running, he felt a little guilty for having engaged in that pursuit for even one season. Twenty years ago he had seen herds of shaggies that reached from horizon to horizon. But these days there were a lot fewer of the beasts, and Renshaw figured it wouldn't be long before the buffalo was just a memory. Just another reminder that the wild country was being tamed—a situation that he deplored, like so many others who had spent their early years in the mountains and the plains, back when there wasn't anything out here but big sky and clear-running rivers and Indians who didn't know for the most part that it was not in their best interests to befriend the white man. So he was not going to contribute any more to the disappearance of the buffalo.

"I don't know," he confessed. "But I'll think of something."

"I know how you can make a lot of money, easy."

Renshaw grimaced. "I can't for the life of me figure out why you'd think I would ever partner up with you and your crew again, Dooley.

"I have new partners now, Red."

"Really. How come?"

"Because I'm in a new line of work, that's why."

"And what might this new line of work be?"

"Bounty hunting."

Renshaw stared. "You? A bounty man? Don't make me laugh, Dooley."

Dooley was scowling now. "I know you think I'm a coward. But you're wrong."

Shrugging, Renshaw said, "It doesn't matter. You can always shoot him in the back."

"Why don't you come outside and meet my new partners?"

"Why would I want to do that?"

"Because then you might feel better about joining up."

"I doubt it, but lead the way."

He followed Dooley out of the cantina, taking his bottle of tequila along with him, blinking at the brightness of the midday sun after the relative darkness of the establishment's interior. Two men were standing idly in the striped shade under the pole ramada that fronted the cantina—and Renshaw knew instantly that they were Comancheros, cut from the same cloth as the pair Gordon Hawkes had killed ten days ago. One looked like a pure-blood Spaniard, his features hawkish, his dirty yellow hair hanging long down to his shoulders. The other one appeared to be a half-breed, dark and swarthy, with a disfigured nose that looked like it had been smashed with an ax handle or rifle butt many years ago. The former wore the concho-studded trousers and short jacket of the *vaquero*, while the latter was clad in grime-blackened buckskins. These were hard-edged men, about as trustworthy as sidewinders, and twice as dangerous.

"This is the man I was telling you about," Dooley told the Spaniard as he gestured in Renshaw's direction.

The Spaniard sized Renshaw up. "You know Gordon Hawkes."

Right then Renshaw knew what this was all about. He glared at Dooley. "You are a damned fool," he muttered.

Dooley grinned nervously. "Maybe, maybe not. The other day, when you told me to leave you alone, I left—but I didn't go far. I was looking in through the door, and saw you talking to Hawkes. Right after he killed those two men."

"Who happened to be friends of mine," said the Spaniard.

Renshaw seriously doubted that the Spaniard had, or even wanted, friends. But he knew that while Comancheros were men who did not live by many rules, they were as a rule inclined to stick together. That was necessary since they were society's outcasts, hunted like dogs by the Mexican government and clashing sometimes with the Indians of the southern plains. It was in the best interests of men like the Spaniard to nurture the idea that if you killed a Comanchero, you would pay dearly for it.

"It was obvious that you knew Hawkes," continued Dooley. "But did you know he's a wanted man? I hear a person can collect ten thousand dollars for him back East. Dead or alive."

Renshaw took a deep breath and tried to think—wishing now that he hadn't spent the last hour drinking tequila. It tended to slow down the thought processes. But not so much that he didn't understand his predicament.

"I'd heard the rumors, like everybody else," said Renshaw. "But even if what you say is true, Dooley, you're a day late and a dollar short. The law's got Hawkes now."

"Yeah, that's true," said Dooley. "But they can't keep him locked up in that jail forever. Sooner or later they'll have to move him back East to stand trial. That's when we'll get him."

"Get him now? If that happens he'll be in the custody of U.S. marshals, I reckon."

"Marshal can die like any other man," said the Spaniard.

Renshaw stared at the Comanchero. "Are you in this for the money? Or just for vengeance?"

"Revenge," replied the Spaniard readily. "But it won't hurt to make a profit off it."

Renshaw turned his attention back to Dooley. "So why are you telling me all this? What makes you think I'd want any part of such a plan?"

"I've seen how you can shoot, Red. I've never seen a better man with a rifle. That might come in handy. My new partners here, well, their specialty is killing up close, you might say."

Renshaw glanced at the Comancheros again. He could believe that. Both the Spaniard and the Breed looked to him like men who would take special pleasure in getting their hands bloody.

"And what's your specialty, Dooley?" asked Renshaw. "Why would we need you for a job like this?"

Dooley suddenly looked more than a little uncomfortable. "Well, I—I can find out things, without raising suspicion. My new partners aren't the kind of men who can linger in a place without drawing attention to themselves. Me, nobody pays me much attention. I can find out more about what the law aims to do with Hawkes than they can."

Renshaw had to admit that this was probably the case. Dooley was an easy man to underestimate. It was doubtful that the Taos sheriff or a United States marshal would be overly concerned if he saw Dooley anywhere in the vicinity.

"So what do you say, Red?" asked Dooley. "Are you game?"

"You want me for some long-range killing, I take it. You aim to do a little bushwhacking if you get the chance."

"Call it whatever you want."

"And what abut Hawkes? Does he get bush-whacked, too?"

"He's wanted dead or alive, like I said before."

"He makes less trouble for us dead," added the Spaniard.

"I see," said Renshaw, thinking fast. "Well, you'll have to let me think on it."

Dooley shrugged. "Sure, Red. Just don't take too long."

"I won't."

Renshaw started to turn away, but the Spaniard spoke up.

"One more thing," said the Comanchero, with a quiet menace. "Don't even think about telling any-body about our plans. That would be a mistake."

"You didn't have to tell me that," said Renshaw, and went back inside the cantina.

When he was sure the Comancheros and Dooley weren't going to come in after him, he breathed a sigh of relief. But the relief was short-lived. He had a real problem, because he had misled those three. He had no intentions of buying into their scheme. But he'd known better than to turn them down out of hand. The Comancheros wouldn't think twice about killing him if they thought he might give them away. Somehow he had to warn the Taos sheriff—and Gor-don Hawkes—without getting his throat cut for his trouble. The only other option was to wait until dark and ride like hell out of Taos without talking to any-body. But that idea just didn't sit right with him. He didn't owe Gordon Hawkes a thing, but somehow he still felt obliged to give him warning. Maybe it was because he felt a kinship with Hawkes. They had both lived in the wild country back when it had been truly wild. They were cut from the same cloth. And like Comancheros, old frontiersmen had to stick together.

Besides, he just flat-out didn't like that conniving bastard Dooley.

Chapter Nine

At six o'clock every evening the Taos lawman made sure that food was brought over from a nearby restaurant for his prisoners. He counted on getting reimbursed for this expense with his portion of the fines that the local judge usually saw fit to impose on the visitors to his cell block. The fare wasn't anything special, but it was better than bread and water, and while the sheriff didn't think law-breakers should be mollycoddled, neither did he think they deserved to be starved.

Hawkes had noticed that the sheriff usually made sure he was the first one to get his plate, but tonight all the prisoners in the other cells got their food before he did. When everyone else was busy wolfing down their dinner, the sheriff returned to the mountain man's cell. And he didn't have a plate of food with him.

"Are you ready to get out of here?" asked the Taos lawman, keeping his voice low so that none of the other residents of the cell block could hear.

Hawkes had been sitting on a narrow cot. Now he stood up and moved to the cell door. "I've been ready," he said.

The Taos sheriff cast another look around and nodded. He unlocked the cell door and stepped aside, gesturing for Hawkes to proceed with him into the office adjacent to the cell block. A few of the other prisoners looked up from their meals to see what was going on. But no one said anything. No one complained that they were deserving of freedom, too. They were too hungry to make much of a ruckus—which was exactly what the lawman had anticipated.

Once out in the office with the door to the cell block closed behind him, the sheriff motioned toward his desk, and Hawkes saw a plate of food there.

"If you want to eat before you go, have at it," said the sheriff.

Hawkes shook his head. "Thanks, but I'd rather skip supper, if you don't mind."

"I kind of figured you'd say that. There's a horse in the alley beyond that wall."

"Whose horse?" asked Hawkes.

"Yours, now. Don't worry. It's been paid for. Fair and square."

"You pay for it?"

The Taos lawman nodded. "You can reimburse me someday. Oh, and here." He turned to the gun rack hanging on one wall, unlocked it, took out a Hawken Plains rifle that looked very familiar to the mountain man. "I believe this is yours." He tossed it across the room, and Hawkes caught it readily. "You hocked it to pay off the doctors, as I understand. Well, you're going to need it where you're going."

Hawkes looked the rifle over for a moment, then glanced at the sheriff. He wasn't very good at expressing himself, even to those he knew well, and much less to strangers. "Why are you doing this?"

The sheriff chuckled. "You could have just said thanks."

"Thanks. But why are you doing it? Seems to me you'll likely catch a lot of hell for helping me this way. You're letting a man wanted for murder just ride out of town, scot-free."

"Yes, I know exactly what I'm doing. You don't need to remind me. And you're right. I'll catch hell because of it. But I don't care. I'm not sure I can even explain it, but it just feels like this is the right thing to do. I could be wrong."

Hawkes slowly shook his head. "You're not. I didn't kill that gentleman down in New Orleans. Or the lawyer in Missouri."

"Then you are a man who has gotten more than his fair share of bad luck, I'd say."

"I've had some good luck along the way," murmured Hawkes. "Take tonight, for instance."

"Yeah, well, you better get going. If I were you I would ride through the night, put as many miles between me and Taos as I could before daybreak. Might be that once the town finds out I let you go, one or two men—or more—might get a notion to go after you, and I might not have a chance to stop them."

Hawkes nodded. "I'm obliged. And I will pay you back."

"Fair enough. Oh, I almost forgot." The sheriff reached into his coat and pulled out the letter Hawkes had written to his daughter. "I reckon you might as well deliver this in person. Now go. Hope you don't mind if I sit down to your dinner."

"No, I don't mind at all."

The sheriff went to the door, opened it and stepped out into the night to take a careful look up and down the street. Seeing nothing out of the ordinary, he motioned for Hawkes to emerge from the jail. The mountain man did so—and paused to breathe free air for the first time in entirely too many days.

"Get going," said the Taos lawman.

Hawkes felt as though he hadn't said enough in expressing his gratitude to the sheriff, but he couldn't think of any more words to get that accomplished—so, instead, he slipped around the corner of the adobe building into the alley. As the sheriff had promised, a horse was waiting for him there, a sorrel gelding with a blaze on his face and one white stocking. In a glance, even in the dark, Hawkes could see that this was no broomtail hag, but rather a cayuse with spirit and stamina. Just how much spirit and stamina remained to be seen. Climbing into the saddle, Hawkes goaded the horse out of the alley. The Taos lawman was still standing in front of the jail, framed in the lamplight spilling out of the open door behind him. The sheriff merely nodded. Hawkes tapped the gelding with his heels, and the horse responded, carrying him down the quiet street and out of Taos at a rapid clip.

Though he was aware that the sheriff's advice regarding putting some distance between himself and the town was sound, he couldn't help but make one stop. At the edge of town was the cemetery—the final resting place for the woman he had loved so fiercely for thirty years. It was impossible for him to ride past without stopping. Leaving the sorrel at the gate in the low perimeter wall fashioned of stones, he moved through the tombstones to the place where Eliza laid. A small wooden tombstone had been erected there—Hawkes had wished he'd been able to afford one of stone, but that had not been the case.

For a long while he stood there, staring at the mound of earth. He still couldn't quite believe that she was gone. And he couldn't yet figure out how he was supposed to get through life without her. At least for the moment he had a purpose, a reason to go on living. Something he hadn't thought possible ten days ago. Grace was in jeopardy, and he was going to make sure she remained safe. But after he had accomplished that mission, then what? He didn't have an answer for that.

Kneeling beside the grave, Hawkes laid a hand on the mound of earth, digging his fingers into it. "I sure hate to leave you," he whispered. "I left you so many times before. So much time we spent apart—I wish I had spent those days with you. I—I wish a lot of things had been different . . ."

He wiped a tear from his eye, choking on emotion. Unable to say anything more, he rose and turned and walked away, finding it hard to walk upright, feeling like he wanted to double over, so severe was the pain welling up inside him. Reaching the sorrel, he blindly pulled himself into the saddle and rode away.

Crossing the desert plain north of Taos, he could see mountains to the northwest. The Rockies. The high country he had called home for all his adult life. His refuge, his sanctuary. But they weren't anymore. Bathed in the silver moonlight, those snow-capped peaks merely looked lonesome and forbidding to him now. He didn't know if he could set foot in those mountains again, now that Eliza was gone. Because that had been their home. Not just a cabin in some remote valley, but the whole magnificent, wild sprawl of it. And without her to share them with, Hawkes found those mountains distinctly unappealing. Empty inside, he rode on alone, serenaded by coyotes, watched over by the stars—a man with only one thing left to do before he died.

When someone started pounding on the door of the shack in which Red Renshaw slept with the Mexican woman who had been his companion nightly since his arrival in Taos, he came instantly awake and reacted instinctively by groping for the pistol that lay on top of a pile of clothing beside the narrow bed. The woman woke, too, with a start and a stifled gasp, but Renshaw cut short any further noise from that source by clamping a big hand over her mouth. Besides, until he knew with certainty who was on the other side of that door, he wanted to keep the woman close beside him. He'd heard of plenty of cases where such women were in cahoots with one or more male accomplices, with their scheme being to relieve an unsuspecting pilgrim of his money—if not his life. Renshaw didn't have very many pesos left, but he had kept this information from her, so he realized that she might possibly think he was still worth robbing.

There was a pause—and then more pounding on the door, more forcefully this time. So forcefully, in fact, that Renshaw began to wonder if the door would stay on its old leather hinges. The shack, located in an alleyway behind the cantina, wasn't the flimsiest structure Renshaw had ever seen, but it was close. The plank walls had warped and weathered, so that there were slits through which the wind could whistle and the cold could infiltrate the interior; the roof had a hole in it through which one could see the stars in the sky. Precisely because the walls were so full of gaps, Renshaw didn't dare light the lamp that stood on a small table in the corner—the only other piece of furniture, if you wanted to call it that, in the room save for the narrow bed he and the prostitute had been sharing a moment before.

"Who the hell is it?" asked Renshaw gruffly. "You've got three seconds to identify yourself before I start shooting."

"It's me—Dooley. For God's sakes Red, keep your finger off the trigger."

Renshaw cursed under his breath—wishing, and not for the first time, that he had never made the acquaintance of that buffalo runner.

"Go away," he growled. "Leave me alone, god-dammit."

"We got to talk, Red. It's about Hawkes. Open the damn door."

Renshaw thought it over. Then he removed his hand from the woman's mouth and pushed her, none too gently, onto the bed. "You stay there," he murmured, "and don't move an inch until I tell you to. *Comprende?*"

She nodded, eyes wide, and pulled a soiled sheet up under her chin to at least partially conceal her nakedness. Which was an odd show of modesty, mused Renshaw, as he moved cautiously toward the door, for a woman who had sold her body to untold numbers of men. But then he had never pretended to understand women.

Still gripping the pistol, Renshaw lifted the door latch and swung the portal open, stepping to one side so that all Dooley could see when he looked into the shack was the pistol aimed right at him.

"Are you alone, Dooley?" asked Renshaw.

"Yes."

"Where are your new partners?"

"They're waiting out front of the cantina."

Renshaw stepped into view, peering out to make sure that Dooley was indeed by himself. Dooley blinked, more than a little surprised by Renshaw's nakedness. But his attention was focused for the most part on the big horse pistol aimed right at him.

"What are you waiting out there for?" asked Renshaw. "It's the middle of the night."

"We just found out, a little while ago, that Hawkes is gone."

"What do you mean, gone?"

"The sheriff let him go."

Renshaw couldn't believe his ears. "And how did you find that out?"

"One of the other prisoners. He was in a cell next to Hawkes. The sheriff arrested him yesterday for disorderly conduct. His friends bailed him out this evening. I was waiting outside the jail, just watching over things, when he come out. So I followed him. He went to the nearest saloon. I bought him a drink. And he told me that the sheriff had let Hawkes go right after sundown."

"Now why would he do a thing like that?"

"How the hell would I know? But the Spaniard, he says we'll find out."

Renshaw didn't like the sound of that. "I wouldn't tangle with the sheriff, if I was you."

"But he's the only one who might know what direction Hawkes took when he rode out of town. And besides, the Spaniard insists on it. You going to tell him not to?"

"I never said I was a party to this," reminded Renshaw.

"Well, you better make up your mind," said Dooley.

"And what if I say no?"

Dooley's smile was as cold as a blue norther. "The Spaniard seems to think you need to come with us, now that you know what our plan is. I ain't too sure he would leave without you."

Renshaw knew what that meant. Dooley didn't have to spell it out. It was what he had been worried about from the very beginning—that Dooley and his new partners might not want to risk leaving him behind, in case he had a notion to tell someone else about their scheme.

"You don't need me anymore," he said, hoping against hope that he could talk his way out of the dilemma. "Hawkes is on his own. Now you and your friends can try to bring him down. Don't need someone who can make a long shot to bring down some U.S. Marshal."

"You better come along, Red," advised Dooley. "The Spaniard is the last man I'd want to cross, was I you."

"You haven't met Gordon Hawkes yet."

Dooley shrugged and began to turn away. "Suit yourself. Don't say I didn't warn you, though."

Renshaw hesitated only a fraction. "Hold on," he growled crossly. "Tell 'em I'm coming. But I got to get my damn clothes on first."

Dooley nodded, and Renshaw shut the door in his face. Lighting the lamp and turning it down low, he dressed quickly. The woman sat on the edge of the bed, watching him intently.

"You go away?" she asked.

"Looks that way, don't it?"

"I will wait for you, if you want."

Renshaw stared at her—then threw his head back and laughed heartily. "No, that's okay. I couldn't afford it." He knew what she was after—more money. Trying to get him to believe that if he paid her well enough she would save herself for his return. As though any man in his right mind would buy that.

She stood up, and let the sheet drop, and Renshaw had to admit that she had a body built to lure a man to his doom.

"If you must go, then make love to me one more time," she said, using her most seductive voice.

"I'd love to," he said, grinning wolfishly. "But this one will have to be on the house."

"What do you mean?"

"I mean I'm one broke son of a bitch, so it'll have to be a free ride."

Her expression suddenly cold, she grabbed up the sheet and wrapped it around her body and sat down on the bed. "Go away," she said flatly.

Chuckling, Renshaw finished dressing. Without another glance in her direction, he stepped out into the night, shutting the rickety door behind him.

As he came around the corner of the cantina he saw Dooley and the two Comancheros standing in the dark shadows against the adobe wall of the establishment. Their horses were tied to a rail nearby. Renshaw didn't fail to notice that his horse was also tied there. Dooley knew his cayuse, so Renshaw figured it was the buffalo runner who had located the animal in a livery down the street. As far as the livery owner was concerned, Dooley and Renshaw were still partners in the buffalohide enterprise, so it wasn't all that surprising that the man would give Dooley custody of the horse. Still, Renshaw was more than a little annoyed.

"Looks like you figured I wouldn't say no," he told Dooley, nodding at the horse.

Dooley smiled dryly. "No, I thought all along you'd see reason—and know what was in your best interests."

"Besides," said the Spaniard coldly, "we would have taken your horse anyway."

"Over my dead body," was Renshaw's quick retort. Then, belatedly, he understood what the Spaniard meant. "Which was the idea, right?"

"Let's go," said the Spaniard curtly. He went to his horse, gathered up the reins, and began walking up the street. The Breed fell in beside him. Dooley and Renshaw brought up the rear. They walked up the street two blocks, then turned onto one of the town's main thoroughfares. Another block, and they were nearing the jail. Lamplight gleamed in the office window. The Spaniard secured his horse to the post in front of the jail, and the others followed suit. The door opened and light spilled out around the shape of a man standing on the threshold. Renshaw recognized him—it was the Taos sheriff. He had heard them.

"Who are you and what do you want?" asked the lawman.

Renshaw realized that the sheriff's eyes had not yet adjusted to the night, and that he hadn't identified any of them—yet. The Spaniard knew this, too, and saw it as a momentary advantage. He stepped forward—and jabbed the barrel of his pistol into the sheriff's midriff.

"Back up," said the Comanchero.

The Taos sheriff stepped back. As soon as the Spaniard was through the door he smashed the barrel of his pistol across the lawman's head. The sheriff went down, stunned and bleeding from a deep gash across his temple. Instinctively he groped for the pistol in the holster on his hip, but as soon as he had cleared leather the Spaniard kicked the weapon out of his hand. The gun skidded across the floor of the office and came to rest beneath the desk.

Dooley went in behind the Spaniard. Renshaw hesitated, hoping that the Breed might make a mistake and step inside, too—giving him an opportunity to make a break for it. But the Breed was no fool. With a sneering grin, he gestured for Renshaw to precede him, and Renshaw had no choice but to do so. The Breed came in last, and shut the door.

"You bastard," muttered the Taos sheriff, glaring up at the Spaniard and blinking away the blood that trickled into his eye. "You'll pay for that."

"Where did Hawkes go?" asked the Comanchero, manifestly indifferent to the lawman's threat.

"Hawkes?" The sheriff looked at each of them in turn. His gaze came to rest on Renshaw's grim features. "What is this all about?"

"We want to know where Hawkes went," said Dooley. "If I were you, I'd speak up."

The sheriff did not move his gaze from Renshaw's face. "I thought you were a friend of his."

Renshaw sighed. He was in a bad spot, and he had no idea how to get out of it. But he decided that the more important matter, at least for the moment, was trying to get the sheriff out of his own predicament.

"Just tell them what they want to know," he said.

"I have no idea where he went."

"You're lying," said the Spaniard—and kicked the sheriff in the ribs, so quickly and unexpectedly that Renshaw jumped. Groaning, the sheriff tried to roll away, but as he did so the Comanchero kicked him again, this time in the small of the back, a blow that left the lawman writhing in pain. Holstering his pistol, the Spaniard drew his knife and glanced at the Breed. "Get him up."

The Breed moved in and pulled the sheriff roughly to his feet, pinning his arms behind his back. The Spaniard stepped up and placed the point of the blade against the lawman's throat, just below the left ear—and pressed slightly. The razor-sharp point pierced the man's skin.

"Damn it," muttered Renshaw. "Just tell him, for Chrissake!"

"Hawkes rode north," said the sheriff, through clenched teeth. "North to Powder River country."

"Powder River?" asked the Spaniard. Clearly he had no idea where the Powder River was located.

"Sioux country," said Renshaw. "I hear they're having a little war up there between the Indians and the Army."

"Why is Hawkes going there?" asked Dooley.

"His daughter is married to a cavalry officer," said the Taos sheriff. "Hawkes wants to make sure she's safe."

"Okay," said Renshaw. "So now we know where Hawkes is headed. Let him go."

The Spaniard looked at him with eyes that were as lifeless as a shark's. He smiled faintly—before driving the blade deep into the Taos sheriff's neck and, with a vicious horizontal stroke, cutting the lawman's throat. He stepped back as bright red blood spewed from this gaping wound. Horrified, frozen in place, Renshaw heard the sheriff make a horrible sound, his body thrashing. The Breed let him go, and he fell, writhed for a moment, and then lay still.

"Jesus," muttered Dooley, staring at the dead man in shock.

The Spaniard wiped the knife's blade clean on a trouser leg, then sheathed it. He was watching Renshaw. "Now you will *have* to ride with us."

And Renshaw knew the Comanchero was right. Because now he was an accomplice to murder—the murder of a law officer. Just like Gordon Hawkes, he would be a fugitive from justice.

The Spaniard extinguished the lamp that provided illumination for the room. Moving to the door, he opened it, scanned the street carefully before stepping out into the night. The Breed followed, as did

Renshaw and Dooley, neither of whom had any inclination to linger in the jail. They mounted up and rode north out of Taos. Renshaw thought it odd that while the night was warm he felt as chilled to the bone as if he were trapped in the high country in the middle of a blizzard. He wasn't too sure if he would ever warm up again. He was not a man prone to flights of fancy, but he couldn't shake the feeling that Death was riding with them.

Chapter Ten

Gordon Hawkes was making good time. He traveled all through the first night, then spent a few hours resting himself and his horse in a dry wash before pressing on well past sundown. A few hours later he stopped for the second time and made camp, leaving before daybreak and traveling through the day, stopping only a few times to dismount, loosen the saddle cinch and give the sorrel a little water from the canteen the Taos sheriff had thoughtfully provided. Fortunately, he located a spring later that day, and filled the canteen, which by then was empty.

Renshaw, Dooley, and the Comancheros traveled through their first night out of Taos as well. The Breed picked up what he believed was Hawkes's sign, and this they followed, while keeping a close eye on their back trail. Renshaw expected the Taos sheriff's death would result in the formation of a posse. Question was, would the posse pick up their trail? Had anyone seen them at the jail that night? Had anyone witnessed their departure out of town? If not, there was little to worry about. Renshaw worried anyway. Taos was a bustling town, and a lot of people came and went all the time. So would anyone connect his sudden disappearance—along with the

departure of Dooley and the Comancheros—with the
sheriff's death? Only time would tell.

It was after sundown on the third day that they
finally caught up with Hawkes.

Renshaw was surprised to see that the mountain
man had started a cook fire. Sitting his horse, along
with the others, on some high ground almost a quarter of a mile to the south, he could see the pinprick
of light that marked the location of the fire. Hawkes
had picked for his camp a site at the base of a rock
outcropping that curled like a snake about two hundred yards east and west. At such a great distance,
in the dark, they could not identify the occupant of
that camp, but they didn't have much doubt that it
was Hawkes. This was lonely country, and they
hadn't seen a sign of any other human since leaving Taos.

"That must be him," said Dooley, putting their
thoughts into words. "So, what are we waiting for?
Let's go down there and finish him off."

"Sure you don't want to wait here?" asked Renshaw dryly. "Would be safer for you, that way."

Dooley just scowled at him, trying to come up with
a retort. Before he could, the Spaniard spoke.

"No, we will wait until daybreak."

"But why wait?" asked Dooley. "That's him.
Bound to be. Ten thousand dollars down there, gentlemen. For the taking."

"No," said the Spaniard coldly. "If we ride in now,
he might slip away in the darkness. We wait until
first light." He glanced at Renshaw. "And then you
will kill him, at long range."

Renshaw made no response. They dismounted and

settled down into a cold camp. The Breed took the first watch, keeping an eye on the distant fire. Renshaw rolled up in his blanket, reins tied around one wrist and a hand resting on his rifle, and tried to get some sleep. He was bone-tired after three long days in the saddle. But sleep wouldn't come. He couldn't stop thinking about what the morning might bring. He didn't think he could bring himself to shoot Hawkes. But if he didn't, the Spaniard would kill him. And he couldn't get the image of the Taos sheriff's terrible last seconds out of his mind. It was either him or Gordon Hawkes. There didn't seem to be any other option available to him. It wasn't that Hawkes was a good friend, or even much of an acquaintance. It wasn't like that at all. So why, Renshaw asked himself, was he having so much trouble justifying a long-distance killing shot? He'd done a great many things that he wasn't proud of in the past. But he had never shot down a man in cold blood. He had never committed murder. And he didn't know if he could do it now, even to save his own life.

It was a long night of mental anguish for Renshaw—but when the first shreds of daylight colored the eastern sky he found himself regretting that it hadn't been longer. His moment of truth fast approached. He lay there in his blankets, feigning sleep, until the Spaniard stirred, rose, and came over to nudge him with a booted foot.

"It's time," said the Comanchero.

Renshaw got up. Following the Spaniard to the high ground from where they had seen the distant camp the night before, he noticed that the mountain man's fire had gone out. He could scarcely locate

Hawkes's camp at this distance. The Spaniard had a spyglass, which he used to scan the base of the rock outcropping. After a moment he handed this to Renshaw, who quickly located the camp. It appeared that Hawkes was still sleeping, wrapped in a blanket. A sorrel horse stood nearby. A wisp of smoke rose from a pile of ash in a circle of stones a few feet away from the sleeping man.

"Make the shot," said the Spaniard. "Do it now, before he gets up."

"It would be better to wait."

"Do it now."

"I have to get closer. Or wait until there's better light."

The Spaniard stared at him for a moment, his dark, hawkish features impassive. Renshaw had no clue what the man was thinking—but he was sure he wouldn't like it.

"How much closer?"

"A few hundred yards, at least."

The Spaniard thought it over. Finally he nodded. Telling the Breed and Dooley to stay behind, he motioned for Renshaw to proceed. "I will come with you," he said.

Toting his rifle and cartridge pouch, Renshaw trudged toward the distant rock outcropping. It was open ground, arid and rocky, and slightly rolling, so that now and then the distant camp was out of sight. Renshaw hoped against hope that Hawkes would suddenly awake and notice them. But the form in the blankets did not move.

"Okay," said the Spaniard. "This is far enough."

Renshaw checked his rifle's load, then got down on

one knee. He preferred shooting from that position, resting the elbow of his extended arm on his knee. He estimated the wind and range and lined up his shot. There was only one thing left to do. Pull the trigger. And in that instant he made up his mind. he knew what he would have to do.

Just as Renshaw was about to squeeze the trigger, the Spaniard grabbed the barrel of the rifle and wrenched it upward.

"You're not going to do it," said the Comanchero flatly.

"What?"

"You're going to miss, on purpose."

Renshaw noticed then that the Spaniard had his knife in hand—the knife that he had used to cut the throat of the Taos sheriff.

"I don't know what you're talking about," he said, trying to keep his voice steady.

"Yes you do. You'll miss on purpose, and claim it was an accident."

Renshaw jerked his rifle out of the Spaniard's grasp and stood up. "Fine," he said curtly. "Then go kill him yourself, if that's what you think."

The Spaniard glanced at the mountain man's camp, then back at Renshaw, and the latter thought he knew what the Comanchero was thinking. The man was debating the merits of killing Renshaw right here and now or waiting until the business at hand was concluded. Renshaw decided that it was in his best interests to help the Spaniard make up his mind—and leveled his rifle at the man.

"Go ahead and try it," growled Renshaw. "Now I know what you're thinking. You might kill me, I'll grant you that. But I sure as hell won't go quiet."

The Spaniard realized his mistake. He had drawn the knife because killing with a blade was a quiet way to kill, and he did not want to alert the sleeping mountain man. But suddenly he found himself at a distinct disadvantage. He had a pistol in his belt, but he had to assume that if he reached for that weapon Renshaw would shoot him.

He nodded curtly in the direction of their own camp. "We go back," he said.

For a moment Renshaw considered making a break for Hawkes's camp. But if he tried that the Comanchero would resort to his pistol—there would be no reason not to, with the prospect of Hawkes being alerted to their presence anyway. Better yet, he could kill the Spaniard and then make a break for it. He glanced quickly behind him, toward the high ground where they had left the Breed and Dooley. And it was then that he saw the Breed standing there, a few hundred yards away, rifle to shoulder. Renshaw knew he was in the Breed's sights.

The Spaniard was wearing that cold smile of his. "We go back—or you die here."

"After you," muttered Renshaw.

The Comanchero shrugged and started walking.

Renshaw didn't know what else to do but follow. If he didn't, the Breed would shoot. He was certain of that. And while he was a dead man anyway sooner or later, he much preferred later.

When they reached the others, Renshaw just kept walking—straight to his horse.

"Where the hell are you going?" asked Dooley.

"I'm leaving. Riding out."

The Breed had lowered his rifle—now he began to

raise it again, and there was little doubt in Renshaw's mind that this time he would shoot. Except that the Spaniard restrained him.

"I want no part of this," said Renshaw, aiming his remarks at the Spaniard. "Now, the three of you can try Hawkes on for size if that's what you want to do. But I'm not in this game."

"If you approach his camp we will shoot you," warned the Spaniard.

Renshaw swung into the saddle. "You don't think I know that?" he asked caustically.

The Spaniard merely nodded—and Renshaw jerked on the reins, spinning his horse around and riding due east. He didn't look back. Didn't need to; he figured the Breed was keeping him in his sights as long as he was in range.

When at last Renshaw was out of range the Spaniard turned to his horse. Mounting up, he ordered Dooley and the Breed to do likewise.

"We will ride in slow. Get as close as we can. If Hawkes makes a move, we close quickly and finish it."

Dooley nodded, without enthusiasm. He had hinged his hopes on a long shot from Red Renshaw to bring Hawkes down, and he hadn't thought he would have to get involved in the actual killing. It wasn't at all to his liking, but then what choice did he have now? If he tried to back out he would lose his share, for sure—and, quite possibly, his life. He noted with dismay that his hands were shaking slightly as he checked his pistol. The two Comancheros were already on the move, holding their horses to a walk, advancing on the distant camp.

Dooley fell in alongside the Spaniard. He figured that at any moment Hawkes would hear their approach and spring into action. But the form in the blankets never moved. Dooley could scarcely believe it. They were actually sneaking up on the legendary mountain man! Maybe Gordon Hawkes wasn't everything he was made out to be, after all.

When they were about a hundred yards from the camp, the Spaniard checked his horse, and in a glance Dooley could tell that the Comanchero was getting suspicious. Dooley looked again at the blanket-wrapped form. Could it be . . . ? There was only one way to find out.

He raised his pistol and fired. The bullet struck the ground inches from the sleeping man—much to Dooley's chagrin, as he had aimed for the man and not the ground. Startled by the gunshot, Dooley's horse began to fiddlefoot, which made hitting a target from the saddle that much more difficult, but Dooley gave it a try anyway. This time, more by accident than by design, he hit the blanket-wrapped form.

"I got him!" he shouted, exultant.

A second later he was dead.

The bullet hit him in the head, entering one temple and exiting the other side, taking half of Dooley's face with it in an explosion of blood and bone. Even as he tried to control his prancing horse, and at the same time spot the source of the killing shot, the Spaniard had to admire the marksmanship of Dooley's killer. Dooley's corpse flopped to the ground. His horse tried to flee, but in death Dooley had held on to the reins, and now the hand holding those reins was trapped beneath the weight of his body. A second shot rang out—and this time the Breed's horse made a grunting sound and went down abruptly. The Breed was just able to jump clear. Seeing this, the Spaniard leaped from his own saddle, but not before drawing his rifle from the leather sheath strapped to the hull so that it ordinarily rode beneath his right leg. The Spaniard's horse took flight. A third shot killed Dooley's horse. This time the Spaniard, seeking cover with the Breed behind the carcass of the latter's cayuse, saw the puff of smoke. It came from halfway up the rock outcropping, above the mountain man's camp. Cursing profusely, the Spaniard got off a quick shot, even though he knew it was probably just a waste of ammunition. Hawkes was dug in deep among the rocks and had them pinned down.

He felt the vibration in the ground beneath his body before he heard the thunder of hooves—and the Spaniard rolled over on his back and looked behind him to see Red Renshaw charging right at him on his galloping horse. Drawing his pistol, the Spaniard took aim and fired, just as Renshaw brought his rifle to bear. But the Comanchero knew from experience just how difficult it was to make a shot from the back of a hard-running pony, and he didn't even flinch as Renshaw's bullet plowed into the ground a few feet away. He didn't miss his own shot, and with great satisfaction saw Renshaw somersault over the back of his horse. Renshaw hit the ground hard, and the Spaniard was confident that he wouldn't get up again. So he was quite amazed when Renshaw struggled to his feet.

The Breed, wanting to be the one to finish Renshaw off, made a mistake of his very own in that instant—rising up to take careful aim at the wounded man, and exposing himself momentarily to Hawkes. Before the Spaniard could issue a warning, the bullet struck the Breed squarely between the shoulder blades and hurled him to the ground. He lived just long enough to reach out and claw at the sandy soil, as though he were trying to crawl away. A single violent shudder racked his body—and then he breathed no more.

Still stumbling forward, Renshaw fumbled for the pistol in his belt. The Spaniard shot him down. Again Renshaw fell, toppling backward, and this time he didn't get up. Renshaw's horse was veering off as it approached the Breed's dead pony, and the Spaniard saw his one chance. He didn't hesitate, leaping to his feet and lunging at the horse, getting a hand on the saddle horn as the cayuse thundered past. He swung aboard, staying low, gathering up the reins and steering the cayuse around. He heard another gunshot, but neither he nor the horse under him was hit, and he kicked it into greater effort and was quickly out of rifle range.

Red Renshaw wasn't sure how long he laid there, flat on his back, staring up at the sun-bleached blue expanse of sky above him and feeling his life slowly leak out of him. He couldn't move—it was entirely too painful. Hell, it was hard enough just to breathe. He figured the best thing to do was just to lie there, as still as possible, and wait until Death came to claim him. How many breaths were left to him? He tried to count them. Tried not to think about anything else besides counting.

He was nearing fifty when a shadow fell over him, and he realized that he had been slipping away into a kind of half-conscious daze before the movement of the shadow snapped him out of it. He tried to focus on the shape that loomed over him, but couldn't quite manage until the man knelt down beside him. Only then did Renshaw recognize Gordon Hawkes. Renshaw would have uttered a curse, except that he didn't have the strength. He'd hoped that he wouldn't have to face Hawkes. It hardly seemed fair that the last emotion he would ever have was intense shame. That made him angrier than the fact that he had been killed by the Spaniard.

"I'm sorry," he mumbled, his voice hoarse, the words slurred.

"Forget it," said the mountain man.

"I'm dying, I reckon."

Hawkes looked at him for a moment, his features as expressionless as stone. "That depends on you. Do you want to live?"

What kind of question was that? "Hell, yes."

"Then make up your mind that you're going to live, and you just might." Hawkes took a look around, and his eyes settled on the mountains to the west.

"I've got two bullets in me," said Renshaw. "I just don't know where. But it sure feels like they ain't in a good place."

"You were hit in the shoulder and the hip. You're bleeding pretty badly, but we can slow that down. With any luck we can be in the Absaroke summer camp by late tomorrow."

"The Absaroke?"

Hawkes nodded. "Last I heard, they were sum-
mering in the mountains due west of here."

"I don't think I'll make it to the mountains."

"I'll rig up some saddles as a travois of sorts," said
Hawkes, "and I'll take you to the Absaroke. They'll
tend to you. That's all I can do. It's up to you
whether you live long enough to get there."

"I'll try."

Hawkes nodded, and Renshaw thought he
glimpsed the ghost of a smile haunt the corner of the
mountain man's mouth. "Good. I'd hate to go to all
this trouble for nothing."

He rose and moved out of Renshaw's view. Renshaw closed his eyes and concentrated on breathing.
It was funny, he thought, how you took such important things as breathing for granted.

Chapter Eleven

Gordon Hawkes felt his spirits lift when he came down out of the pass and into the sheltered valley and saw the skin lodges arrayed along a stream that meandered through fields of luxuriantly deep grass interspersed with stands of timber. Many times he had come down out of the mountains to visit the Absaroke, and in the vast majority of those occasions he had been welcomed by the Crow. He and the Absaroke had a long history, stretching back thirty years, back to the time when he had first ventured west with an expedition launched by the Rocky Mountain Fur Company. Over time they had come to accept him as one of their own, and among some of the other tribes he was also known as White Crow.

Nearing the village, Hawkes glanced behind him at Red Renshaw. He had taken the saddles from the two horses he had killed in his clash with Renshaw's companions and strapped them together using rope. Upon this makeshift travois he had laid the wounded man—and had then proceeded to drag the saddles for two days, across the plains and into the mountains. It had not been easy going, especially the negotiation of the high pass that now lay behind them, and Hawkes was frankly amazed that Renshaw was still alive. He wasn't sure, though, how much longer that would be the case. Renshaw had lost a lot of blood, and he had been slipping in and out of consciousness—more out than in of late.

Several braves rode out to greet him, but as soon as they got within a hundred yards Hawkes was recognized, and immediately one of the Absaroke checked his pony abruptly, wheeled it around, and galloped back to the village to spread the news of his arrival. The other two rode up and greeted the mountain man with friendly smiles, while gazing curiously at the wounded man—and the rig upon which Renshaw was laid out. Several more riders approached from the village, and beyond them Hawkes could see that the Absaroke were gathering among their skin lodges to observe. One of the riders was someone very familiar to Hawkes: He Smiles Twice, one of the mountain man's closest friends. He Smiles Twice had ridden with Cameron Hawkes to rescue his father from the Dakota Sioux some years ago. Now he was a chief of this Crow band.

"It has been a long time, my brother," said He Smiles Twice, immensely pleased.

"Too long," said Hawkes. He dismounted and used his knife to cut the rope that attached the saddle-rig to his own hull. Then he undid the bindings that lashed Renshaw to the rig. He'd had to tie the wounded man down during the long climb to the pass and the subsequent descent. He Smiles Twice motioned for two of the braves to dismount and bade them carry Renshaw the rest of the way to the village. He didn't have to inquire whether the wounded man was a friend of Hawkes—that was evident, just as it was clear why the mountain man had brought him here. Gathering up the sorrel's reins, Hawkes followed the two braves. He Smiles Twice dismounted and walked alongside of him. The other braves brought up the rear of this procession on horseback, leading the ponies of the pair who were transporting Renshaw.

"Two winters have passed since we have seen you last," He Smiles Twice said. "Why have you not come to visit?"

"Eliza was sick for a long while," said Hawkes. "She's dead now."

He Smiles Twice was shocked. He had known Eliza well. Often Hawkes and his wife would spend many summer days among the Absaroke, and they would bring their children, Cameron and Grace, with them. His own wife and Eliza had become friends, just as the mountain man's children had been befriended by his young sons and daughters. The news of Eliza's passing was unsettling. Though slight of build, Eliza had been a very resilient woman, and He Smiles Twice had been completely unaware of any illness. It saddened him to think that she was gone to the other world. But it saddened him even more to think of the torment her passing must be causing his good friend. The grief did not show, but He Smiles Twice knew it was there, running deep and strong inside Hawkes.

"And your daughter?" asked the Absaroke.

"As far as I know, she's still alive. But she may be in danger." And Hawkes proceeded to tell He Smiles Twice what he knew of the situation Grace was in, concluding that concise narrative with the news that he was on his way north to the Powder River country.

"The Sioux will remember you," said He Smiles Twice.

Hawkes nodded. His daring escape from the Dakota had become legend in the Sioux nation, as had his fight to the death with the famed war chief Long Horse, which had occurred as a part of that escape. As a result, his scalp would be highly prized among the Sioux. Any warrior who killed him would be greatly honored. It was, in a way, very flattering that the Sioux considered him one of their greatest enemies, respecting his prowess as they did that of few white men. Hawkes knew what He Smiles Twice meant to convey with that comment. It was a warning.

"I don't have any choice," he replied. "I have to go."

He Smiles Twice knew Hawkes well enough to know that this was so, and he had no intentions of trying to talk the mountain man out of it.

"Stay until the sun rises tomorrow," he suggested.

Again Hawkes nodded. He had been on the move almost constantly since leaving Taos and had gotten very little sleep for days. And the sorrel needed time to graze. Tomorrow, he decided, would be soon enough to be on the move again.

Hawkes was welcomed into the lodge of He Smiles Twice and given a good meal. Afterward, he and his friend sat around a fire outside the entrance to the lodge and smoked a pipe. Numerous Absaroke braves as well as many children came by to welcome the mountain man. Hawkes was deeply moved by the genuine affection these people showed him. But they were, after all, *his* people, much more so than his own kind. He had long felt this way.

That night he slept in the chief's lodge, and slept well. Very early the next morning he rose and went to the lodge where Red Renshaw was located. The Absaroke woman charged with caring for Renshaw had cleaned his wounds and placed poultices on them to draw out the poison of infection. He seemed to be resting peacefully, and not wanting to disturb him, Hawkes turned to go. At that moment Renshaw's eyes flickered open.

"Hawkes?" His voice was weak, barely more than a whisper. "That you, Hawkes?"

"Yes." It was still fairly dark in the lodge, and Hawkes assumed that Renshaw could not see him clearly. "How are you feeling?"

"Where am I?"

"You're in an Absaroke village. They're taking good care of you."

"You brought me here? I don't remember anything after that bastard shot me."

"What do you know about that man?" Hawkes was more than curious about the Comanchero who had gotten away. He needed to know what kind of man he was.

"They call him the Spaniard. He's a Comanchero. A mean son of a bitch, too. He killed the Taos sheriff. Cut his throat. Murdered a man in cold blood and didn't even blink."

Hawkes grimaced. The Taos lawman had been a fair and decent man to whom he'd felt a great obligation.

"I didn't want no part of it," continued Renshaw. "You got to believe that, Hawkes. But the Spaniard would have cut *my* throat if I hadn't gone along. I was just lucky that I got away with my life. I got the drop on him, and he had to let me go. If he tried to stop me it would have alerted you. But then, you were already alerted. How did you know we were there?"

"Just a hunch," said Hawkes. He had seen no evidence of pursuit after leaving Taos, but that wasn't reason enough not to take precautions. To that end, he had arranged his camp so that it appeared he was sleeping in his blankets next to the fire, and took up a position in the rocks above to keep an eye out for interlopers. From that vantage point he had seen Renshaw and the Spaniard approaching his camp on foot, and he had seen the confrontation that then took place between them, one that had culminated in Renshaw's departure. He had seen it—though he hadn't known for certain what it all meant.

"But damn me if I didn't have to come back," said Renshaw. "Don't ask me why. There was just something about the whole deal that rubbed me the wrong way. Guess this is what I get for sticking my nose in somebody else's business." He peered curiously at Hawkes. "How come you saved my life?"

"Not sure I did. You could still die."

Renshaw smiled. "Maybe not. So how come you done what you done? After all, I was a member of that bunch that was bound and determined to kill you. You could have just left me there to die, and been within your rights."

"I guess because you came back."

"You better keep an eye peeled for that Spaniard, Hawkes. I don't think you've seen the last of him."

"Why is he so dead set on getting me? Is it the bounty?"

"More to it than that, I think. Has to do with you killing those other Comancheros. They're vermin, but a close-knit bunch of vermin."

Hawkes nodded. "Well, you're going to stay here for a while, until you heal up. The Absaroke will take good care of you."

As he turned to leave the skin lodge, Renshaw said, "Good luck to you up north."

Hawkes walked out without acknowledging. He Smiles Twice was waiting for him. The Absaroke village was just now beginning to stir. Children were going down to the stream to collect fresh water. Women were resurrecting last night's fires. Some of the braves were gathering to discuss a hunting trip. He Smiles Twice held the reins of the mountain man's sorrel gelding, and as Hawkes emerged from the skin lodge, he extended them toward the mountain man.

"When you are done," said the Crow chief, "you will come back and live with us."

Hawkes mounted up, quickly considering the offer. It occurred to him that he wasn't likely to get a better one. He could not return to the remote cabin where he had spent the last few years with Eliza. There were too many memories there. As a fugitive from justice all these many years, his options had always been very limited. But perhaps among the Absaroke he could make a new home. Not that he really expected to come back from the Powder River country alive. Or cared if he did.

"That sounds good," he said, and reached down to clasp the hand of He Smiles Twice in his own. No further words passed between them. Sometimes, words between good friends were superfluous.

He Smiles Twice watched the mountain man ride out of the village. Only when Hawkes was out of sight did he turn away, going to a nearby skin lodge and speaking briefly to a young woman who was adding wood to a fire before passing inside. Two other young women were inside, preparing bread. Seeing He Smiles Twice, one of them stood up quickly, a question in her eyes. The chief nodded grimly.

"He is gone." He watched her closely, glimpsed the anguished regret that passed briefly across her features.

"Thank you for not telling him," she said.

He Smiles Twice looked at her for a moment, well aware of the connection that existed between this Oglala Sioux woman named Pretty Shield and his friend White Crow. She had first met Hawkes when he was taken captive by the Sioux—and she had fallen in love with him, helped him in his escape. She had helped him, as well, when Hawkes had sought vengeance against the men of Gilder Gulch for the death of his son, Cameron. Then she had gone away, because her presence was a problem for Hawkes. He Smiles Twice did not know what Hawkes felt where Pretty Shield was concerned. It was a subject never broached between them. But he could guess. His sense was that Hawkes had loved this pretty, slender Sioux girl. But the mountain man had also loved Eliza. Sacrificing her own happiness, Pretty Shield had tried to resolve that dilemma for him. He Smiles Twice admired her greatly because of her actions. For that reason he had gone to considerable lengths to make sure the Mountain Crow accepted her. In the years since she had come to live among them, bearing the wampum belt that the Absaroke had long ago bestowed upon Gordon Hawkes, symbolic of their eternal friendship, Pretty Shield had attracted a lot of attention from the young braves. But not once had she expressed the slightest interest in any of them. He Smiles Twice was convinced that she never would, her love for Hawkes was that strong. So now she lived with several Absaroke maidens, young women who, for one reason or another, had no family with which to reside.

"Why did you not want him to know that you were here?" asked He Smiles Twice. "You heard that his woman had died."

Pretty Shield nodded. The news had been a heavy blow. She had always admired Eliza, even while she had envied her. Eliza had shown her every kindness, in spite of the fact that her husband had lived with Pretty Shield for many months. And while no one had ever mentioned it, Eliza had *known*—the way women knew these things—that she and Hawkes had slept together, and that the two of them shared strong feelings for one another.

"You might have comforted him," continued He Smiles Twice. "I think he would have been happy to see you."

"Perhaps," said Pretty Shield, struggling to maintain her composure. She had *wanted* to go to Hawkes, wanted to comfort him, wanted to feel his arms around her once more. Every night she dreamed of being with him again, forever. And yet she simply couldn't go through with it.

He Smiles Twice shook his head. Women were impossible to understand.

"When he has done what he has to do in the land of the Sioux," said the Absaroke chief, "he will come back to live among us. Then you will get another chance, I think."

"Unless my people kill him," said Pretty Shield, in a barely audible whisper.

"Many have tried." He Smiles Twice turned and left the skin lodge.

Stepping outside, Pretty Shield looked at the mountains to the east, where the high pass was located—the pass through which Hawkes would leave the valley. Floundering in second thoughts, she struggled against the urge to go after him. To look into his eyes one more time, just in case he *didn't* come back. She was struck—not for the first time— by how alone she was. The Absaroke had been kind to her, and she had a few friends in the village, but she was still very much alone. She would always be an outsider. There was only one person who could cure her loneliness, and she had just let him ride away because she had not wanted to intrude on his grief. Eliza was dead, but she remained with him, she was still in his heart, still monopolized his thoughts. Pretty Shield had come between them once before. She would not do so again, no matter how much it cost her.

Chapter Twelve

As was his custom, Captain Brand Gunnison arose early—before his wife awakened—and dressed very quietly so as not to disturb her slumber. Slipping out of the quarters that he and Grace had recently been able to move into, he took a look around the parade ground. Before long the bugler would sound reveille, and Fort Phil Kearney, now completed after months of work, would come to life. But for now only a few people stirred, apart from the sentries who moved along the banquettes at the perimeter wall. It had been quiet last night, with no disturbances that Gunnison was aware of. This had been the case for a couple of weeks now, whereas before hardly a night had passed without some gunfire. Following the ambush of Fetterman's command, the Sioux had become emboldened and had proceeded to harass the soldiers as the latter rushed to finish the fort. Slashing forays by bands of warriors had been the norm, and they had come with such nerve-wracking consistency that everybody in the garrison was on edge. But suddenly, inexplicably, all the hostile activity had ceased.

Gunnison noted that there was a nip in the air, and he checked the sky. A line of dark clouds to the north was becoming visible as the sun prepared to

rise in the east. Having lived on the high plains for
more than a half-dozen years, Gunnison knew the
seasons. Knew that those clouds might signify the
first wave of cold weather, and that before long winter storms would begin to sweep across this country.
Provisions for the winter were supposed to be coming up the Bozeman Trail. In spite of that, Bridger
and Gunnison and others had prevailed on General
Carrington to give some thought to dispatching hunting parties to harvest the wild game abundant along
the river. Other detachments were busy cutting timber to use as firewood. The winters up here were
long and bitter as a rule, and it paid to be prepared
for them.

This line of thinking reminded Gunnison that he
needed to tell the sergeant that the walls of his quarters needed some additional chinking. The barracks
and officers' cabins had been constructed of green
wood, and already in places the ever-present wind
whistled through spaces that had appeared between
the square-cut logs. When that wind came out of the
north it could cut to the bone, and Gunnison's foremost concern was his wife's comfort. Grace had not
seemed well these past few weeks. Of course, whenever he asked if she was feeling poorly she would
emphatically deny that anything was wrong. But he
could tell. She seemed wan, listless at times, and certainly lacking the energy she usually exhibited. Gunnison was worried, and her health was constantly in
the forefront of his thoughts.

He headed for the barracks where his men were
housed. A few of the troopers were lounging in front
of the long, rectangular building, and one of them

was the sergeant who, upon seeing Gunnison approach, went inside, appearing a moment later with a cup of coffee, which he offered to the captain. Gunnison took it and sipped the strong brew gratefully.

"Make sure the hunting party gets an early start, Sergeant," he said.

"They're getting ready to go now, Captain."

"Good. And have someone tend to the walls of my cabin, if you don't mind."

"They'll be good as new before the day is out." The sergeant threw a quick look around and then leaned forward. "Captain, I've heard rumors that the general is thinking about sending the women and children back down the trail to safety before the first snow comes. Any truth to that?"

"There had been some discussion along those lines, as a matter of fact." Gunnison peered curiously at the noncom. "Why? You didn't bring anyone along."

The sergeant grinned. "Why, no. I ain't found a woman yet who could put up with me long enough to get hitched. Me and some of the other boys were just wondering, that's all."

Gunnison thought it over. "This has something to do with Laura Denning, doesn't it?"

The sergeant nodded. "Can't put one over on you, can we, Captain?"

"No. Not that you haven't tried," joked Gunnison.

"Just that we're all pretty worried about Mrs. Denning. She doesn't seem to be doing too good. Some of us wonder if she would make it through a winter stuck in this . . ." The sergeant peered bleakly at the outpost, searching for an appropriate word.

"Hellhole?"

The sergeant chuckled. "That's just about right."

Gunnison nodded. He wasn't surprised to learn that Laura Denning had become the subject of conversation in the barracks. Ever since her husband's death, Laura had been in bad shape. She seemed to have lost the will to live. Talk among some of the officers was that she appeared despondent enough to even contemplate suicide. Gunnison wasn't willing to discard that notion, and, like his peers, had begun to keep a close eye on the woman.

"Well," he said, "there's no denying she would probably benefit from a change of scenery. I'm told she has family back east. But the issue is whether it would be safe to transport the women and children down the trail."

"Looks to some like the Injuns have lost interest in us," remarked the sergeant.

"What do you think?"

"I think it might look one way and actually be just the opposite."

Gunnison nodded agreement. Finishing his coffee, he handed the empty cup back to the sergeant and left the barracks, bent on completing his early morning rounds of the fort before a staff meeting scheduled for this morning at post headquarters. Normally, he paid close attention to his surroundings, but this morning he found himself too preoccupied to do so. Thoughts of Laura Denning—disturbing thoughts in and of themselves—gave way to disturbing ruminations about the death of her husband and the reason for that death. Try as he might, Gunnison could manufacture very little animosity towards the Sioux. True, they were ruthless enemies, prone to torturing their captives—on several patrols Gunnison had himself borne witness to the atrocities they could inflict on those unfortunate enough to fall into their hands. They had claimed the lives of nearly one-fourth of his entire company, and those twenty-odd men had been more than just numbers to Gunnison; they were men who, for the most part, he had led through several campaigns, and had come to know and respect. And yet he could not hate the Sioux with the passion that he saw in so many other whites. The Sioux nation was fighting for its very survival, and Gunnison could hardly fault them for that. They knew that with every white man that came west their future was dimmed that much more. Were the situations reversed, Gunnison knew his own kind would fight just as desperately to stave off the inevitable, and in that desperation might resort to brutality.

Thoughts of Laura Denning also brought Grace to mind. His wife had been much subdued since the tragedy of Lieutenant Denning's death. Laura was her best friend at the fort, and she hated to see the despair and pain in the widow's eyes. More than that, mused Gunnison, Laura's unhappy fate had Grace wondering when her day would come—the day that she would find herself in Laura's position, grieving the loss of her own husband. In all their time together, Gunnison had appreciated the fact that while Grace might have preferred that he pursued another, less dangerous line of work, she had recognized his commitment to the Army and had never pressured him to leave it. Not that she had changed to the point where she was now applying that pressure. At least not intentionally. But she no longer seemed inclined to *pretend* to support him in his career. She hated the Army and the threat it posed to her future happiness and she wasn't bothering to hide it anymore. This had put a terrible strain on their relationship. At times Gunnison wished that he had not allowed her to accompany him. Quite apart from the perils involved, he now had something else to be afraid of—namely, that this experience, should they both survive it, would damage their marriage, perhaps irrevocably.

As he drew near the stables, Gunnison noticed that the hunting party—six of his cavalrymen under the command of a corporal—were preparing to leave the fort. They would venture south by west a few miles until striking Clear Creek, a major tributary of the Powder River. There were numerous pine-sheltered draws along that stream that were favored by game. Gunnison was relieved to see that Jim Bridger was mounted up and waiting for the troopers, intent on joining them.

"Thanks for going along," Gunnison told him. "Even though we haven't seen much of the Sioux lately, I'll feel better knowing you're out there keeping an eye peeled for trouble."

"I'll do it," said Old Gabe through a wad of chewing tobacco. "But I ain't tagging along to nursemaid your soldier boys, Captain. I've had a hankering for a nice juicy venison steak for some time now. Those beeves you brought along with you are as tough as leather. I lost a tooth trying to chew my supper the other day, and damn it, I ain't got enough teeth to spare these days."

Gunnison laughed. "Good luck in your hunt, then."

Arms folded and with one leg hooked over his pony's neck in front of the saddlehorn, Bridger peered down at Gunnison, clearly debating whether he should broach a subject he wanted to address. Finally, he said, "I hear tell the general is thinking about going ahead with his plans to build two more outposts along the Bozeman."

"That's what I've heard, too."

"Well, since I ain't going to be at the meeting this morning to voice any objections to such a hare-brained scheme as that, I trust you'll fill in for me."

"I'll do my best. Though I don't get away with back-talking Carrington like you do, Gabe."

Bridger grinned. "I'm thinkin' he's beginning to regret bringing me along on this little picnic."

"Thank God he did, that's all I can say."

The troopers were ready to depart, so Bridger gathered up his rein leather and gave Gunnison a quick nod before wheeling his horse about and joining the rest of the hunting party as it slipped out the water gate at the south corner of the compound.

Gunnison finished making his rounds and arrived at Carrington's quarters moments after the bugler had blown reveille. The post headquarters was a two-room cabin southwest of the parade ground, near the main gate. Carrington used one room as his personal quarters, and the other for business. The latter room contained a long trestle table flanked by benches along with a single chair, and several smaller tables lined the walls—all handmade by artisans in the expedition. There was a big stone hearth in one wall, and someone had built up a fire within its blackened belly. Carrington's personal steward had prepared some coffee in a large urn standing on one of the smaller tables, and some of Gunnison's fellow officers were helping themselves. He passed on the java, spending his time studying a recently drawn map of the area, including a good portion of the nearby Bozeman Trail, that hung on the wall opposite the fireplace. A few moments later, Carrington emerged from his private quarters and everyone snapped to attention. The general gestured for them to be at ease. Gunnison noted that, as usual, his commanding officer looked impeccable in a fresh uniform adorned with plenty of gold braid. One of the benefits, mused the cavalryman, of having a personal steward on hand.

Carrington took the chair at the head of the long table and accepted a cup of coffee while most of the other officers seated themselves on the benches. Gunnison chose to remain standing beneath the map. The general turned his attention to the cavalryman first.

"Did your patrol yesterday turn up anything, Captain?"

"No, sir. We found no fresh sign of the hostiles."

"That's because they've given up," said Captain Fetterman bluntly. "Once we finished this fort they knew it was hopeless. They've tried to run us off and failed, General. Now is the time to strike, and strike hard, while their morale is low. Give me eighty good men and I will drive Red Cloud right out of the Powder River country."

Gunnison stared at Fetterman—and tried not to laugh out loud. "I'd like to remind the captain," he said coolly, striving to keep the disdain from his voice, "that a recent scout by Jim Bridger indicated that Red Cloud was still up on the Powder, with about fifteen hundred lodges. That means at least five thousand warriors on hand."

"If he's got five thousand warriors, then what is he waiting for?" asked Fetterman. "It'll be winter soon, and we all know that Indians don't fight in the snow. His time is running out if he intends to launch an attack against us."

"I doubt he will attack this position," said Captain Powell. "It is too strong."

"I agree," said Carrington. "And Captain Fetterman brings up a point worth considering. Winter will be here before we know it. If we are to accomplish anything else this year, then we had best act quickly. We must proceed, I think, with plans to build an outpost on the Tongue River. And we must decide whether it would be wise to take the women and children out of here."

"Pardon me, sir," said Gunnison, "but I have to say that, in my opinion, that's just the kind of thing Red Cloud is waiting for. He isn't going to waste his men on forays against small patrols. He's waiting for you to send out a sizable detachment. Defeating that detachment will give him a much-needed victory, and will boost the morale of his braves. And it will also whittle down our numbers. And that's what he wants to do. We have six hundred able-bodied men in this garrison. That's more than enough to defend the fort against an attack by a few thousand Sioux. But if we lose very many more men before we are reinforced—which I understand will not occur until the spring—then we are closer to the point where we are no longer adequately able to defend this position."

"Sounds to me," said Fetterman, "as though Captain Gunnison would prefer that we hide behind these walls, do nothing and wait for help to come." He didn't bother trying to keep a mocking tone from his voice.

"That's pretty much my opinion," agreed Gunnison.

"Well, Fetterman," said Carrington, "we can't ignore the fact that Captain Gunnison probably has more experience fighting Indians than any of us in this room. However"—he turned a steady gaze upon the cavalryman—"that experience is confined to campaigning against small bands of marauding Cheyenne and Arapahos. Red Cloud has an army. And fighting him requires more than familiarity with field tactics. Besides, we cannot lose sight of the fact that we were ordered to establish three posts along the Bozeman Trail. To date we have established only one. I fully intend to obey the instructions that General Sherman personally conveyed to me."

Fuming at the slight Carrington had aimed at him, Gunnison kept his mouth shut. It was, he thought, one of the more unfortunate aspects of life in the Army—one had to learn to suffer fools gladly.

"As to sending the women and children away," said Captain Brown, "I'm not sure that would be the wisest course, for several reasons. One, of course, is the risk involved. What would it do to the morale of *this* command if something happened to them? And, it seems we are all in agreement that as long as they remain within the walls of this fort, they are safe from harm. Thirdly, to send them away might send the wrong signal to Red Cloud. It might lead him to believe that we are not confident of our ability to successfully hold this position."

"On the other hand," said Powell, "they would be safer elsewhere. There is no denying that."

"General Sherman suggested that we bring our families along as a way of demonstrating to the nation—and to our enemies—our confidence in the success of this endeavor," Carrington reminded them. "And while I was unable to bring my family, I trust it is safe to say that the presence of loved ones has improved the outlook of those in this command who did."

"But in fact," said Gunnison, "having them here is as much a burden as a blessing, sir."

All the officers looked at him, wondering if this meant that he was advocating the removal of the women and children—this, in spite of the fact that he had just advised against sending out a detachment to construct a post on the Tongue River. Gunnison could tell that this was precisely what General Carrington was thinking.

"There is one woman in particular," added Gunnison, "who may not survive the winter here. That is Lieutenant Denning's widow."

"Nonsense," said Fetterman. "I venture to say that by the time the snow melts she will have taken up with some other, previously unattached officer."

Gunnison was stunned. Then, in the grip of a sudden, violent surge of fury, he advanced on Fetterman, fists clenched. "You son of a bitch," he muttered. "How dare you . . . ?"

"Captain Gunnison!" snapped Carrington.

Gunnison didn't seem to hear. Fetterman leaped to

his feet, taking a step backward, preparing to meet the cavalryman's advance, but Powell and Brown both interjected themselves, the latter restraining Gunnison while Powell kept a wary eye on Fetterman.

"You had better take back those words," rasped Gunnison, "or be prepared to defend them!"

"That's enough!" roared Carrington, on his feet now. "Both of you, stand down! I will not tolerate this. And this quarrel will not be continued elsewhere. Captain Fetterman, your remark was unworthy of a gentleman, and completely uncalled for under any circumstances. You will apologize for it at once."

Fetterman hesitated, his features twisted with anger and resentment. But the stern expression on Carrington's face bought him to his senses.

"I apologize. It was a . . . a thoughtless comment on my part."

"Good," said Carrington. "There will be no further discussion of this incident, either here and now, or elsewhere in the future. Resume your seats, gentlemen."

Fetterman, Powell and Brown sat back down, and Gunnison returned to the wall beneath the map. Still standing, Carrington said, "I do not think it would be wise to send the women and children down the trail at this time. They should be perfectly safe within this fort. But we will proceed with plans to send a detachment to the Tongue River. Captain Fetterman, you will be in command. Unless there is something more, you are dismissed."

Carrington returned to his private quarters while

the rest of the officers filed out of the room. Gunnison was the last to leave, and as he paused just outside the door, watching the others disperse, he was approached by the sergeant.

"Captain, I think you better come with me."

"What's wrong?"

"The hunting party just got back."

"Already? What happened?"

The sergeant threw a quick look around to see if anyone was within earshot, and when he was convinced that there wasn't, said, "They brought somebody in. Somebody that Jim Bridger says you need to talk to."

"Who is it?"

The sergeant shrugged. "I don't know. But they're over at the stables."

Gunnison bent his steps in that direction. When he arrived at the stables, Old Gabe met him at the entrance.

"You'll never believe who we turned up, Captain."

Before Gunnison could ask the identity of the person that was causing such a furor, Bridger turned away, leading him and the sergeant to a stall near one end of the long building. The rest of the hunting party was congregated there—and among them was a bearded man in buckskins that Gunnison recognized immediately.

Gordon Hawkes.

Chapter Thirteen

Gunnison was astonished, but he swiftly gathered his wits about him. He knew that Bridger was aware of his father-in-law's true identity; in fact, Hawkes and Old Gabe were good friends and had been for more years than Gunnison had been alive. But he wasn't sure if any of the troopers present knew that this was the notorious Gordon Hawkes. Sadly, much of the Second Cavalry had fallen in an ambush sprung by Cheyenne Wolf Soldiers a couple of years ago; those that had survived had been in a detachment led by Gunnison—a detachment accompanied by Hawkes. But most of those men had left the Army since, or been reassigned to other companies or units within the regiment. But even if none of these men knew Hawkes by sight, if they heard the name it was likely that they would know his history. It was increasingly difficult, these days, to find anyone west of Mississippi who didn't know at least some of the important aspects of the man's story, particularly that he was wanted on a couple of murder charges, and had been wanted in Colorado for several cold-blooded killings at a gold camp—though technically he had received amnesty for those alleged crimes, an amnesty that had not officially been revoked. Still, Gunnison was painfully aware that the first thing that came to mind for most people who heard the name Gordon Hawkes was that he was a fugitive from the law, and by association a desperate character.

So the immediate question for Gunnison was whether the troopers present had heard Hawkes's name, and until he knew that he couldn't be certain how to react to the man's presence. All he could do was turn and look at Bridger, wanting to ask the question that might direct him out of the dilemma he found himself in, but uncertain how to phrase it. Old Gabe, though, was a very intuitive man, someone who was still alive precisely because he had the ability to accurately assess a situation at a moment's notice.

"Captain, I reckon you remember my old pard, Henry Gordon."

Gunnison nodded. So that was it, then. Bridger had the foresight to use Hawkes's alias in front of the cavalrymen.

"Yes, we've met." Gunnison extended a hand to Hawkes. "How are you, Mr. Gordon?"

Hawkes wore a bemused expression beneath his unkempt, sandy beard. "Call me Henry, Captain. And I'm still above snakes. That's about all the good I can say."

Gunnison turned to the corporal in charge of the hunting detail. "I suggest you return to Clear Creek and finish what you started. Mr. Bridger, do you intend to accompany them still?'

"You bet. Henry, we'll shoot the breeze when I get back. Come on, boys."

Gunnison waited until Old Gabe and the detail

were gone. A nod to the sergeant sent the noncom out of the stables, too.

"What are you doing here, sir?" asked Gunnison. "The last news I had, you were in Taos, with Eliza. How is she, by the way?"

"She's dead."

Gunnison was stunned. His thoughts flew to Grace—and how this terrible news would affect her. Then he realized how difficult it must be for Hawkes. He could scarcely imagine what it would be like to lose Grace. She was the center of his universe, and his world would come crashing down around his ears if anything ever happened to her. How did a man survive such a blow as that?

"How . . . ?" Gunnison hesitated, aware that this was a subject that had to be intensely painful for Hawkes, and one the man might not want to dwell upon.

"It was just her time," said Hawkes flatly. "While I was down there I heard what was going on up here. Heard that you'd been assigned to this expedition— and that you had brought my daughter with you."

Gunnison nodded. "I know what you're thinking. Believe me, I've had second thoughts about it. I'm not sure it was the best course of action."

"It's pretty damned clear to me what the best course would have been."

"I understand. But, partly, it was a moment of weakness on my part. I couldn't bear to think of spending no-telling-how-many months apart from her. And then there's Grace herself. You know how she is. She made up her mind that she was coming with me, and when she makes up her mind . . ."

Hawkes shook his head. "That's no excuse. You never should have let her come along and you know it. It's too dangerous."

"Well, it's too late to change that decision now. It's been made, for better or worse. So is that why you've come? To make sure she's safe, and stays that way?'

"That's about the size of it."

Gunnison couldn't help it. He bristled. "Don't you think I'm capable of taking care of my own wife?"

Hawkes gave Gunnison a long look from top to bottom. He couldn't blame the cavalryman for resenting the implication that he was not adequate to the task of seeing to Grace's safety. But he was keenly disappointed that Gunnison had put his daughter in peril in the first place. He didn't know Gunnison that well. They had met during that bad business at Gilder Gulch, and back then Gunnison had been his enemy—a man with orders to bring law and order to a volatile situation, orders that meant he had to try to prevent Hawkes from wreaking his vengeance on the men who had taken his son's life. Gunnison had even placed him under arrest, and had fully intended to haul him off to the nearest Army outpost, where his fate would most certainly have been sealed. They had met again a couple of years later, when the Colorado Volunteers had threatened to destroy Black Kettle's peaceful band of Southern Cheyenne. And while Gunnison had objected to the injustice of that situation, he had waited until the last minute to come around to the right side of things and become an ally. In short, as far as Hawkes was concerned, his daughter's husband was a decent man who had a sense of fairness about him, but he did not always follow the right course. In other words, a man whose judgment was suspect. And this latest stunt—bringing Grace to the Powder River country when he must have known that there was going to be all-out war with the Sioux—was further proof of that.

"I'm thinking you won't object," said Hawkes, picking his words carefully, "if I volunteer to help you with that."

Gunnison took a deep breath, trying to check his temper. Hawkes had lost his son, and now his wife was gone, and Grace was all that he had left. It was something the cavalryman thought he should try to keep in mind.

"That suits me," he finally said. "Let's say we introduce you to the rest of the command as Henry Gordon. I'm sure Grace and Mr. Bridger will go along with the subterfuge, and hopefully no one else at the fort will know your true identity. But even if we manage to pull that off, you'll still be expected to serve as a scout for the Army. How do you feel about that? Means you'll be placed in a situation where you might have to fight the Sioux. And last I heard, you were determined never to take another life."

"I killed two men in Taos, and two more on the way up here," said Hawkes bleakly. "I guess you could say I've gotten over my scruples about killing."

Gunnison was curious to know under what circumstances Hawkes had taken the lives of four men, but decided to save that topic for another conversation. There were more pressing matters to be concerned with at present.

"As for fighting the Sioux, I've done that before," continued Hawkes.

"Very well, then," said Gunnison. "I'll introduce you to General Carrington."

Staying outside the cabin while Gordon Hawkes went inside to tell his daughter that her mother had died was one of the most difficult things Gunnison had ever done. He wanted desperately to be with her in this, her moment of need. In fact, he couldn't imagine a situation where she would need his support more than this. On the other hand, this was an intensely private moment for both Grace and her father, and Gunnison didn't want to interfere with that. So he waited outside, pacing restlessly, straining his ears to hear any sound from within—a cry of anguish, a calling of his name—that would end this agonizing exile and prompt him to rush to his wife's side. But the cabin was quiet. Too quiet, and Gunnison wondered what was transpiring between Hawkes and his daughter. A few minutes later—it seemed like hours had passed—Hawkes emerged. The mountain man looked drawn and haggard, yet relieved as well.

"How is she?" asked Gunnison. "How did she take the news?"

Hawkes looked at him bleakly. "She's her mother's daughter," was all he said, and walked on by.

Gunnison watched him go, marveling yet again at how Hawkes was holding up under obvious strain, wondering if he himself could be that strong under similar circumstances. He couldn't begin to comprehend the toll that telling Grace about her mother's passing must have taken on the mountain man.

Bracing himself, the cavalryman quietly entered

the cabin. Grace was sitting at the rough-hewn table that was the centerpiece of the one-room quarters. She sat very rigidly in the chair, a handkerchief twisted tightly in her fingers. Tears had made silver trails on her cheeks. He came up behind her chair and placed his hands on her shoulders, squeezing gently.

"I'm sorry, darling," he said softly. "I know you wish you had been with her."

Grace sighed, a forlorn sound. "I will always wish I'd been there to tell her how much I loved her. And to tell her good-bye." She placed a hand over one of his. "But I am where I belong. With you."

Gratified, he bent down to kiss the top of her head. "Your father is going to stay around," he said. "Did he tell you?"

She shook her head. "My poor father. How will he managed now, without her?"

"He has you."

She only nodded.

"I expect this will be difficult for you to do," he said, "but you'll have to act as though you do not know him well. It's pretty much common knowledge these days that you are the daughter of Gordon Hawkes. He will be using the alias Henry Gordon, and he will be scouting for us. This, in order to stay as close as possible to you."

Again she nodded. "I understand. And I'll do my part."

"I'd better take him to see Carrington. Unless you want me to stay . . . ?"

"No, go ahead. I would actually prefer to be alone right now."

"Okay." He bent down, and this time kissed her softly on the cheek, tasting the salt of her tears. He felt tremendous sympathy for her, and great admiration at the same time. She was so strong, truly, the product of Gordon and Eliza Hawkes. Gunnison felt helpless—wishing that there was something he could do to ease her pain, but realizing that there was nothing to do. Only time would ease that pain.

Stepping outside, he looked around for Hawkes. He was standing some distance away, looking at something across the parade ground. Gunnison followed the mountain man's gaze and saw Laura Denning, walking slowly, head down. He knew she wasn't going anywhere in particular. That was what she did—walk aimlessly about the fort, and he wasn't even sure that she was aware of where she was, or what she was doing.

"Who is that?" asked Hawkes, as Gunnison approached within earshot. "And what's the matter with her?"

"She's the widow of one of my officers. He was killed some weeks ago."

Hawkes nodded. He had sensed that the woman was a lost soul. It was remarkably easy to identify someone suffering the identical torment as he was having to endure himself.

"Some of us are worried that she won't make it through the winter," said Gunnison. "She seems to have lost the will to live."

"Sometimes you're forced to live," said Hawkes flatly. "Even when you would rather not. So, are we going to see your commanding officer now?"

"Yes, we'd better. He would find out you were

here sooner or later, and wonder who you were. It's this way."

As they crossed the parade ground, Gunnison continued to speak. "I better tell you a little something about our situation. We're up against Red Cloud, and he's got probably five thousand warriors at his beck and call. Mostly Sioux, but some Northern Cheyenne and Arapaho Dog Soldiers, as well. They gave us a lot of trouble early on. Hit us hard, and often. We lost a lot of good men. But once we got this fort completed the attacks became much less frequent. Now we hardly see a hostile anymore. Which has led some of my fellow officers into overconfidence, I'm afraid."

"Including Carrington?"

"That's my impression."

Hawkes digested this news and then said, almost to himself, "It sure seems to me that the men they send out here to command their armies are unadulterated fools, for the most part."

"I don't think Carrington is a fool. But he doesn't know much about fighting Indians. Though we have a fool or two among us. Captain Fetterman, for example. He barely survived a Sioux ambush. Lost nearly half of his command. And yet that didn't appear to have a sobering effect on him. Not in the least. In fact, he said this morning that with eighty men he could ride straight through the Sioux nation."

"If it's any consolation," said Hawkes dryly, "such men tend to get themselves killed early on, and cease to be a problem."

They arrived at the headquarters building, and Gunnison paused just outside. "Let me do most of the talking," he advised.

"That suits me."

Gunnison knocked on the door, and Carrington's voice from within bade him enter. Stepping into the office where, earlier that morning, he had nearly come to blows with Fetterman, Gunnison found the general and the very infantry captain who had become his nemesis, poring over maps spread out on the long table. Looking up from his work, Carrington glanced at Gunnison, then past the cavalryman at the buckskin-clad Hawkes.

"What is it, Captain?"

"This is Henry Gordon, sir. The hunting party came across him just a little while ago. He's a friend of Jim Bridger's. And I know him, too. He did a little scouting for us against the Arapaho."

Hawkes looked at Gunnison, his features betraying nothing—least of all that he was struck by the ease with which the cavalryman could lie. He had never scouted against the Arapaho, or any other tribe, for that matter. He had ridden for a time with the bluecoats during the recent unpleasantness in Colorado, but that had been to protect the Southern Cheyenne from the Colorado Volunteers. The idea of scouting for the Army had never appealed to him. He really couldn't say that he was on the Army's side in the first place. In fact, it would have suited him just fine if the Indians were still running the show west of the Mississippi. The westward tide of pioneers did not bode well for him. He had never looked forward to the day when his own kind conquered the wild country, because the wild country had always been his refuge.

Carrington gave him another, longer, look. Judging him, sizing him up. Apparently the general liked what he saw, and nodded. "That's fine, Captain. If you and Bridger vouch for him, then we'll put him on the payroll."

"I would like to have him assigned to my command, sir. He could ride with my patrols."

Carrington pursed his lips, mulling over the request. "Captain Fetterman and I are discussing his march to the Tongue River. I feel he could better use a scout, under those circumstances."

"I respectfully disagree, General," said Fetterman. "I don't trust any of these civilians. Especially not after what happened with Bob North."

"Bob North?" asked Hawkes.

"One of our scouts, Mr. Gordon," said Carrington. "He betrayed us to the Sioux. Led Captain Fetterman into an ambush from which he narrowly escaped. North is a traitor to his own kind, and I relish the day when I see him hanged for what he's done. What are your feelings about the Sioux?"

"I know a little something about them," replied Hawkes. "They don't much care for me, nor I them."

"If we can defeat them here and now, we will have done our country a great service. It will mark the end—or at least the beginning of the end—of the Indian wars. The West will be open to civilization then. It will be a great day in our nation's history."

"Beating the Sioux won't be easy," said Hawkes. "It's a big nation, and they are fierce fighters."

Fetterman shook his head. "They are no match for the United States Army, Mr. Gordon. I can assure you of that."

With a glance at Gunnison, Hawkes said, "If you say so, Captain."

"Will any of my men be assigned to Fetterman's expedition, sir?" Gunnison asked Carrington.

"No. I will need your men to continue their present duties. The captain will hand-pick twenty of his best men to serve as a mounted force to screen the advance to the Tongue."

"Yes, sir." Gunnison was careful to mask his skepticism. Why was it, he wondered, that infantry officers thought it was a simple matter to transform a foot soldier into a cavalry trooper? It was related, he suspected, to the fact that the infantry had a certain degree of disdain for the cavalry. It had always been so. Generally, they thought horse soldiers were poorly disciplined rowdies, and that, in Gunnison's opinion, was a textbook case of not giving credit where credit was due. Cavalry tactics were fundamentally different from infantry tactics, and for that reason he believed that this whole notion of putting foot soldiers on horseback was folly. But then, he was beginning to think this entire endeavor was folly, as well. Needless to say, these were sentiments he could not very well share with Carrington, so he said nothing more.

Carrington dismissed him and turned back to his maps. Gunnison escorted Hawkes outside.

"I see what you mean about Fetterman," said the mountain man. "He is a fool. But I think you're wrong about the general. He's one, too, right along with Fetterman."

"Carrington thinks the Sioux have given up. That's why he is willing to split his command and send Fetterman to the Tongue in order to establish an outpost there."

"If the Sioux ever give up I'll be surprised. I reckon Red Cloud is just sitting out there, keeping a close watch on things, hoping that you soldierboys do something stupid. He needs a victory to keep his warriors in line. That he set a trap and failed is something he has to compensate for. And this time he can't afford to fail."

"You think they'll attack Fetterman's command?"

Hawkes shrugged. "Wouldn't you?"

Gunnison thought about it and didn't take long to arrive at an answer. "Yes," he said grimly, "that's exactly what I would do in Red Cloud's place."

Hawkes was surveying the fort, and Gunnison thought he knew what the mountain man was thinking. He was worried about just one thing. Not Fetterman, not Carrington, not these soldiers—certainly not the advance of civilization. Grace was his sole priority. And he was wondering—as Gunnison had—at what point Carrington's steadily dwindling command would no longer be able to hold Fort Phil Kearney.

Chapter Fourteen

At least once a week, General Carrington had dispatched a wood train west, where there was abundant timber on the high ground no more than two miles from the fort. Though construction was completed, a lot of wood was still required for heating and cooking purposes The train sent out two days after Gordon Hawkes arrived on the scene had consisted of ten wagons and fifty-five men. It set out at daybreak, and a few hours later a lookout spotted a signal from the Pilot Hill heliograph. Instantly the garrison was in commotion. There was no mistaking the signal—the wood train was under attack by the Indians. Officers congregated at the headquarters building. Carrington assigned command of the rescue to Captain Powell, and ordered Gunnison to support the infantry. Gunnison announced that since he already had a patrol out that day, he could muster about thirty men for the job at hand. Carrington authorized Powell to take fifty men from the Eighteenth Infantry and march at once to the aid of the beleaguered wood train. At that moment, Fetterman stepped up to ask for the command in Powell's place. He was, after all, the Eighteenth's senior captain. The general was in no mood to argue and acceded to Fetterman's wishes. Captain Brown requested permission to accompany the rescue party, and Carrington approved that, too.

Returning to his quarters, Gunnison found his subordinates, Lieutenants Grummond and Hillier, awaiting him, along with the ubiquitous sergeant. He succinctly relayed the information he had to them.

"Will you be leading the detail, Captain?" asked Hillier.

At that moment Grace emerged from the cabin just a few feet away, well within earshot, curious to know what the commotion was all about. Gunnison glanced at her—and shook his head.

"No. Lieutenant Grummond, you will take the detail and cooperate fully with Captain Fetterman."

"Yes, sir!" Enthusiastic, Grummond dashed off in the direction of the stables.

Joining his wife at the cabin doorway, Gunnison watched Grummond go, and Grace could detect the concern etched into his features.

"I don't like the feel of this," he muttered.

"What do you mean?" she asked.

"This could be a trap."

"And you think you should go yourself," she said. "I know that's what you're thinking. And why aren't you?"

He glanced at her, realizing that she was well aware of his reasons. He wasn't leading the detail himself out of deference to her. It had been a snap judgment on his part—until he had seen her standing here, he'd had it in mind to ride out with his men. He didn't like it that he felt as though he were shirking his duty—and letting down his men—because of his concern for her. But she was deathly afraid of losing him, and wasn't it his responsibility as a loving husband to take that into consideration? He was torn between his duty to the Army and his duty to his wife.

"Grummond can handle it," he said, avoiding the truth.

"Where is my father?"

"He rode out first thing this morning with the patrol."

"Do you think he's all right?"

"I'm sure he is, darling. I think your father is just about indestructible."

She didn't smile, as he had hoped that she would. "No," she replied, somberly. "He's just an ordinary man. You should go, Brand, if that's what you feel like you should do."

"No. As I said, Grummond is capable of handling this."

She touched his arm, a deep sadness emanating from her, and Gunnison wondered if its source was solely the loss of her mother and sympathy for her father, or if there wasn't more to her melancholy. Something that had to do with him.

Trying to crowd these concerns to the back of his mind, he went to the stables to see Lieutenant Grummond off. He noticed that two scouts, Fisher and Wheatley, were preparing to accompany the rescue force. Even Fetterman's fifty foot soldiers were mounted, as in this case, time was of the essence in reaching the wood train. Carrington was there, as well, and Gunnison heard the general reiterate his orders to Fetterman with, in the cavalry officer's opinion, significant modification.

"Relieve the wood train, Captain," said Carrington, "and drive the Indians back, but under no circumstances are you to pursue the hostiles. Do not proceed past Lodge Trail Ridge."

Gunnison thought this was prudent of Carrington. It was a common Indian tactic to use a small band of warriors as a decoy to lure their enemy into an ambush that would be sprung by a much larger force. And if Fetterman were to go beyond Lodge Trail Ridge he would be completely out of sight of the network of lookouts that had been established on high ground all around the fort.

It was obvious that Fetterman did not approve of the restrictions that had been placed upon him. He and other officers had come to believe that Carrington was entirely too cautious. But he assured the general that he understood his orders, and thereupon led the eighty men in his command out through the water gate.

There were two routes that Fetterman could take to arrive on the scene where the wood train was under attack—south around the Sullivant Hills or the more northward option, which would take him along Lodge Trail Ridge. He chose the latter, and within an hour had reached that high ground. It was then that he saw the heliograph signal from the lookout post on Pilot Hill—a signal that informed him that the hostiles had quit the assault on the wood train. Fetterman wondered in which direction the Sioux and Cheyenne were withdrawing. He didn't have to wonder for very long. A handful of warriors suddenly appeared along the western base of Lodge

Trail Ridge. They were moving north on hard-run war ponies, but when they spotted the bluecoat column above them, they whipped their horses around and fled in the opposite direction. Fetterman couldn't resist. He ordered his men to give chase, without giving thought to the fact that in doing so the column would vanish from the sight of the lookouts, and that he would be disobeying Carrington's direct orders. Fetterman hoped that the ten fleeing warriors were just an advance party of the group that had attacked the wood train, and that by following them he would be led directly to the main force.

A few minutes into the chase, the ten warriors split into two groups, veering away from one another and then suddenly altering course and crossing paths. Seeing this, the scout named Wheatley shouted at Lieutenant Grummond that they were riding into a trap. Before Grummond could respond, hundreds of warriors poured out of several draws on either side of the ravine down which the pursuit had taken the bluecoats.

Fetterman called a halt. Warriors were rushing toward him from directly ahead and either flank. A quick glance behind him revealed that another large contingent of hostiles was blocking escape. Shouting orders to dismount and form a defensive square, Fetterman realized that his commands were being drowned out by a sudden crashing din of gunfire. The Indians were firing into the milling clot of soldiers, emptying saddles at an alarming rate.

Lieutenant Grummond instinctively led his cavalry up a steep slope, trying to reach high ground, and assumed that the mounted infantry would follow his lead. In a glance he realized, to his horror, that they weren't going to be able to. The warriors had swiftly converged on Fetterman's men, who fell beneath an onslaught of lances, tomahawks and clubs—the weapons preferred by the Plains Indian when time came for close-quarters killing. Grummond didn't have an opportunity to watch the slaughter for more than a few seconds; a shout of alarm from one of his troopers brought his attention to the top of the ridge, where yet another large detachment of Sioux warriors had suddenly appeared to block their path. These warriors swept down upon them, the air splintered by their war cries. More hostiles charged up the slope to close in on the troopers from behind. Grummond had just enough time to realize that he was doomed—and then a lance driven through his chest killed him instantly. Within sixty seconds, the rest of his command was slain.

For a few moments the victorious Indians raised their voices in cries of pure, joyous triumph. They then proceeded to the business of gathering up the Army horses that were still alive, as well as the weapons of the fallen bluecoats. Some of them paused long enough to take scalps for trophies. This bloody work done, they withdrew to the west, and a deathly stillness fell over the ravine littered with corpses.

Fetterman's disobedience—and the disappearance of his command down the far side of Lodge Trail Ridge—was immediately made known to the men within the walls of Fort Phil Kearney, thanks to the alert heliograph operator at the lookout post on the crest of Pilot Hill. A few minutes later another signal came from the post, indicating that fierce gunfire could be heard from the far side of the ridge, indicative of a desperate battle being waged.

Like the other officers, Gunnison made haste to the headquarters building. Carrington told Captain R. Ten Eyck to take a full company of the Eighteenth, with every man mounted, to Lodge Trail Ridge. Gunnison asked for and received permission to go along. As he raced to the stables for his horse, the cavalryman felt a knot of dread form in his belly.

They rode in haste westward to Lodge Trail Ridge, and when they reached the crest of that high ground and looked down into the ravine below at the bodies of eighty-one men, the sight stopped them dead in their tracks.

"Jesus Christ," muttered Ten Eyck under his breath, staring in horror at the carnage.

There was not a single Indian body to be found, but that didn't surprise Gunnison. The Plains Indians collected their dead whenever possible so that they might be given a proper ceremonial send-off to the other world—and to prevent them from being mutilated by the enemy. They believed that in the other world the warrior would remain in the same physical condition that he was in at the time of his death.

Ten Eyck dispatched patrols to either end of the ravine, with orders to keep an eye out for the hostiles. Only then did they proceed to the gruesome task of checking the bodies, hoping against hope that they would find a survivor or two.

Gunnison was stunned by the loss of nearly thirty of his men. He had never suffered such a setback. He had lost men before, but never to this extent. He dismounted and walked among the piles of bluecoat dead on the long slope where Grummond and his command had been cut down. He knew the name of every single man who lay here. They were more than just troops to him. In a sense, they were like family. He'd been told by some fellow officers, who did not approve of the rapport that he had gone to great pains to establish between himself and the soldiers who served under him, that to become too familiar with the ranks was a perilous thing to do. From their perspective, familiarity bred contempt, and Gunnison risked losing the respect of his men. Gunnison had never bought into that argument, and had never had reason to regret the camaraderie that had developed. But now he realized that there *was* a risk involved. The risk of this very situation, standing among the corpses of men whom he had come to know quite well. He had heard them talk about their lives, about their families if they had any and of their hopes and aspirations. And now they were gone, never to see those families again, never to realize those aspirations, never to stand around another campfire drinking coffee and chewing tobacco and shooting the breeze with their comrades. It was a shocking loss—and Gunnison was shaken to the core.

Ten Eyck called him from down below, at the bottom of the ravine where another collection of bluecoat bodies lay. When he reached Ten Eyck he looked down at the corpses of Captain Fetterman and Captain Brown, lying side by side. Each had a bullet hole in the temple. A pistol was still clutched in Fetterman's hand, while Brown's pistol was a short distance away.

"It looks to me," said Ten Eyck, "as though they killed themselves."

Gunnison looked at him and nodded, trying to give the implications of this discovery time to sink in. To commit suicide in the face of the enemy was, perhaps, understandable—especially when all hope was gone and the enemy were the Sioux. But understandable or not, it was not an honorable thing to do.

"Brown thought killing Indians would be a lark," muttered Ten Eyck. "Like some kind of damned hunting excursion." He shook his head. "I guess he lived long enough to realize how wrong he was about that." He glanced at Gunnison, a question in his eyes.

"That's what it looks like," said Gunnison. "But we can't be sure. And I see no reason to impugn the honor of these two men based solely on a supposition."

Ten Eyck nodded gratefully. "I concur wholeheartedly. You're a good man, Gunnison. I confess, I wasn't too sure about you. Fetterman was certainly no friend of yours, and yet you walk away from a golden opportunity to besmirch his reputation."

"He's dead," said Gunnison flatly. "I think he was a reckless fool, but he's already paid the ultimate price for that recklessness." He let his gaze stray to the other bodies strewn across the ravine bottom. "Damn him, though. Damn him for leading these good men to their deaths."

"We had better get them back to the fort," said Ten Eyck. "There's no telling when the Sioux might come back."

Gunnison's intuition told him that the Indians were long gone—well on their way back to the village on the banks of the Powder River, carrying news of their great victory to Red Cloud, and carrying the trophies of that triumph as well. Many fresh scalps would hang from the lodgepoles tonight. The warriors would celebrate through the night, recounting great deeds of valor around a council fire. Red Cloud had his much-needed victory now. And that meant his warriors would be encouraged, and by the morrow they would be itching for an assault on the fort.

"I'll ride for the wood train," he told Ten Eyck. "They can't be more than a couple of miles from here. We'll transport these bodies back to the fort in those wagons."

Ten Eyck nodded his approval of this plan, and Gunnison strode to his horse, suddenly in a hurry to put this grisly, tragic scene behind him.

They returned the bodies of Fetterman's ill-fated command to Fort Phil Kearney without mishap. Gunnison was relieved to see that the morning patrol had returned. He spotted Gordon Hawkes, standing a little apart from the men who gathered at the gate to watch in grim silence as the wagons loaded with the dead trundled into the post. He wanted to talk to the mountain man, because the disaster at Lodge Trail Ridge had changed everything. Now that Red Cloud had his victory, and the garrison had been diminished, Gunnison wasn't as sanguine about their ability to withstand a concerted effort by the Sioux to take the fort. His foremost concern, therefore, was his wife's safety. And on that subject he couldn't think of anyone better to talk to than Hawkes.

Dismounting, he made his way through the press

of soldiers to reach the mountain man, but before
he could speak, one of General Carrington's aides
approached to tell him that the general wanted to
see all the officers at once.

"You better come with me," Gunnison told Hawkes.

Hawkes nodded and followed him across the parade ground to the headquarters building. As Gunnison and his colleagues gathered around the long table,
the mood was solemn. At least, mused the cavalryman,
no one was going to make foolish comments about
how easy it would be to drive the Sioux out of the
Powder River country. It had to be clear to everyone
concerned, now, that the Indians were going to fight
to the death. And at the moment it looked as though
they might actually prevail.

Spotting Jim Bridger leaning against the wall in
one corner of the room, arms folded across his chest,
Hawkes walked over to join Old Gabe.

"I don't know what it is about you," Bridger said.

"What do you mean?"

"Somehow you always manage to be in the middle
of things when things go from bad to worse."

Hawkes had to smile. "Just lucky, I guess."

"I reckon."

Carrington emerged from his private quarters.
Hawkes didn't know the general, having met him
only once, and then briefly, but it was clear that Carrington was shaken to the core by what had happened. This was the moment when he had to prove
what he was made of, and Hawkes was curious to
know if he would follow a pattern set by entirely too
many other Army commanders on the frontier, when
their fondly held belief that their command was su-

perior to any Indian force was shattered. A lot depended on what a man did once his illusions were stripped away.

Seating himself in the chair at the head of the table, Carrington peered at the other officers. For a moment, no one said a word. They knew, as Hawkes did, that their survival might well hinge on what the general did in response to this setback.

"Today," said Carrington, at last, his voice hollow, "we lost about twenty-five percent of our effective fighting force. And we now know that Red Cloud is far from finished. He has proven himself to be a . . . a formidable foe." Carrington paused—and Hawkes could tell that this admission was one the general had been very reluctant to make. "The question now is what he will attempt next."

"And whether, if he attacks the fort, we can hold it," said Captain Powell.

Carrington glanced at Bridger. "What do you think Red Cloud will do?"

Bridger shrugged. "Hard to say. His warriors will want to finish us off. But Red Cloud has to look to the future. If he had his way you'd abandon this fort and walk away. He'd probably let you, too. That way he's at least bought some time. But he knows that even if he can destroy this command that won't be the end of it. There'll be more soldiers to fight next year. And more the next one after that. So he knows he can't afford to lose a lot of men. Not if he has to continue the fight."

"And the first big snow will be coming," said Ten Eyck. "Indians don't like to fight in the winter, anyway."

"That may be true under certain circumstances," said Hawkes. "It's true that a war party usually won't ride in winter. For one thing, it's too easy to track them. But none of that applies in this case. They aren't worried about getting away after the fighting is done."

With pursed lips, Carrington stared at his hands, which rested on the table in front of him, the fingers splayed.

"I am not willing to even consider abandoning this fort," he said. "Not without orders to do so. On the other hand, it's obvious that we cannot go forward with plans to establish two more outposts along the Bozeman trail. We will have our hands full just holding on to this position through the winter. That must be our priority. We could use reinforcements. So we need to get a message through to Fort Laramie." Once again he glanced at Bridger. "Can you do that?"

Hawkes looked at Old Gabe. Bridger was impassive, and he didn't hesitate in responding.

"I'd have a better chance than most, I reckon."

"Red Cloud will probably anticipate this," said Gunnison.

Bridger nodded. "Of course he will."

"What are the odds?" asked Captain Powell.

"Fifty-fifty, at best," replied Bridger.

"Those aren't the best of odds," said Carrington.

"They are in this country," said Old Gabe.

"Then I'll improve them by sending more than one messenger." Carrington's gaze turned to Hawkes. "Are you willing to take the chance, Mr. Gordon?"

Unlike Bridger, Hawkes hesitated. He had no desire to make a bid for Fort Laramie. It wasn't that he was afraid of the odds. He'd faced steeper ones than that on many occasions in the past. But his first instinct was to stick close to Grace, especially since she was now in more danger than ever.

"I don't need any company, thanks anyway, General," said Bridger. He knew perfectly well why Hawkes was hesitating. But of course his friend could not voice his reasons—not without giving away his true identity.

"I would expect the two messengers to travel by separate routes," said Carrington. "Chances are that at least one of you would get through."

Hawkes thought it through. What action could he take that would give Grace the best chance at survival? As hard as it would be to leave her at a time like this, it would be to go to Fort Laramie and bring back reinforcements, so that Fort Phil Kearney could be held.

"I'll go," he said.

Chapter Fifteen

Telling Grace that he was going to leave her, and putting himself into great jeopardy just days after having informed her of the death of her mother, was not something Hawkes looked forward to. It wasn't as difficult to do as imparting the news he had previously had to present to her, but the mountain man was well aware of his daughter's vulnerability at this moment in time. She would not like it that he was putting himself at risk, and the fear that she might lose him so soon after the loss of her mother would be a terrible burden on her.

When he and Gunnison reached the cabin where the cavalryman and his wife resided, they found that Grace was in the company of the woman Hawkes had seen wandering aimlessly across the parade ground a few days earlier—the woman Gunnison had identified as the widow of an officer who had recently been slain by the Sioux. She jumped in her chair as the door opened and they entered, jerking her head around to stare at the two men, and as soon as she identified them her expression changed dramatically, from hopeful expectation to dull rejection. It occurred to Hawkes that she was still waiting for her husband to return to her. That hinted at madness, but he didn't judge her because of it.

Seeing Gunnison, Grace leapt to her feet and flew into his waiting arms. "I heard what happened," she whispered. "Thank God you decided not to go." She looked at Hawkes, smiled bravely and reached out to grab his hand, and she didn't have to say anything for the mountain man to know that she was equally grateful that he had come back alive from the morning patrol.

Gunnison felt a little uncomfortable with this display of affection in front of Laura Denning, considering that she would never again be able to greet her own husband in the way that Grace had just welcomed him.

"Laura," he said, detaching himself from Grace, "I would like to introduce Henry Gordon. A friend. Henry, this is Laura Denning."

Laura looked at Hawkes. Her eyes met his but very briefly, and then she looked down at the floor. It was long enough, though, for Hawkes to ascertain that there was no life in her, no hope, no dreams. His heart went out to her. He knew what she was going through. But he also knew that a show of sympathy was not always the most helpful thing to receive when you were grieving deeply, as Laura obviously was, so he said nothing.

"Carrington has decided to send word to Fort Laramie regarding what's happened here, and our situation," Gunnison told Grace. "Old Gabe has agreed to deliver that message. And . . . and Henry here has agreed to do the same."

Grace looked at her father with growing alarm, and both Hawkes and Gunnison wondered if she would remember to maintain the charade regarding his identity. Not that exposing him in Laura Denning's presence would do much harm. The latter seemed to be lost in a world of misery, paying no attention to what went on around her.

"The general figures that by sending two men there's a better chance of the message getting through," said Hawkes. "I reckon you can't argue with that."

"How long will it take to get there and back?" asked Grace. Watching her closely, Hawkes could tell that she was striving to remain strong.

"About a week there," he said. "If the weather holds."

"More snow is coming soon," she said flatly. "I can tell."

Hawkes nodded. His daughter had been born and raised in this country, and she knew how to read the weather as well as he did.

"There's no better solution," said Gunnison. "After what happened today . . . well, there's just no guarantee that we could hold this fort without reinforcements."

She looked at her husband then, gazed deeply into his eyes, and saw the worry there, and even anticipated what was coming next from him.

"In fact," he said, taking her hands in his and looking at them, so small and delicate and light against his palms, "I've been thinking you might be more safe going with him."

"No," she said sternly. "I'm staying here with you." She glanced at Hawkes, almost apologetically.

The mountain man smiled and nodded. He'd already considered what Gunnison had in mind—and rejected it, precisely because he had known without a shred of doubt what her response to that suggestion would be.

"Grace . . ." Gunnison was going to protest her decision, but she placed her fingers against his lips and silenced him.

"I am staying right here with you, where I belong," she said softly, but firmly. "But I do think Laura should go with you, Mr. Gordon."

"What?" Gunnison was taken aback.

"Yes." Grace glanced at her friend. She didn't know if it was right and proper to be talking about this in front of Laura, but then this was hardly the time to worry about such niceties. "Look at her. She's not going to make it if she stays here, Brand. You *know* that's true. And you know I'm not the only one who has come to that conclusion."

"No, you're not," he admitted.

"She needs to get away from this place. She has family back East. And if she can get to Fort Laramie, she could get home."

"Yes, probably. There's a stage company that runs from Laramie to the railhead now."

"And I have the utmost faith in Mr. Gordon," continued Grace. "I am certain he will get through to Fort Laramie."

Hawkes knew her too well to be fooled. She wasn't nearly as confident as she was making out to be. In fact, she was worried sick about him. That aside, however, she had concluded that Laura Denning's only chance was to get away from Fort Phil Kearney. If she stayed here she would be dead before the winter was out. If she left with Gordon Hawkes she

would at least have a chance. But Hawkes wasn't
sure he wanted to be a party to this. It would be a
big job just getting himself to Fort Laramie all in one
piece, much less with a woman in tow. For Grace's
sake he might have accepted the additional burden,
even though he wasn't convinced that she would be
safer going with him. But to take the Denning
woman was something else entirely. For one thing,
it was clear she was barely able to fend for herself. At
least Hawkes knew that his daughter was a person of
great stamina, indomitable will, someone who could
shoot nearly as well as he could, could read sign,
build a fire, hunt game, someone who was accustomed to the vagaries of the weather on the high
plains. He knew nothing about Laura Denning, but
his first impression was that she was not made of
the same stern stuff as Grace. She would bring no
assets to the venture, only liabilities.

Grace could tell that her father had serious doubts.
"She is my friend," she said. "I care about her a great
deal. And I just can't bear to stand by and watch her
die a little more every day. I don't know that she
will ever be able to overcome. But I have to believe
that if she were back home, with her friends and
loved ones, that perhaps they might be able to do
what I haven't been able to. They might be able to
convince her that there is a reason to live."

Hawkes drew a long breath. There was simply no
way he could deny his daughter's earnest plea.

"Okay. If she wants to go, I'll take her. But I won't
drag her out of here kicking and screaming."

"If Carrington gets wind of this, he'll try to stop
you," predicted Gunnison.

Hawkes nodded. "I realize that. His first priority is to hold this fort, like he said. He's hinged everything on getting word through to Fort Laramie. And my taking her along makes the odds of that happening even worse than they already are. But if it's what Grace wants, then it's what will happen."

Grace had returned to Laura's side, sitting on her heels beside the chair in which the young widow sat. "Would you like to go home, dear?" she asked, placing her hand over Laura's hands, which were folded in her lap. "Would you like to see your family again?"

Laura raised her head and looked at Grace, and as far as Hawkes could tell there wasn't a glimmer of interest in the poor woman's face. She hardly seemed to understand what Grace was trying to convey.

"This man," said Grace, gesturing at Hawkes, "is going to Fort Laramie. He will take you with him, and you will be quite safe in his care. From Laramie you will be able to go home. Though of course I will miss you terribly, there is no reason for you to stay here any longer. In fact, I think it would do you good to be with your family. Don't you?"

"I suppose so," said Laura, without enthusiasm.

"Then it's settled," said Grace. She rose and turned to look again at her father. "When will you leave?"

"Tomorrow, after sundown," said Hawkes. "I need a little time to get some things together. And to get past the scouts I'm sure Red Cloud has watching the fort, we'll have to travel under cover of darkness, at least for a while." He hesitated, still besieged by doubts. And clearly he wasn't the only one. Neither Gunnison nor Laura Denning herself seemed too sure about this scheme. But Grace was sure, and for that reason he decided to keep his doubts to himself from now on.

He stepped outside. It was nearly night, and bitterly cold wind knifed his flesh. Glancing to the north, he saw an ominous line of clouds in the distance. Grace was right, of course. There was foul weather coming. But the weather, no matter how foul, did not concern him. He had lived through the worst this country had to offer. In fact, he thought it might actually be an advantage to him in his upcoming attempt to slip past the Sioux scouts. If he could pull that off, then he expected little trouble in reaching Laramie. But that was a very big "if," and he knew it.

Later that night he found Jim Bridger in the stables checking the hooves of his horse. Seeing that no one else was around, Old Gabe dug into his possibles bag and broke out a jug of whiskey, which he invited Hawkes to share—an invite Hawkes happily accepted. They found an empty stall and sat down in the straw and passed the jug between them a few times until they had stoked a nice warm liquid fire in their bellies.

"Gordon," said Gabe, "tell me why it is that we are getting older but no wiser."

Hawkes smiled. "I've often wondered that myself. What are you doing here, anyway? Don't you have enough to keep yourself busy without volunteering to work for the Army every time they ask you?"

"Well, I could say I did it 'cause I'm a patriot. But you wouldn't believe me. Fact is, I get bored. Hell, why did we come out here in the first place, old son?

For the adventure. And Lord knows we got plenty of that, didn't we?"

"More than enough to last one lifetime," agreed Hawkes.

"Maybe it's because I *am* old," said Bridger wistfully. "And I miss the old days something fierce. Miss living every day to the fullest on account of not knowing if I'd have another one. Maybe I'm trying to recapture my lost youth."

Hawkes chuckled. "Believe me, Gabe, it's gone for good."

Bridger sighed. "Yeah, I know. And there's another reason."

"Yeah. Because with you around there might be some lives saved."

Bridger grimaced. "That's how I was thinking. I suppose some would say that was mighty conceited of me."

"No, I don't think so."

"Well, I haven't been doing a very good job of that in this case."

"This is a special case. This is the Sioux nation we're talking about. We all knew they wouldn't go down without a fight. And it would be a fight unlike anything any of us had ever seen."

"True enough." Bridger took another long pull off the jug and passed it to Hawkes as he wiped his mouth with the sleeve of his buckskin jacket. "I'm thinking that the odds are stacked against us ever seeing Laramie, Gordon."

"We've faced steeper odds."

"Maybe." Bridger didn't sound convinced. "But you know, even if you get there all in one piece, you

might still be in danger. Might be that somebody
there will know who you really are. Fort Laramie has
changed a lot since you've seen it last, I reckon. It's
a busy place. Lot of different folks from all over coming and going."

Hawkes shrugged. "I don't care about that. All I
care about is getting reinforcements here."

"Well, the first man there has to buy the other one
a drink."

Hawkes gazed fondly at his old friend. "Then you
better make sure you have some money on you,
pard."

Old Gabe laughed. "And you better make sure you
still have your scalp on you, pilgrim!"

The first task on Hawkes's agenda the next morning was to find a suitable horse for Laura Denning.
The sorrel that the Taos sheriff had provided him
had turned out to be an animal with plenty of bottom, a mustang that he knew he could depend on.
He had to find one just as dependable and durable
as that for his companion. Gunnison assured him
that he could have any horse he selected, as long
as it wasn't one of General Carrington's Thorough-
breds. The mountain man assured him that it would
be no thoroughbred and, indeed, his final choice
was a shaggy dun that didn't look like much at all.
The animal belonged to one of the civilian teamsters
who had accompanied the expedition. True to his
word, Gunnison acquired the horse, though he
could not refrain from telling Hawkes that he
thought he'd paid at least twice what the broomtail
was worth. Hawkes assured him that the horse was

worth the price, and while he remained dubious, Gunnison didn't argue the point. One had to assume that a man of Gordon Hawkes's experience could tell what horse was best suited to travel in this country, in the prevailing conditions.

Those conditions had taken a turn for the worse during the early morning hours, and the morning dawned with an ominous sheet of blackish-gray cloud blocking the sun. By noon it had begun to snow, and a few hours after that the snow was coming down pretty fast. The temperature plunged to well below freezing. Carrington summoned Hawkes and Bridger to his quarters and asked them how much the weather would hamper their attempt to reach Fort Laramie.

"Shoot, General," drawled Bridger, "this ain't so bad. Certainly nothing to write home about. I've seen northers blow through that could freeze a horse clean through in less than an hour."

"Truth is, I hope it keeps snowing through the night," said Hawkes. "It will help us. The Sioux scouts might be huddled in their camps. And even if they're not, they will have a hard time seeing us."

"And new falling snow will cover our tracks," added Bridger. "Makes it less likely they will cut our trail and follow us on the morrow."

Carrington was visibly relieved. "The two of you are courageous men. Whether you succeed or not, the United States will owe you both a tremendous debt of gratitude."

"Oh, we'll succeed," said Bridger confidently. "Don't you fret about that, General."

Once they were outside the headquarters building,

Bridger took Hawkes by the arm and said, "This didn't occur to me until Carrington said all that about a debt that would be owed us."

"What didn't occur to you?"

"This might be a chance to get those old murder charges off your back, Gordon."

Hawkes shrugged. "Maybe. It doesn't really matter."

"Yeah, I know, nothing really matters to you, except your daughter's safety," said Old Gabe, slightly exasperated. "You don't really care if you live or die. I reckon I can understand that, 'cause I know what Eliza meant to you. But damn it, hoss, Eliza would hate to see you this way. And even if you don't care about living for yourself, you should give some thought to staying alive for Grace's sake. She's already lost her brother and her mother. You want her to lose her father, too?"

Hawkes stared at Bridger for a moment, and try as he might, Old Gabe could not fathom his old friend's expression.

"Why don't we worry about collecting that debt after we get to Laramie," he said, finally.

Bridger nodded. He wasn't sure if that response meant that he had gotten his message across, but he was willing to accept it for now.

Hawkes proceeded with his preparations. Since it was unlikely that he would be in a position to risk a campfire, he needed to take along prepared food—hardtack and smoked beef. He also needed plenty of blankets, an oilskin, a hatchet, flint, some rope, powder and shot and an additional pistol. He wanted a heavy blanket coat or capote for Laura, as well as sturdy boots. In fact, he wanted her

dressed in men's trousers; a dress would not only
be useless, but possibly a hindrance, as frostbite
was a very real threat. He made sure all the metal
on the saddles that he and Laura would use were
blacked with charcoal. If the sun came out during
their trek he did not want its light to reflect off
anything.

They waited until late in the night, when the fort
had quieted down, and only the sentries patrolling
the walls could be seen. Grace and Gunnison delivered Laura Denning to the water gate at the south-
east corner of the compound, where Hawkes was
waiting with the two horses, and Gunnison assured
the mountain man that he had spoken to the sergeant
of the guard and that no mention would be made of
the fact that Hawkes was not alone as he left Fort
Phil Kearney. As the cavalryman helped Laura into
the saddle, Hawkes said good-bye to his daughter. It
was a difficult parting, but he was proud of the fact
that she did not make it harder than it had to be by
becoming emotional.

"Just come back to me," she whispered, embracing
him, and resting her head against his chest.

He stroked her hair. "I always do, don't I?"

"You always have in the past."

Reluctantly he pulled gently away and climbed
aboard the sorrel. Gunnison wished him good luck.
Hawkes refrained from telling the cavalryman to take
care of Grace until he got back. Gunnison was, after
all, her husband, and clearly loved her as much as
the mountain man did. He would die for her, if need
be. And Hawkes could scarcely asked for more
than that.

Gunnison nodded at the guard at the gate, and the heavy timber portal swung open. Hawkes took up the reins to Laura's horse and rode out into the snow-swept night.

Chapter Sixteen

Hawkes knew that Fort Laramie lay several hundred miles to the south. He had no stars to guide him that night, and while Gunnison had provided him with a compass, the mountain man did not feel the need to consult with that device. He was endowed with a nearly infallible sense of direction, an asset honed over thirty years in the wild country. And, on this first night at least, he was not so much concerned with the direction he traveled as he was with keeping as much as possible to the timber found mostly on the slopes of ridges, confident that he was moving in generally the right direction throughout.

The snow fell for most of the night, sometimes gently, sometimes more thickly and sometimes the wind out of the north would pick up, and sudden gusts would encase them in a cocoon of white. The cold was bitter and bone-biting, and while Hawkes was relatively impervious to discomfort, he remained mindful of the threat of frostbite, especially where Laura Denning was concerned. Frequently he would pause and ask her how she fared, if she had feeling in her hands and feet, and she would tell him that she did, that she was okay. The mountain man wasn't convinced that she would voice a complaint even if she had one. He wasn't sure she cared if she froze to death or not.

Keeping to the high ground where the timber was thick, they made slow but steady progress. Hawkes kept all his senses attuned to any indication that there might be Indians in the vicinity. At one point he caught a whiff of woodsmoke, very faint but distinct, and he paused for a moment, peering into the night to windward, wondering if a camp of Sioux scouts was close at hand. He doubted that in this weather the scouts would be on the move, but he didn't want to stumble into one of their camps, either.

They pressed on through the long, cold night, and about dawn Hawkes got the impression that they were being followed. Again he stopped, pulling Laura's horse alongside his, and twisting in the saddle to peer into the snow-draped darkness behind them. Finally he saw them—a pair of glowing eyes, then another, and another, and yet another—and he knew then that a pack of wolves had picked up their trial. The wolves were on the hunt, and while they tended to avoid men, the scent of the horses had attracted them. Hawkes drew the Plains Rifle from its leather sheath and checked the percussion cap, just in case. The wolf pack got in close, but then veered off, circling their position, near enough so that the mountain man could see their swift, fleeting shapes through the trees. Hawkes glanced at Laura, wondering if she saw the lobos, wondering too what her reaction would be. There was something about wolves that triggered a primal reaction in most people, a fear so strong that it amounted to abject terror that could result in blind panic. In all his years in the high country, Hawkes had often crossed paths with wolves, but had never had any trouble with them. He doubted Laura had anything like that much experience with the predators. But the woman, though she saw the pack, watched them with only mild curiosity. Hawkes wasn't sure if her composure was due to courage or indifference.

Once he was sure that the wolves did not intend to attack the horses—that their caution had overcome their hunger—Hawkes pushed on. The wolves shadowed them for an hour more, and then, as the night began to fade away before the slow onslaught of daylight, the pack vanished. The mountain man began looking for a good place to camp, and soon found it—a rocky ravine enclosed by thick timber, on the eastern slope of a ridge and so partly sheltered from the winds blowing in from the northwest. He put the horses on a short tether, and then rigged a shelter using the oilskin, lashed to several tree trucks with rope. Into this shelter he deposited his weapons, possibles bag, all the blankets and Laura Denning. He figured they had made about ten miles during the night, and while that was probably far enough to put them beyond the range of Red Cloud's scouts, he wasn't going to take any chances, and so was reluctant to build a fire. The first order of business was to make sure Laura didn't need one, and with her permission he took off her boots and stockings and checked her feet, massaging them with his hands, and determining that she still had feeling in her toes. He checked her hands as well, and was satisfied that she was all right. He bundled her up in blankets and offered her some food. She ate a little, thanked him and then lay down to sleep. Hawkes draped a blanket around his shoulders and sat cross-legged under the oilskin shelter, listening and watching and waiting. He was tired and tense from the difficult night passage they had just made, but he could go without sleep for days.

He let her sleep for about four hours, and then saddled the horses, gathered up the gear, and they were on their way again. The snowfall had lessened, and the sky was getting lighter, and Hawkes thought that by nightfall it would begin to clear. Already the sun was trying to pierce the layer of gray clouds in places. If anything, the coming night would be even colder than the one before, but Hawkes had hopes of covering enough distance before they stopped again so that he could feel more sanguine about building a fire to provide life-sustaining warmth for his companion. His attention turned now to making the best possible time and less to avoiding Red Cloud's scouts, which he felt confident were behind them now. Still, he took all due caution, even while it became increasingly difficult to remain in cover as the terrain began to flatten out and the timber became less abundant.

They came to a river which Hawkes believed to be the Little Powder. If it was, he knew it pointed due south straight at Fort Laramie, and that once he reached its headwaters he would then cross the Belle Fourche and the Cheyenne rivers and reach his destination. He stuck as much as possible to the wooded high ground along the western bank of the river. At times, though, they had to cross open ground, and Hawkes realized they were leaving a trail now that the snow had ceased to fall and the wind had died

down. But there was no help for it. Sometimes the
route took them along a rocky crest beyond which
was a steep drop to the river fifty or a hundred feet
below. The rambunctious river rolled northward over
and around jumbled rock and sheets of blue ice. At
times the going was rough, but Hawkes knew that
soon the land would level out, and he was confident
that their sturdy and surefooted horses would come
through for them. Laura Denning seemed to be holding up well—better, in fact, than he had anticipated.

But then, in the afternoon of the second day out
of Fort Phil Kearney, Hawkes began to check their
back trail more and more. He had a sudden feeling
that they were being followed. He had nothing to
base this on. There was no sign of pursuit. But he
had a gut instinct, and he knew that it would be a
mistake if he failed to heed it. Often before he had
had this same kind of feeling. He couldn't explain
where it came from, but he was aware of the fact
that it had saved his life on more than one occasion.

To his surprise, the Indians first appeared ahead
of them. They seemed to appear out of thin air, three
warriors—Northern Cheyenne by the looks of their
attire and war paint—sitting on their ponies among
the trees about fifty yards in front of Hawkes and
Laura. She saw them at the same time, and the
mountain man was pleased to note that she made no
sound, gave no sign of panic. He wondered for a
moment if the three braves had mistaken her for a
man, given her clothes. Was that why they hesitated
to attack? He was quickly disabused of that notion,
however, as a war cry shattered the cold stillness of
the afternoon—a sound coming from behind them,

and Hawkes twisted in the saddle to see several more warriors closing in. Then another war cry, this one from down the steep, wooded slope to his left, and Hawkes spotted two more Northern Cheyenne. Now he understood. Somewhere along the way, this war party had crossed their path, and while three followed, the others pressed on, circling around to cut in front of their prey.

Hawkes quickly assessed the situation—and realized immediately that there was no hope of coming out on top in a fight. There were too many of them. Their only chance was to escape. But there were Indians on three sides, and a very steep drop of about a hundred feet to a rock- and tree-strewn river bottom on the fourth. It was a descent that would be impossible for the horses, and very perilous for humans. But not as perilous as staying put.

The trio of warriors who blocked their advance began to move in, and Hawkes made his decision. Without a moment's hesitation he drew his Plains Rifle from its sheath, swung down off the sorrel and helped Laura off her horse.

"You've got to trust me," he told her, "and do what I tell you without hesitation. Will you do that?"

She nodded, her lips pressed tightly together, her eyes bright with . . . fear? Hawkes didn't think so. He didn't think she was afraid, even here and now.

"Come with me, then," he said, and, taking a firm grip of her hand, turned and launched himself over the edge of the cliff.

He landed feetfirst in deep snow, but the angle of the slope was so steep that he could not stay upright, and toppled forward, losing his hold on Laura's hand, and concentrating thereafter merely on holding on to his rifle. He tumbled down the slope, and then the ground fell out from beneath him as he rolled over a rock overhang, and he plummeted through the air for several seconds, bracing for an impact. It wasn't as bad as he'd expected; more deep snow cushioned his landing. He lay there a moment, catching his breath, or trying to, as snow dislodged by his precipitous descent rained down on him. Getting unsteadily to his feet, he took a look up at the ridge high overheard, somewhat amazed that he'd been lucky enough to survive the fall without any broken bones. Then he noticed Laura, lying facedown in the snow about twenty feet away—and lying there very still.

Alarmed, he went to her, struggling through a snowdrift that was so deep that he sank nearly up to the thigh every time he took a step. Reaching her side, he turned her over on her back, gently brushed the snow from her face, and then laid his head down between her breasts to listen for a heartbeat. She was alive. He checked her head for injuries, and found none. That was all he had time to do, for suddenly a bullet smacked into the snow right beside him. He looked up again—and this time saw several of the Northern Cheyenne at the edge of the cliff. A puff of smoke was followed by the report of a long gun, and another bullet screamed through the air inches from his head. Hawkes slung his rifle over a shoulder, hooked his arms under Laura's, and dragged her closer to the base of the cliff, so that they were sheltered from the gunfire by the rock overhang. It was hard going in the deep snow, but being shot at was a great motivation, and he got them both under cover in a matter of seconds.

The shooting from above ceased immediately. All Hawkes could hear was the raspy heaving of his own labored breath and the soughing of the winter wind in the bare limbs of the trees that lined the nearby river. Then he heard something else—a low moan. Laura was coming around.

"You're okay," he said, as her eyes fluttered open. "We made it."

"Are they . . . gone?" she asked, her voice the barest of whispers.

"I don't know," he said. "They might be satisfied with the horses and go on their way." He decided on the spur of the moment not to lie to her. "But it's more likely that they'll try to find a way down into this canyon so that they can finish us off."

She looked him in the eye, and Hawkes wondered what she was thinking. There was still no panic, and why should there be? Laura Denning wasn't afraid to die. But there were worse things than death, mused Hawkes. He fumbled under his coat for one of the pistols that—thank God—was still in his belt. He checked the pistol's percussion cap and load, and handed it to her, butt first.

"You don't want to fall into their hands," he said flatly.

She looked at the pistol for a moment. He was fairly sure that suicide was something that had crossed her mind in the days since her husband's death, so his suggestion did not shock her.

"What do we do now?" she asked quietly.

Hawkes took a long look around. "Wait. This is as

good a place as any for that. If they get down here
before dark we're done for, I reckon."

"And if not? If they come down after dark?"

"Then we might have a chance."

"I know who you really are," she said.

He stared at her, startled by this admission.

"Grace told me right before we left the fort. She
has been a good friend to me. I don't know that I . . .
I could have gotten through these last weeks without
her friendship."

"We need to get to Laramie," said Hawkes. "It
might be your only hope."

"You're lucky, you know."

"How's that?"

"At least you had something to live for when you
lost your wife. My husband and I . . . we had not
been married very long. We planned on having children, and . . ."

"You do have something to live for," he said
firmly. "You say my daughter was a good friend to
you. Now you can return the favor. You can help me
get to Laramie so that reinforcements are dispatched
to Fort Phil Kearney."

She looked at him again, and this time smiled
faintly. It was the first time he had seen anything
remotely resembling a smile from her. "Don't worry.
We'll get there."

He nodded, encouraged by her demeanor under
these circumstances, and only wished that he could
feel as confident about their survival as she sounded.
He'd been in plenty of tight spots before, but none
much tighter than this. The way he saw it, they had
little choice but to stay right where they were—at

least until he could be sure that the Indians on the ridge above were no longer in position to shoot them down once they emerged from the cover of the rock overhang. It really was a question of how long it took the warriors to make their way to the river bottom— assuming they were coming at all.

An hour passed. The day began to darken. And Hawkes began to think that maybe, just maybe, they'd gotten a lucky break—that perhaps the Northern Cheyenne had been satisfied with the horses after all. He decided to take the risk of stepping out from under the rock overhang, Plains Rifle cocked and ready. He saw no one on the ridge above him. No gunfire greeted his appearance.

"Are they gone?" asked Laura.

"Maybe. We better get moving."

They walked south, along the river, and Hawkes turned his thoughts to the distance that lay between him and Fort Laramie. They had no provisions, no blankets and, worst of all, no horses. Even so, he was certain that he could make the journey under such adverse conditions. He wasn't sure about Laura Denning, though. She had courage and she had stamina—but did she have enough of both for the ordeal that lay ahead?

The sun had set, the shadows of night began to gather—and Hawkes headed into a thick stand of timber with thoughts of making camp there for the night. Even though it was risky, he felt as though a fire was in order. They would require its warmth to get through the night. But just as they entered the stand the distant whicker of a horse grabbed his attention, and he dropped into a crouch at the edge of the woods, pulling Laura down beside him. About two hundred yards to the north, a mounted warrior came into view, emerging from the rocks and trees that covered a slope. No, make that three mounted warriors—and Hawkes could only assume that they were members of the war party that had made its presence known earlier. Where were the others? That was the crucial question. Because Hawkes decided then and there that he was going to go for the ponies these Northern Cheyenne were riding. He had to get to Laramie, and quickly, and he couldn't do that on foot with Laura slowing him down, and he certainly couldn't abandon her. So his options were severely limited, and those Indian ponies looked like his best hope.

Two of the warriors rode close together, while the third was a straggler, coming along some distance behind his companions. All three appeared to be very alert, scanning the ground and then their surroundings—obviously they were looking for something, or someone, and Hawkes was pretty sure he knew what. The mountain man realized that he would have to save his long gun for the man who rode apart from the others—the one who was farther away. That left him with a pistol and a knife to deal with the two who rode together, as he was not prepared to take the other pistol away from Laura Denning. Especially since, with the odds standing at three to one against him, there was at least a fair chance that he would fall in the action he was about to commence.

Motioning for Laura to stay put, Hawkes drew the pistol from under his coat and waited until the two warriors were as close as they ever would be, passing within thirty feet of his position. One of the Cheyenne scanned the trees that concealed the mountain man, then looked away, only to look back again—and Hawkes wondered briefly if the brave had seen something, or if it was just something instinctive, a premonition of danger. Hawkes didn't wait to find out. He rose to his feet, stepped out from behind the tree, and, drawing a quick bead on the nearest warrior, fired the pistol.

The bullet struck its mark, and the warrior let out a sharp cry and toppled sideways off his horse—falling toward the pony of his companion, and spooking the animal, so that Hawkes saw that he had a few seconds at most to devote to the third rider, the straggler. Dropping the empty pistol, the mountain man grabbed up his long rifle and put stock to shoulder. The third Cheyenne was riding forward at a gallop, the hooves of his horse throwing up a plume of snow, and he let out a war cry as he bent low, his cheek very nearly resting against the neck of his mount, making himself a smaller target. Hawkes muttered a curse, for this forced him to take a few more precious seconds to draw a more careful bead before squeezing the trigger. The Plains rifle boomed and the bullet slammed into the Cheyenne's skull, blowing out the back of it, so that the man was dead before he pitched backward off his still-running horse.

Those few extra seconds Hawkes had spent in killing the second Cheyenne cost him dearly, for it gave the surviving warrior the time he needed to get his spooked pony under control and kick it into motion. He rode straight at Hawkes, unlimbering his long gun and getting off a shot just as Hawkes slew his

companion. The bullet plowed into the trunk of the
tree beside the mountain man, and a splinter of wood
gashed Hawkes right above the eye. He spun away,
startled by the pain and confused for an instant, wondering if he had been shot. Yet he had the presence
of mind to drop the Plains Rifle and grope for his
hunting knife. Blinking at the blood that blinded him
in one eye, Hawkes spun to see the Cheyenne warrior bearing down on him. The warrior had thrown
away his now-empty rifle and was drawing a tomahawk; as he drew near he launched himself at the
mountain man with a savage cry. Hawkes tried to
sidestep, but the snow was deep enough to slow him
down, so that the warrior's body struck him a glancing blow and knocked him off his feet. They both
scrambled to regain their footing. The Cheyenne was
a shade quicker, and lunged as he lashed out with
the tomahawk, a lateral stroke that, had it connected,
would have gutted Hawkes. But the mountain man
managed to avoid that blow, albeit clumsily. Off balance, he fell backward into the snow. The Cheyenne
saw his chance, and moved in for the kill, raising the
tomahawk, a fierce light of triumph gleaming in his
dark eyes.

And then Laura Denning shot him dead.

The Cheyenne's corpse sprawled across the mountain man's legs. Hawkes kicked it off and got up,
wiping the blood from his face and looking at Laura,
who stood ten paces away, the pistol in both hands,
smoke curling from its barrel. He half expected to
see a horrified expression on the woman's face. But
he saw a fierce elation there instead. The Cheyenne
she had killed, of course, hadn't had anything to do

with her husband's death. But he was an Indian, and as far as Laura Denning was concerned, that made him fair game.

Hawkes stepped forward, pried the pistol from her grasp, and set about reloading all the weapons, anxiously scanning the river, anticipating the appearance of the other Cheyenne in the war party. But none appeared. He couldn't figure out why that was the case, but he didn't waste a lot of time mulling it over, turning instead to the task of catching the Indian ponies. He got the first easily enough, but the other two were skittish, and shied away from him. He mounted the one he had in hand and steered it towards the nearest of the other two, holding it to a walk. In this way he was able to get close enough to gather up the reins and lead the second pony to Laura. He did not waste time on the third horse; instead, he helped Laura aboard her pony and then led the way out of the trees, turning south, intent on riding well into the night.

Chapter Seventeen

As Old Gabe had said, Fort Laramie was much changed from the frontier outpost Hawkes remembered. It had become a major frontier crossroads, and a tent city had sprung up around the stockade. There was even a medium-size Indian village—about seventy lodges—nearby. Even this time of year there was considerable traffic to and from the fort. The arrival of Hawkes and Laura Denning might not have drawn all that much attention except for the fact that they were riding Indian ponies painted for war—and the fact that Bridger had made it to Laramie first. As they passed through the tent city, a man that Hawkes took for a trader by his garb stepped up to walk alongside the mountain man's horse for a moment, peering curiously up at the rider.

"You from Phil Kearney by any chance?" he asked.

Hawkes nodded. "How did you know?"

"Old Gabe Bridger got here yesterday. Said there was another messenger coming—maybe. And that he had a woman with him." The trader glanced curiously at Laura Denning. "Pretty rough trip for a woman, I'd say."

"She did okay," said Hawkes, and rode on as the man veered off to join a cluster of other civilian onlookers. The mountain man figured it wouldn't take long before the word had spread that he was the second messenger sent by Carrington. And he had to wonder, among all the people congregated in and around Fort Laramie, if there wasn't at least one among them—besides Bridger—who would know his true identity. But Hawkes couldn't worry about that now. Bridger had made it through, and no doubt told the commanding officer of the garrison here about the plight Carrington was in. The mountain man's first priority was to find out if reinforcements had already been sent to Fort Phil Kearney—and if not, why.

His path was blocked by a pair of sentries at the main gate, and he identified himself as Henry Gordon, scout for General Carrington, with an urgent message for their commander. They let him pass. One of the first sights that greeted Hawkes as he entered the stockade was the wiry figure of Old Gabe hastening across the parade ground. Apparently Bridger had been alerted to their arrival by one of the soldiers up on the wall.

"By God you made it!" roared Bridger, delighted. "But not without some trouble along the way, I see." He studied the Indian ponies. "Cheyenne, by the looks of those markings."

"That's right. A war party caught us along the Little Powder five days ago. I'll tell you all about it—as soon as you buy me that drink."

Bridger laughed. "Fair enough. And how is Mrs. Denning?"

"I'm fine," she said.

Old Gabe was startled by the fact that she had

addressed him so readily, accustomed as he was to a Laura Denning who had been impervious to what was going on around her, wrapped up in an impenetrable swuddle of grief. But the Laura Denning he saw today was looking at him with a very direct gaze, and he concluded that somewhere between here and Fort Phil Kearney she had emerged from that cocoon.

"Good, good," he said, nodding. "I have welcome news for you, ma'am. They're expecting a stage in here tomorrow or the next day, coming out of Dallas and headed to points east. You'll be on your way home in no time."

She glanced surreptitiously at Hawkes. "I see," was all she said, and it didn't escape Bridger's notice that, contrary to his expectations, his information was not all that welcome.

"What about the reinforcements for Carrington?" Hawkes asked as he dismounted and then helped Laura to the ground. "Are they already on their way?"

"Not yet," said Bridger—and held up a hand as Hawkes shot him a sharp look. "Now don't get those damned hackles of yours up just yet, hoss. The man in charge here, a general by the name of Merritt, seems like a good man and he is willing to dispatch two companies of the Second Cavalry to Carrington's aid."

"Then why hasn't he?"

"Looks like they'll be leaving first thing in the morning. You know how the Army is. Or maybe you don't. It's a lot of hurry up and wait. Preparations have to be made, and they have to be made by the book. Putting a column in the field in two days is quick work, if you ask me."

"I'll take your word for it. Are you riding with them?'

Bridger nodded. "Someone's got to lead 'em there. And you can figure that if Red Cloud finds out we're coming he'll try to stop us before we get to Fort Phil Kearney."

"I'm going, too," said Hawkes.

"That don't surprise me. Well, come on, I'll introduce you two to Merritt."

They proceeded to the post headquarters, and Bridger made the introductions. Merritt greeted Hawkes warmly.

"Mr. Gordon, you're a brave man, and you've done your country a great service that will not soon be forgotten. As for you, Mrs. Denning, Mr. Bridger here has told me something of your circumstances. Let me offer you my most sincere condolences. The Army lost a fine soldier when your husband fell, but that loss is nothing when compared to what you have suffered. My wife and I insist that you stay here with us until you leave Fort Laramie. We have the room, and you are welcome to remain here for as long as you wish."

Laura thanked him.

"General," said Bridger, "my friend and I made a bet before we left Fort Phil Kearney, and I've been waiting on that drink for two hours now, so if you don't need us anymore . . ."

Merritt chuckled. "No, not at the moment. Mrs. Denning, if you'll come with me, I would like you to meet my wife, Harriett."

As Hawkes turned to follow Bridger out the door, Laura stepped forward and reached out to touch his arm.

"You . . . you won't go without saying good-bye, will you?" she asked shyly.

Surprised, Hawkes said, "Well, no, I reckon I'll see you again before we leave."

Once they were outside Old Gabe gave Hawkes a curious glance. "What was all that about?"

"Damned if I know," said Hawkes.

"Well, I think maybe I do. Looks to me like Mrs. Denning has found a reason for living again."

"I don't know what you're talking about."

"Now, hoss, you need to stop pulling my leg. You two been through an ordeal together. If that don't tear people apart, then it tends to bring people closer."

"I don't want to talk about this, Old Gabe."

"Just saying that I think she cottons to you, that's all."

Hawkes gathered up the Indian ponies and dragged them along as he headed across the parade ground in the direction of the main gate, Bridger at his side. Once out in the tent city he was able to sell the Cheyenne ponies for forty dollars apiece inside of fifteen minutes. He could have sold them quicker than that to a Chinese man who ran an eatery, but Hawkes wasn't particularly keen on the idea of the ponies ending up in tomorrow's stew. The eventual buyer was an Indian trader who thought he could use the animals for barter with the peaceful band of Southern Cheyenne who had erected their winter lodges in the fort's vicinity.

"You reckon the Army will make me the loan of a good horse for tomorrow?" Hawkes asked Bridger.

"The way General Merritt was talking, I think you can count on it."

Hawkes nodded. "Good. Then you can buy me that drink now."

Bridger chuckled. "At least one! Come on, I know just the place."

Hawkes followed Old Gabe to a tent saloon that was packed with customers. Bridger assured him that this was the only place within three hundred miles that you could buy real whiskey, not watered-down snakehead. That, said Old Gabe, was precisely why you had to fight your way through the press of traders and wolfers and mule skinners and assorted riff-raff just to get to the bar and order. The bar was made of planks appropriated from a wagonbed, laid across big water barrels. Storm lanterns hanging from nails driven into stout poles holding up the canvas roof let off a smoky yellow glow. There was no floor, just churned up mud with planks laid across it here and there. A half-dozen tables cobbled together from more cannibalized wagons were strewn randomly about the establishment. All in all, Hawkes mused, this place made that seedy Taos cantina he'd been lingering in a few weeks back look like a palace.

Making their way to the bar, Hawkes and Bridger ordered shots of whiskey, and when they got their glasses, Old Gabe raised his in a toast.

"Here's to us, hoss. We got here all in one piece. Now we got to get back the same way."

"We'll get back," said Hawkes resolutely, thinking about Grace. "We have to."

He knocked the drink back, gasping at the searing fire of the liquor—and then a hand came down hard on his shoulder, pulling, spinning him around, and he found himself looking into an all-too-familiar face.

"Talbot," he muttered.

"I'll be damned," breathed the dark-bearded man with ice-cold blue eyes who stood facing Hawkes, fists clenched. "I thought it was you. The one and only Gordon Hawkes. You've got some nerve walking around bold as brass like this, after what you've done."

The customers standing within earshot all turned their attention to Hawkes and Talbot, sensing trouble, and trying to give the two men some room.

"Looks like you two know each other," drawled Bridger. "You mind introducing me to your friend, Gordon?"

"Talbot here is no friend of mine," said Hawkes.

Talbot barked a short laugh. It had a sharp and bitter note. "Not hardly. Hawkes killed some of my men down in Colorado a few years back, when he was trying to set free some Cheyenne bucks I'd taken prisoner."

"He was with the Colorado Volunteers," Hawkes informed Old Gabe. "That outfit had more than its fair share of butchers and Indian haters, but I'm inclined to think Talbot was the worst of the lot."

Talbot grinned tautly. "I'm of a mind to kill you where you stand, Hawkes."

"You can try."

Talbot unclenched his right hand, and Bridger watched it move closer to the pistol holstered at his side. He reached out a hand to grab Talbot's arm.

"Now hold on there, mister," he said.

Talbot lashed out, a backhanded blow that caught Bridger by surprise, striking him in the face and knocking him backward against the bar. The crowd scattered then, and pandemonium reigned in the tent saloon as men pushed and shoved and elbowed each other in a concerted attempt to clear out before the shooting started.

But Hawkes didn't give Talbot a chance to draw his pistol. He plowed right into the man, driving him back into a table. Talbot ricocheted off the table and lost his balance and went down, and Hawkes held on, going down with him, plucking the pistol from the man's holster and laying the barrel across Talbot's skull, a hard blow that knocked him unconscious. It happened so quickly that Talbot didn't have a chance to defend himself—which was precisely what the mountain man had intended.

When he was sure that Talbot was going to stay down for a while, Hawkes got to his feet and looked around at a circle of grim, weathered faces. Talbot had spilled the beans where his true identity was concerned, and he was sure enough people had heard the name that it would spread quickly through the tent town. How many of the residents of this community knew the history behind that name remained to be seen, but it didn't appear that anyone in this bunch was inclined to move against him. So he dropped Talbot's pistol and turned back to the bar to check on Bridger.

"I'm okay," said Old Gabe. "Lot better than he appears to be." Bridger looked at Talbot and ruefully shook his head. "I must be gettin' old, hoss," he sighed. "In better days he never would have . . ."

"I know." Hawkes motioned for one of the bartenders to come over, which the man did, albeit hesitantly. There was plenty of elbow room now, and the mountain man thought he ought to take advantage of it. "Two more shots," he said. The bartender nodded, and provided the whiskey. Hawkes handed one to Bridger. This time he was the one to raise his glass in a toast. "Here's to better days."

Bridger had to smile. "You don't seem to be slowing down all that much."

Hawkes knocked back the shot, waited until Old Gabe had done the same, and then suggested that they take their leave. Bridger was ready. Outside, Old Gabe paused and glanced back at the tent saloon.

"You don't reckon you ought to do something about that pilgrim?"

"Like what?"

Bridger shrugged. "I don't rightly know. But strikes me that he has a real bone to pick with you."

Hawkes nodded. "At least he's not wearing a uniform anymore."

"I heard the U.S. Army took over those Colorado Volunteers, turned 'em into a regiment of regulars, and in the process they got rid of a lot of the bad element. I wouldn't be surprised if that man in there was one of the men they turned out."

Hawkes shrugged. "I'm leaving in the morning. If Talbot wants to follow me up into the Powder River country, then so be it."

Bridger shook his head. "You know what your problem is? You've just gotten too damned accustomed to men being after you."

"Well, doesn't seem to be much point in holding

on to this Henry Gordon alias anymore, Old Gabe. Guess I better go tell General Merritt who I am. He's going to hear about it from someone, and it might as well be me."

"You're right. I'll go along with you."

"Might want to reconsider. Because if they try to arrest me I'll put up a fight. My daughter is up there at Fort Phil Kearney and I aim to get back to her."

"Maybe it won't come to that. But there's only one way to find out."

Hawkes started for the main gate, and Bridger fell in step alongside.

General Merritt sat behind his desk, ramrod straight in the chair, elbows resting on the desk and fingers laced together as he listened to the story Gordon Hawkes told him. He was intent and solemn, and the mountain man couldn't tell what the officer was thinking. But Hawkes didn't let that stop him. He mentioned everything he thought was relevant to the two murders he had been accused of committing, as well as the situation that had arisen in Colorado a couple of years earlier, during which he and the Colorado Volunteers—not to mention Colorado's governor—had been at odds. He talked about the killings that he had been involved in at Gilder Gulch, and flatly explained that he had fully intended to exact a full measure of revenge in that instance for the death of his son. He didn't make excuses, only stated facts. And when he was finally done with the narrative, Merritt sat there for a moment, impassive as a statue, and Hawkes figured the man was trying to assimilate everything he'd just been told.

"If all that you say is true," said Merritt, finally, "you've had the worst string of luck of any man I know, Mr. Hawkes."

"It's true," said Bridger, standing alongside Hawkes. "And it's true I ain't been present at any of these killings, but I do know one thing: Gordon Hawkes has never told a lie to my knowledge."

"I've lied," said Hawkes. "But I'm not lying now. Those are the facts, General, plain and unvarnished. I had nothing to do with those two murders back east. But I did kill some men at Gilder Gulch, and I did try to free the Cheyenne braves being held prisoner by the Colorado Volunteers, and while men died that night, I'm fairly sure it wasn't by my hand."

Merritt nodded. "I know a good deal about that mess in Colorado, and I do not approve of what Governor Evans tried, and certainly I condemn the actions taken by Colonel Chivington at Sand Creek. As for this man Talbot, I know about him. He's been hanging around the fort for a couple of months now, and he's nothing but a troublemaker. I was not aware of his service with the Colorado Volunteers, but I'm not surprised that he rode for Chivington, nor am I surprised that he was cashiered when the Army took over that unit. Beyond that, though, I must confess I am not sure what you would have me do."

"Don't expect you to do anything, General," said Hawkes. "Just wanted you to hear the truth from me. I figured you'd hear about me soon enough from some other source."

"I see." Merritt pushed his chair back and got up, paced over to the hearth, where a roaring fire provided the room with heat, then came back to the desk. "I suppose I would be well within my rights to place you under arrest, Mr. Hawkes, given that you are a fugitive from justice. After all, it's not up to me to determine your guilt or innocence. That is a job for a jury of your peers."

"My daughter is trapped in Fort Phil Kearney," said Hawkes. "She's the wife of a Captain Gunnison, who's with the Second Cavalry."

"Yes, I know the captain. A good officer."

Hawkes hesitated, wanting to pick his words carefully. "I'm not inclined to sit in a jail cell here while my daughter is in danger."

Merritt stopped pacing and looked at the mountain man, the faintest of smiles touching the corners of his mouth. "I take that to mean you would resist arrest."

"I'd have to."

"What about that great service he did for his country, General?" asked Bridger. "And I don't just mean what he done recently, bringing word from Carrington. If it wasn't for my friend here, there could have been another Sand Creek Massacre in Colorado. Thanks to him, Black Kettle and the Southern Cheyenne weren't wiped out by the Colorado Volunteers."

"I understand," said Merritt. "But as you know, there are still a lot of people in this country who don't share your sentiments. They would point out that it was the Cheyenne Wolf Soldiers who wiped out about half of the Second Cavalry."

"That was in self-defense," said Bridger. "Governor Evans had declared martial law. He assumed overall command of all military forces in Colorado, and sent the Second Cavalry against the Southern

Cheyenne—an action, as I recall, that the War Department later condemned."

Again Merritt nodded. "That's true." He sat back down and took a sheet of writing paper from a desk drawer, dipped a pen in an ink bottle and began to write. Hawkes glanced at Bridger, brows raised, and Old Gabe just shrugged. He had no idea what Merritt was up to. All they could do was stand there and wait until the general was done. When he had finished, Merritt reviewed what he had written. Then, apparently satisfied, he folded the paper, sealed it with wax, and handed it across the desk to Hawkes. "There's no way to know how many men are going to be after you when word of your identity spreads through that tent town out there, Mr. Hawkes. But there are some tough customers in that crowd, and some who wouldn't mind trying to collect on the rewards placed on your head, I'm sure. So I don't know how much that letter will aid you. But I have written that you are a scout on a special mission under my direct orders, and that you are not to be hindered in any way in the pursuit of that mission. And I intend to write to the War Department, recommending that the President of the United States issue you a full amnesty from any and all charges that may have been made against you in the past, as consideration for the service you have done this country. I'm afraid that's all I can do."

Grateful, Hawkes looked at the paper in his hand, and wasn't quite sure what to say. "That's—that's much more than I ever expected."

"But I have a feeling it's not more than you deserve. I believe your story, Mr. Hawkes. And the fact that Jim Bridger vouches for you holds a lot of weight with me. I cannot, however, guarantee that you'll get that amnesty."

"I gave up expecting guarantees a long time ago, General."

"I suggest you stay in the fort until the relief column leaves in the morning."

Hawkes nodded. "I'll do that. Thank you, sir."

Merritt stood up and extended a hand to both of them. "Thank you, gentlemen, and good luck."

Early the next morning, Merritt's relief column began to assemble on the parade ground. Hawkes and Bridger shared breakfast with the soldiers in the mess hall and then went to the headquarters building, where Hawkes was introduced to the officer the general had put in command of the column, a Major Furness. In a brief meeting on the porch of the building, Merritt reiterated the importance of the column getting through to Fort Phil Kearney, and warned Furness that he could expect stiff resistance from the Sioux. Hawkes was glad to see that the major's response lacked bravado. Furness simply said that he and the men in his command would do their best to carry out the orders they had been given. It inclined Hawkes to be hopeful, at least, that Furness was not underestimating the difficulties that lay ahead.

As the column mounted up with the appropriate fanfare, Hawkes and Bridger went to their horses. Hawkes was checking his saddle's cinch when Old Gabe said, "You're about to have a visitor, hoss."

The mountain man looked across at Bridger, then

followed Old Gabe's gaze to Laura Denning, who was coming toward them.

"Good luck," murmured Bridger. He climbed quickly into the saddle, and set his horse on a canter for the main gate, through which Furness, at the head of the column, was already passing.

Hawkes had to admit that Laura looked fetching. Apparently Mrs. Merritt had provided her with a new dress. She had washed her hair and brushed it out until it shone in the pale winter sunlight. But the greatest enhancement of all was the light in her eyes. She seemed more alive than he had ever seen her. A spirit of life had inhabited her once again. Hawkes was glad to see it. Nonetheless, he felt some trepidation as she approached.

Reaching him, she smiled shyly and looked down at her hands, which were clasped tightly together. "I—I couldn't let you go without saying good-bye."

Hawkes felt a little guilty. Yesterday he had left her with the impression that he would speak to her again before leaving, but in fact he had hoped to get away from Fort Laramie without having to do so. This, because he had a hunch what was on her mind, and he didn't want to hear it. He didn't want to hurt her: She'd been hurt enough already.

"I'm glad you did," he replied, lamely. "And I wish you all the best, Mrs. Denning."

"After all we've been through, I think it would be okay if you called me Laura, don't you?"

"I reckon so. I hope you have a safe journey home, Laura."

She glanced up at him—a glance full of speculation. "I've been thinking . . . thinking that perhaps I could stay here for a while." As she looked out across the parade ground a gust of cold north wind blew tendrils of hair across her face, and she brushed them back, and the gesture struck Hawkes as very girlish. "Yes, I do have family back east. But, well, there isn't really anything back there for me. That's why I came out here, after all. Why I married . . ." She could not yet bring herself to mention her dead husband's name. Summoning up all the courage at her command, she finally looked Hawkes straight in the eye, and blurted, "What I mean to say is that I want to stay here until you come back."

Hawkes almost winced. His worst fears had been realized. Laura Denning had become attached to him. Too attached. She might even think she was in love, though he knew that was not the case. She had needed a reason to live, as well as someone to latch onto, and he had wandered into the picture. Added to this was the fact that they had been through the ordeal of the trek from Fort Phil Kearney together. And now he was faced with the prospect of having to do damage to a heart already shattered by the death of Lieutenant Denning.

"I'm flattered," he said. "Very much so. But you're a young woman, Laura. Not much older than my daughter, I'd guess."

"I'm twenty-three," she said. "I'm not that young."

"Still, you're young. And I'm an old man. Most of your life is ahead of you. Most of mine is behind me. It—it just wouldn't be fair to you."

"Shouldn't I be the one to decide what's fair to me?"

He shook his head sadly. "No. Not in this case."

He watched, with growing horror, as her composure began to melt. Yet somehow she managed to maintain it.

"I understand," she said, her voice a little ragged. "You're still in love with your wife. I realize that. I'm still in love with my husband. But . . . well . . ."

He reached out and laid a hand on her shoulder. "Laura, believe me, I know how it is. I know how you can love someone and yet when they're gone, or very far away, and you know you'll never see them again, you feel the need to be with someone. But right now you need to be alone. It isn't all that bad, really. Sometimes it's necessary."

"And what about you? You'll be all alone."

His smile was tender. "No, I won't be. I have my memories."

She laid a hand on top of his. "You're a good man, Gordon Hawkes."

He shook his head, feeling a fondness for her, a closeness to this woman, that he had not felt before. "No. I'm just a man. I've made a lot of mistakes. I'd be making another if I led you to believe that you should stay here. That I would come back. Because I wouldn't. So go home, Laura. I know it's hard to believe right now, but one day you'll be happy again. That's a guarantee."

She stepped up and gave him a kiss on the cheek before turning quickly away and walking rapidly toward the headquarters building. Halfway there she started to run. Mrs. Merritt was there, arms open to embrace her. The general's wife looked across at Hawkes and nodded. It was a confirmation that he had done what needed doing, and an assurance, as well, that Laura Denning would be taken care of. That assurance made it easier for Hawkes to climb aboard his horse and set out across the parade ground, into the dust not yet settled from the passage of the relief column he had to make sure got through to Fort Phil Kearney.

Chapter Eighteen

It took a while, but after being in the village of the Absaroke Crow for about two weeks, Red Renshaw woke up one morning and thought that just maybe he was going to live after all. For the first time he could actually take a deep breath without suffering intense pain. Once he began to believe, his recuperation was swift. A few days later he was sitting up to eat, and a few days after that he was standing. Within three weeks of his arrival at the village, he left the skin lodge for the first time.

Several Crow women acted as nurses—placing poultices on his wounds, washing him, feeding him, making sure that the fire in his skin lodge never went out. But over time there was one in particular, whose name was Pretty Shield, who paid him the most attention. Renshaw thought she was without doubt the prettiest Indian woman he had ever seen, and in his years as a trader on the Plains he had seen plenty of them. Her features were quite a bit more aquiline than those of most Indians, and he wondered if perhaps she had European blood in her veins. And although he had always managed to resist the charms of the young women with whom he had come into contact, he found himself anticipating Pretty Shield's arrival each and every day. He was perfectly aware

of the fact that if he continued down this path of
infatuation he would be putting his heart at risk—
something he had only done once, many, many
years ago. That situation had turned out badly, and
that broken heart had been the principal reason he
had come west. Since then, whenever tempted, he'd
just resurrect those old memories, and promptly
cured himself of any lovesickness. But this tech-
nique didn't seem to work where Pretty Shield was
concerned. He thought that maybe it had something
to do with the fact that he had come as close as he
ever had to dying. Maybe that had changed the way
he looked at things, particularly how he wanted to
spend whatever time was left to him. But whatever
the reason, he couldn't seem to take his eyes off
Pretty Shield. And so it was that he got up the
nerve to ask He Smiles Twice, who came to check
on his progress on a regular basis, to tell him more
about the girl.

The Absaroke chief was surprised. "You do not
know her?"

"Nope. Why?"

"You are a good friend of Gordon Hawkes, yes?"

"I wouldn't say good friend. I met him some years
back. He and a partner of mine were friends. But
after that I hadn't seen him until the day we met up
in Taos a while back." His head cocked to one side,
Renshaw peered curiously at the Absaroke. "What
does that have to do with Pretty Shield, anyway?"

"Pretty Shield has always loved but one man, and
she will never love another as long as she lives.

Renshaw was crestfallen. "I didn't know she was
taken. Who's the lucky man?"

"White Crow. The one you know as Gordon Hawkes."

Renshaw was stunned. "You're joking."

The grave expression on the face of He Smiles Twice made it clear that the chief was in earnest.

"Well," said Renshaw, trying to pull himself together. "It ain't like I didn't know better than to fall for a woman again." He shook his head with a rueful smile. "So how did it happen that Pretty Shield . . . ? No, I don't even want to know."

He tried to put her out of his mind, but that was more than he could do, especially since he saw her for long periods of time every day. Finally he had to broach the subject—doing so one morning as they walked together along the creek just beyond the village. He had insisted on taking walks every day, to rebuild his strength, and she insisted on following along in case he pushed himself too far.

"I asked He Smiles Twice about you," said Renshaw, right out of the blue, blurting it out.

"Why did you do that?"

"Well, I might as well say it—I'm right fond of you, Pretty Shield. So naturally I was wondering if you were taken. Turns out you are. I didn't know about you and Hawkes. Now I do."

Pretty Shield's smile seemed to freeze, become fragile. "What did He Smiles Twice say to you?"

"That you were in love with Hawkes. And that you would never love another. Is that true?"

Pretty Shield had to look away. "Yes, it is true."

"Then why aren't you with him? His wife is dead. Did you know that?'

"I know. But I can never be with him."

Renshaw shook his head. "Doesn't make any sense to me."

"It is a long story."

"I've got plenty of time. Not like I've got anywhere to go."

"I do not wish to speak of it."

Renshaw grimaced. "I guess what I'm wondering is, whether or not there's any chance for me. You know, where you're concerned."

She met his gaze. Her expression was very solemn. "I will never be with another man," she said flatly.

Renshaw knew then that there was no hope, and he felt that emptiness in his gut that he'd felt only once before in his life, and had resolved never to experience again. He cursed himself for a fool. How could he have put himself in this position? Exposed himself to this kind of exquisite torture again?

"Well," he drawled, trying to put on a brave front. "I'm feeling pretty strong today. Think I'll walk on over to those trees yonder."

Pretty Shield followed his gaze, across the snow-blanketed valley at a wooded slope nearly a quarter of a mile to the east. "That is too far," she said. "You are not strong enough."

"The hell I'm not! And if you don't mind, I'd like to be alone for a spell."

"I should go with you."

"I don't want you to," he said curtly. "Go back to the village." He felt like telling her that he never wanted to see her again. It would be entirely too painful. But he didn't want to come across as ungrateful to her for all that she had done in caring for him during his long recuperation. No, it would be better, he decided, to leave the village. If he could walk to those trees and back again, then that would indicate that he was sufficiently recovered to ride out in a day or two. The sooner the better, as far as he was concerned.

He started off across the valley. The snow lay about a foot deep on the ground, and that made it hard going for a man who had just spent several weeks flat on his back trying to heal after being shot twice, but Renshaw pushed himself. Looking over his shoulder, he was annoyed to see that Pretty Shield was following him. Not trying to keep up, just keeping about fifty paces behind him. He stopped and gestured for her to go back. "I don't want no company!" he said. Pretty Shield stopped and just stood there. "Leave me alone, damn it!" he shouted. But still she did not turn to go. Muttering, Renshaw had no recourse but to continue on his way.

By the time he reached the edge of the trees he had to stop to catch his breath. The long walk had taken a lot out of him; he could scarcely believe that he was still this weak, but there was no getting around the fact that he was a long way from being completely well. Still, he did not want to reveal his weakness in Pretty Shield's presence. He had to at least *look* like he was recovered, so that he would face no resistance when he announced his plans to depart. And then, of course, there was his pride. So he stood there for only a moment, glancing back again to see that Pretty Shield was still coming, following his footsteps in the snow. "Damn stubborn woman," he rasped, and forced himself to start ascending the slope, going deeper into the trees. He had to focus on putting one foot in front of the other to such an extent that he paid little attention to his surroundings. That was out of character for Red Renshaw—and it cost him dearly.

He heard Pretty Shield shout a warning—just seconds before he heard a wild and savage cry that jerked his head around. A man was hurling himself down the slope at him, a Bowie knife in one hand and a pistol in the other, and Renshaw only had time to identify his attacker before the Spaniard plowed into him, knocking him off his feet.

Rolling clumsily away from the Comanchero, Renshaw yelled at Pretty Shield to run, and he managed to catch just a glimpse of her as the Sioux woman started forward, her first instinct to help him. "For God's sake, run!" he roared, and then the Spaniard had him by the hair and was pulling him to his feet, and Renshaw felt the cold, razor-sharp blade of the man's knife biting into the flesh at his throat, and he stopped struggling.

Pretty Shield watched in horror—and realized that she could do nothing by herself to help Renshaw. His only hope rested with the warriors in the village. She whirled and began to run, fleet as a antelope, through the snow, retracing her steps, and shouting at the top of her lungs, though she feared she was still too far from the skin lodges for anyone to hear her.

The Spaniard growled a curse and raised his pistol, drawing a bead on the Sioux woman. But just as his finger tightened on the trigger, Renshaw pushed backward with all his strength. Not that he had much, but it was enough to throw the Spaniard off balance and spoil his aim. The pistol barked, but Renshaw was relieved to see that Pretty Shield did not fall. Uttering a sound of incoherent rage, the Spaniard savagely pistol-whipped Renshaw, gashing his skull open, and Renshaw crumpled, blood streaming down his face. But the Spaniard wasn't done; he drove his knee into Renshaw's face, smashing his nose, and the Indian trader fell facedown into the blood-splattered snow.

"You bastard," rasped the Spaniard. "Don't you die on me yet." He reached down and again grabbed a handful of hair to yank the half-conscious Renshaw to his feet. This time he pushed Renshaw up against a nearby tree trunk, put his face up close to that of his victim, and grinned. "I have been waiting for days for you to come out to see me, Red," said the Comanchero. "As you might guess, I have a debt to settle with you."

"How . . . ?"

The Spaniard laughed, an ugly sound filled with malice. "How did I find you? It was easy enough. Your friend Hawkes left a trail that I could follow here. I grew tired of waiting, *amigo.* I even thought about going into the village after you. But I thought better of it. Hawkes would not have brought you here if he was not a friend of the Crow."

"Hawkes is long gone."

"Ah yes, I know. Gone to the Powder River country. But I will find him. I did not want to leave until I had settled my score with you."

Renshaw looked the Spaniard in the eye—and saw his own death. A sudden calm resignation swept over him.

"Then what are you waiting for?"

The Spaniard glanced in the direction of the village. Pretty Shield was halfway there, and he could tell that her cries of alarm had already stirred up some activity within the skin lodges. In a matter of minutes the Absaroke warriors would be on their ponies and riding this way.

"What a shame," muttered the Spaniard, "that we do not have more time to talk. Just know this, my friend. No one crosses me and lives."

He drove the Bowie knife deep into Renshaw's throat and slashed viciously sideways, nearly decapitating the Indian trader, and then stepped back with a pleased expression on his face—a face splattered with the hot blood of his victim. Renshaw's body flopped into the snow at the base of the tree and the Spaniard spit on the still-twitching corpse for good measure. Then, with one last look at the distant Crow village, he loped up the slope and disappeared into the trees.

A few minutes later, He Smiles Twice and a dozen warriors arrived on the scene. The chief had swept Pretty Shield up on the pony behind him as he rode out of the village—and now she was the first to leap to the ground and run to Renshaw's body. With an angry gesture, He Smiles Twice dispatched the warriors into the trees to follow the trail left by the Spaniard. They kicked their ponies up the slope and He Smiles Twice dismounted to stand at Pretty Shield's side.

"Who would do this?" she whispered, shocked by the brutal way Red Renshaw had died.

"What did the man look like?"

"I only saw him for a moment. He had long yellow hair and the nose of a hawk. He wore leggings that had circle of silvers on them."

He Smiles Twice nodded. "That is the man that White Crow described to me, the one who was hunting him. The one whose companions White Crow killed."

Pretty Shield glanced along the slope. The Crow warriors had disappeared over the crest above them. Would they catch the man who had killed Renshaw? She hoped so. But somehow she doubted that they would. The man had come out of nowhere to attack Renshaw, and she suspected that he would vanish back into thin air. She wondered if he was even human, for how could a human being kill so savagely in cold blood? Whatever he was, he was free now to go after Hawkes. And that thought sent chills down Pretty Shield's spine.

More warriors arrived from the village. He Smiles Twice sent some of them up the hill to join the others in their pursuit of the killer. The others placed Renshaw's remains in a blanket, lashed it into a tight bundle with rawhide, and transported it back to the village. He Smiles Twice urged Pretty Shield to go back, too, but she refused. He Smiles Twice didn't insist. Instead, he mounted his pony, and helped her up behind him again, then proceeded up the slope.

In an hour's time they were on their way back to the village. As Pretty Shield had feared, their prey had simply disappeared. His trail had led them to an icy stream, and then was gone. The warriors had searched both up and down the stream to find where he had emerged, but to no avail. It was as though he had sprouted wings and flown away. Deep in thought, Pretty Shield said nothing during the ride back.

He Smiles Twice convened a council of elders, and it was attended by many of the warriors in the village. The discussion centered on whether to send out a war party to find the killer of Red Renshaw. He Smiles Twice pointed out that Renshaw had been placed in their care and keeping by their brother White Crow, and it was a stain upon their honor that they had failed to protect him from the Comanchero. One of the elders argued that it would be unwise to send out a party, as it was apparent that another winter storm was coming soon to the mountains. But this dissent aside, the general consensus was that He Smiles Twice had made a valid point, and that further effort should be made to apprehend the Comanchero. They owed that much to White Crow.

Preparations were immediately underway. On account of this, He Smiles Twice did not even think about Pretty Shield until some hours later, after the war party was on its way. Only then did he consider how distraught she had been, and went to the skin lodge where she lived with the other maidens. There he was informed that she had left some time earlier. He searched the village for her, to no avail. His concern growing, he employed several braves to assist him in his search. But by nightfall it was evident that Pretty Shield was gone. No one had actually seen her leave the village. Somehow she had slipped away undetected. It was not until the following day that He Smiles Twice learned of the missing pony. The owner of the pony was incensed, and insisted on going after her. But He Smiles Twice said no, and assured the brave that he would be compensated from the chief's own remuda.

There was considerable speculation among the Absaroke as to why Pretty Shield had run away. He Smiles Twice was certain that he knew the answer, but kept his own counsel.

In his opinion there could be only one reason for her sudden departure.

She had gone north—north to the Powder River country—to warn Gordon Hawkes about the Comanchero.

Chapter Nineteen

It took a while, but eventually Bob North realized that there was no point in huddling out of sight in the skin lodge with the hope that keeping a low profile in the Powder River village of the Sioux would improve his chances of staying alive. All of the Sioux warriors knew he was in their midst, and he figured a good many of them weren't happy about it. It boiled down to whether or not they would honor the wishes of Red Cloud and let him live. After a while, he simply could not bear to remain confined in the skin lodge. So one day he ventured out, well aware of the fact that it might be the last thing he ever did. To his amazement, he was allowed to wander freely through the village. He was the recipient of some ugly stares, but no one laid a hand on him. The next day he took another, longer stroll. This time he tested his luck, venturing to the edge of the village and standing there to gaze at the vast Sioux horse herd spread out across the snow-covered valley, the ponies pawing at the snow to get to the grass below. He tried to calculate his odds of getting to one of those horses and making good his escape. Not that he had any destination in mind. Sooner or later word would spread about the way he had betrayed the Army, and no place would be safe for him. But then, neither was this place. The only reason he was still alive was because Red Cloud thought he might be of some use. When he ceased to be of any value, then he would be put to death. Of that he was certain.

But when North turned away from his long perusal of the horse herd he was confronted by a pair of grim warriors. Fully armed, they were just standing there, watching him—waiting for him to make a move. To give them an excuse to kill him where he stood. North's slender hopes came unraveled right then and there. Giving the warriors a wide berth, he walked back into the village, returning to his skin lodge to sit there for the remainder of the day feeling sorry for himself.

Early the next morning, Red Cloud came to visit him. The Oglala chief was accompanied by Spotted Calf. The two Indians sat cross-legged around the fire in the center of the lodge.

"When Spotted Calf brought you here," said Red Cloud gravely, "you said that you agreed to scout for the bluecoats only because you wanted to help the Sioux."

"That's true," lied North. "And I have helped you since I've been here, haven't I?"

"You have done as I have asked," agreed Red Cloud. "Still, there are many in this village who do not trust you. They say, how can we trust a man who would betray his own kind? Does a man who would do that have any honor? If he does not, then he cannot be trusted."

"Don't they remember that I once lived among the Sioux? The woman I loved was one of your people. I came to think of the Sioux as my own people. That is not unheard of. Many other white men have done the same."

Red Cloud nodded. "Ten suns ago, two men left the fort and traveled south. I believe they were messengers sent by the bluecoat general to Laramie. I think the bluecoat general has asked for more soldiers. We wonder, will more soldiers come?"

"It's likely," replied North. "I know the general in command at Laramie. A man by the name of Merritt. I believe he would send every soldier he could spare to Fort Phil Kearney, yes."

Red Cloud glanced at Spotted Calf, and the latter spoke up. "How many soldiers could be sent?"

North shrugged, thinking it over. His last sojourn at Fort Laramie had occurred over a year ago, and he had no idea of that post's garrison numbers. "There would not be that many. Maybe a hundred. But I'm just guessing."

"Even if they are only a hundred, they must not be allowed to reach the fort," said Red Cloud.

"I don't understand what you're waiting for," confessed North. "You have thousands of warriors here. There are only a few hundred soldiers in Fort Phil Kearney. Why don't you attack? You could wipe out Carrington's command."

Red Cloud nodded. "Yes, it could be done. But hundreds of Sioux and Northern Cheyenne would die."

"But it would be a great blow against the Army. It's possible that such a defeat would force them to give up the idea of building outposts in Sioux country. Might be that it would shut down the Bozeman Trail completely."

"You do not know your own people very well if you think they would simply give up," said the Oglala chief, chiding North. "No, they will send more soldiers. And that is why I cannot suffer the losses that would come from attacking the fort."

"Then what do you expect to gain by all this?" asked North, exasperated. At this point he just wanted this situation—an intolerable morass from his point of view—to be resolved, and he didn't much care how it was done, who won or lost, and how many perished in the process.

"It would be better," replied Red Cloud, "if Carrington would leave the fort. If he would take all his bluecoats and go back where he came from."

"Red Cloud believes that if the soldiers leave on their own, some time might pass before they return," explained Spotted Calf. "But if we kill all of Carrington's men, the Army will have to march against us. It would be a matter of honor for your people."

North understood then—and he had to admit that Red Cloud had a point. He just proved, North thought, why this man was chief of the Oglala. He was one smart hombre. Now it all made sense to him. Now he could fathom why Red Cloud had not ordered an all-out assault on the fort. And why he wanted to keep the relief column from reaching its destination. If he could destroy or turn back that column, the garrison at Fort Phil Kearney would be devastated by the news. Morale would plummet. Carrington might feel he had no choice but to abandon the fort. Especially if Red Cloud convinced him in some way that he would be allowed to go unmolested.

"Tomorrow, Spotted Calf will take five hundred warriors," said Red Cloud, "to stop the bluecoats who are coming from Laramie." He pointed a gnarled finger at Bob North. "You will ride with him."

"Me?" North was stunned. "Why me? What for?"

"You say more than once that you are here to help the Sioux, that even when you scouted for the bluecoats that was what you were doing. Now you will be given a chance to prove yourself."

"Haven't I already done that?" asked North, trying to keep the panic out of his voice. "Didn't I lead the bluecoats into an ambush, just as you told me to?"

"You have proven yourself to me. But, as you see, there are many warriors who still do not trust you. If you fight beside them, then they will see with their own eyes that you mean what you say."

Bob North didn't want to fight. He especially did not want to make himself a target for the soldiers, who would pay special attention to any white man who rode with the Sioux. But what choice did he have? The answer was obvious. Unless he continued to do what Red Cloud told him to do, the Sioux would never let down their guard enough for him to escape. He doubted they would ever really trust him. But maybe if he rode with Spotted Calf and managed to stay alive, then they might not watch him so closely. And there was even a slim possibility that he could escape during the fight between Spotted Calf's five hundred warriors and the relief column. Once before, when he had led Fetterman into ambush, he had used the confusion of battle to slip away.

"I would be honored to ride with Spotted Calf, of course," he said, and could only hope that he sounded sincere.

Red Cloud nodded. "That is good. A horse and weapons will be brought to you in the morning."

With that, the Oglala chief rose and left the skin lodge, followed by Spotted Calf. The latter waited until they were beyond far enough away from the lodge so that there was no possibility of North overhearing his words before he spoke.

"Why must I take him?" he asked the chief. "He is a coward. He will be of no use in a fight."

"I know." Red Cloud did not often tolerate anyone questioning his decisions, but in this case he was willing to make an exception, since until a few moments ago Spotted Calf had not been privy to his true motive for visiting North. All Spotted Calf had known was that he wanted to ask the white scout about the garrison at Fort Laramie. The news that North would accompany him when he rode against the relief column had to have been as big a shock to Spotted Calf as it had been to North himself. "Remember," he added, "that two of Carrington's scouts will be riding with the bluecoats from Laramie. They are the bluecoats' eyes. Kill them, and the soldiers are blind."

Spotted Calf pondered this for a moment, trying to figure out what this had to do with Bob North. "You are telling me to use our prisoner to lure the scouts to their deaths."

Red Cloud nodded. "I believe those scouts will take great risks to capture or kill our prisoner, because he has betrayed them." The Oglala chief paused for a moment, frowning as he glanced back at the skin lodge in which Bob North huddled. "It is true that I have deceived that man. As you know, Spotted Calf, I put great store in the truth."

"There is no dishonor in lying to our enemies."

"Yes, there is. But I must do whatever is necessary to defeat the bluecoats, and save our people."

"We will stop the soldiers from Laramie," promised Spotted Calf, "or we will not return."

Red Cloud smiled faintly at this bold talk. "No, you must return, and bring back with you as many of our brothers as you can."

Spotted Calf nodded. They walked a little while in silence before the Oglala chief spoke again.

"But do not bring North back," said Red Cloud.

Spotted Calf understood. Bob North would be a constant reminder for Red Cloud that he had acted dishonorably, according to his own standards, and Spotted Calf thought that sparing his chief this inner conflict would be the least he could do.

Jim Bridger agreed with Hawkes that the closer the relief column got to the Powder River country, the greater the chance that they would be attacked by Red Cloud's Sioux. They never seriously entertained the notion that they could actually reach Fort Phil Kearney before being discovered by the hostiles. Red Cloud was too careful for that, and he had surrounded the fort with a screen of scouts. It was a small miracle that both of them had gotten through. Two companies of bluecoat cavalry would not do so without a fight, of this they were convinced.

Major Furness was counting on them to give him

some warning when the Sioux did come. So it was
that every morning, before the sun was up, and before the camp began to wake, Hawkes and Bridger
rose and stirred up last night's fire and brewed some
coffee and used it to wash down some jerky and
hardtack before saddling their horses and riding out.
Furness had reliable maps and knew how to read
them, so they didn't have to worry about acting as
guides for the column; every evening they would
huddle with the major and become acquainted with
the route he intended to take on the following day.
That way they always knew about where to find
the soldiers.

They usually rode together, but they didn't do so
just so they'd have company. In enemy country, two
rifles were better than one. Few words passed between them as they rode; their job was to keep an
eye out for Indians, and they devoted all of their
attention to the task at hand. For five days they saw
nothing that would alarm them. But on the morning
of the sixth day, when Hawkes calculated that Fort
Phil Kearney—and his daughter—were only about
seventy, eighty miles farther north, they both spotted
something that made them abruptly check their
horses.

"You see that?" asked Old Gabe, peering intently
at a tree-covered slope about a quarter mile to the
northwest of their location.

Hawkes merely nodded. Like Bridger, he had noticed a flock of birds that was winging across the
sky and headed directly for the timber had suddenly
veered off, as though startled. There was something
in those woods. Their first consideration was the fact

that they were nearly within rifle range. To proceed
would place them in jeopardy if the forest were filled
with hostiles, even though it had been their experience that most Indians were not very good long-
range shots. But if they didn't get closer they couldn't
do their job.

Hawkes looked at Bridger—and Old Gabe looked
back at him. They were thinking along the same lines.

"So which one of us goes?" asked Bridger.

"I'll do it," said Hawkes.

"How come you get to have all the fun?"

Hawkes smiled. "You said it yourself, back at
Laramie."

Old Gabe scowled. "What did I say?"

"That you're getting old, but I'm not slowing
down much."

Bridger grimaced. "That's why a person should
never talk much. Your words always come back to
haunt you."

"Just remember why we're here, Gabe," said
Hawkes. "My daughter comes first, for me."

Bridger nodded. He understood what his friend
was trying to convey. If Hawkes got into trouble,
Bridger knew that his first instinct would be to rush
to stand by his side, regardless of the odds. But what
he had to do instead, if there were Sioux in those
woods, was to hasten back to the column and report.
Even if it meant leaving Hawkes to die alone. Because Furness and his soldiers *had* to get to Fort Phil
Kearney. That was more important to Hawkes than
his own life, and Bridger had to respect that.

"Don't go getting yourself killed, hoss," murmured Bridger.

"I'll try not to." Hawkes kicked his horse into a canter and rode on. Old Gabe unlimbered his long rifle, just in case. Though his eyes weren't what they used to be, he figured he might be able to make a shot count even at this distance.

As he approached the timber, Hawkes also drew his long gun. The Plains Rifle normally rode in a leather sheath tied to the saddle beneath his right leg. Now he rested the butt against his right thigh. He knew the rifle was ready—he'd made sure of that just an hour or so ago, prior to leaving camp. He kept his attention on the trees, searching for any telltale movement. He was beginning to think maybe they'd been misled by the behavior of the birds—when suddenly a horseman burst into view. Hawkes checked his horse and brought rifle to shoulder. But he didn't shoot, because the rider was clearly a white man.

The horseman stopped his own mount cold when he spotted Hawkes. He glanced back at the trees, then spun the horse to the north and, low in the saddle, urged it into a gallop. He gave every indication of a man being pursued. But what puzzled Hawkes was that there didn't seem to be anybody chasing him. *And why the hell,* wondered the mountain man, *is he running from me*? It didn't make any sense, and Hawkes hesitated, uncertain what to do next.

Bridger, though, was on the move. Hawkes heard Old Gabe shouting and turned in the saddle to see his friend riding hard. For a moment, though, the distance was too great, and Hawkes couldn't tell what Bridger was yelling. He had to keep his horse under tight rein; the animal was pivoting, fiddle-footed, ready to run, since that was what all the other horses in the vicinity seemed to be doing. But Hawkes was listening to his instincts—instincts honed by many years in dangerous country—and right now they were warning him that something was very, very wrong. The hair at the nape of his neck was standing on end, and that was a signal he was not inclined to ignore.

"It's North!" shouted Bridger. "Stop that son of a bitch!"

Hawkes could hear Old Gabe now, shouting at the top of his lungs while steering his fleet pony in pursuit of the man who had emerged from the trees. He recognized the name. During his sojourn at Fort Phil Kearney, Gunnison had told him all about the scout who had betrayed the garrison. That explained why Old Gabe was acting so impulsively; he had been responsible for all the civilian scouts attached to Carrington's command, and he had taken North's treason very personally. So much so that he wasn't thinking—hadn't stopped to wonder why North had come right out into plain view as he had. The only reason he would have done that . . .

Hawkes turned his attention back to the trees. This time he saw them—horsemen, dozens of them, coming down the slope. The woods were crawling with Sioux braves, their bodies and ponies painted for war.

The mountain man spun his horse around and gave it free rein. The animal responded by leaping into a gallop. Hawkes maneuvered to intercept Old Gabe. Bridger hadn't seen the Indians yet; his focus was on North. Before Hawkes could reach Bridger, the Sioux broke cover. Even as he heard Hawkes yelling at him to run for his life, Old Gabe saw why. Forgetting all about North, he turned his horse and fled, Hawkes right behind him.

A glance back revealed that hundreds of Sioux had now emerged from the cover of the trees. And they were all giving chase. In spite of the circumstances, Hawkes thought it was an awe-inspiring sight. It was as though the entire Sioux nation was after him. He'd faced steep odds before, but nothing like five hundred to two. Whether he and Bridger lived or died depended for the most part now on the horses they rode. The Second Cavalry went to great pains to acquire the best mounts, and for that Hawkes was grateful. The Sioux ponies were wiry and quick, and the mountain man could only hope that they lacked the stamina that his horse and Old Gabe's possessed.

After a mile or two of full-speed flight across the rolling plains, Hawkes noticed that he and his companion were putting a little more distance between themselves and the Indians—or most of the Indians, anyway. About thirty, maybe forty, of the warriors were managing to keep pace, while the balance began to fall behind. A moment later, most of the Sioux had given up the chase. Hawkes couldn't know whether they had done so under orders from the chiefs that led them, or whether it was common consent among the braves that they would not catch their prey. Either way, Hawkes figured they were hoping that the handful of warriors who had pulled ahead could get the job down.

Reaching the top of a swell, Hawkes and Bridger were greeted by a happy sight. There was the relief column not a quarter mile away, and coming straight at them. As though each could read the other's mind, both scouts checked their horses and leaped from the saddle, rifles in hand. Standing calf-deep in snow, they took careful aim at the oncoming Sioux. The warriors were not deterred. In fact, Hawkes surmised that they were cheered to see their prey turn to fight. The swell prevented them from seeing the cavalry column. They thought that a triumph was within their grasp, that in moments they would have two fresh scalps, when in fact disaster lurked just out of sight.

Bridger fired first, when the warriors were about four hundred yards away. It was a long shot, but Old Gabe made it count. A heartbeat later, Hawkes squeezed the trigger of the Plains Rifle, and lightened the load of a second Sioux pony. Both men reloaded with lightning speed and both got off another shot. Two more warriors fell. But the rest kept coming. A quick over-the-shoulder glance assured Hawkes that, having heard the gunfire, Major Furness was leading his troops forward at a gallop. Before Hawkes could finish reloading a second time, and when the warriors were but a hundred yards away and beginning to fire back, filling the air around him with hot lead, the cavalry surged over the swell, thundering past the two scouts on both sides. Caught completely by surprise, the warriors tried to turn their ponies and flee. But in an instant the troopers were on them. For a minute or two the gunfire was a constant din. Soldier and warrior fought hand to hand in a melee of pivoting horses and dying men, a scene of ferocity and carnage partially obscured from Hawkes's view

by a pall of gunsmoke. He and Bridger stood their
ground and picked off several Sioux who managed
to break free of the bluecoat swarm.

And then, abruptly, it was over. Every warrior had
fallen. There were a few more gunshots as the troopers finished off the wounded. Hawkes understood
that this was a brutal necessity. The relief column
could not be burdened with prisoners. Such was warfare on the high plains. You either lived or died—
there was no other alternative.

Major Furness rode back to join Hawkes and
Bridger, wiping the bloody blade of his saber on a
trouser leg before returning it to its scabbard.

"A pretty large scouting party, if you ask me," he
said, his voice hoarse.

Bridger shook his head. "Ain't no scouting party.
Probably three, four hundred more of them just a
couple miles north of here."

"Three or four hundred! Are you certain?"

"At least that many," confirmed Hawkes. "They'll be
riding to the sound of the gunfire, Major. Count on it."

Bridger nodded. "Red Cloud must have known
we'd gotten through to Laramie, and figured reinforcements were on their way to Carrington. So he
sent out a crew big enough to get the job done."

Furness grimly surveyed the countryside, looking
for the strongest possible defensive position.

"Don't do it, Major," advised Bridger, divining the
officer's intentions. "You make a stand out here,
they'll just cut us down."

"Then what do you suggest?"

Hawkes thanked his lucky stars that he was riding
with an officer who wasn't too proud to ask a civilian

for advice when it really counted. He'd met some—
a certain few of Carrington's subordinates up at
Kearney came immediately to mind—who thought
that just because they had graduated from West
Point, or fought in some big battle back East during
the war, that they knew better than any frontiersman
how to wage war against the Indian.

"Take the fight to them, Major," said Bridger.
"Meet 'em head on."

Furness nodded curtly. "Yes. Yes, of course. Good
idea." Spinning his horse around, he shouted for
his lieutenants.

As he and Hawkes turned for their horses, Bridger
said, "Well, here we go, hoss. If we get to Fort Phil
Kearney alive, you buy the drinks this go 'round."

"Done," said Hawkes.

Their horses had demonstrated that they were
well-trained cavalry mounts; ground-hitched, they
stood where their riders had left them, pawing at the
snow to get to the dead mat of grass beneath, un-
moved by all the activity around them.

In short order Furness had his men formed in a
line, two troopers deep. He took his place in the center with the color sergeant, who had passed the regimental guidon to a corporal and was unfurling the
Stars and Stripes which he had taken from its casing.
The troopers were busy loading their Spencers.
Bridger rode for the right end of the line, so Hawkes
went to the left. The two troopers at that end spared
him a glance. One was at least ten years the senior
of the other; he had a sweeping mustache and sun-
faded eyes. The younger looked to be hardly more
than a kid fresh off the farm.

"You two keep an eye on me," said Hawkes. "If I go somewhere, you come with me. Understand?"

The older man nodded. "You can count on it."

"I am," replied Hawkes. He looked at the younger cavalryman. "You been in a scrape with Indians before?"

"Yes, sir," said the kid. "But not like this one is gonna be."

Hawkes smiled faintly. "You'll do."

"Hell yes, he will," said the older confidently. "Besides, Billy, it'll be one hell of a tale to tell your grandchildren."

"Yeah," said Billy, a little breathlessly. "I hope so, Riley. I hope so."

Hawkes understood that he wasn't hoping that what was about to happen would meet the other trooper's qualifications for "one hell of a tale," but rather that he would survive to tell it.

The order came down the line to move out, and the line advanced, mounts held to a walk, the flags at the center snapping briskly in a stout north wind.

"What is that?" asked Billy, glancing skyward.

It sounded like thunder, but Hawkes knew that it wasn't.

A moment later the Sioux horde came into sight, seeming to rise up out of the ground as they swarmed up out of a low spot in the undulating, snow-blanketed plain.

"Lord have mercy," breathed Billy.

Spotting the bluecoats, the Sioux warriors let loose with shrill war cries, an unnerving sound, like the wailing of all the damned sentenced to an eternity of torment. The officers along the line shouted at their men to keep a tight formation and hold their fire. The Sioux surged forward, three hundred yards, two hundred—and then Furness gave the order all the cavalrymen were aching to hear, and even as the lieutenants passed it along the Spencer carbines spoke, a ragged volume, a hundred rifles spewing death into the mass of warriors. The result was dramatic—suddenly dozens of war ponies were without riders. The officers bellowed out orders to keep firing, but this was hardly necessary; the troopers kept slinging lead into the Sioux onslaught, blunting the charge. And as the warriors faltered Furness brandished his saber, the blade gleaming in the pale winter sunlight, and the blue line rushed forward. It was, thought Hawkes, impeccable timing. They crashed into the formless mass of Sioux, many of whom scattered like quail. Some stood their ground and hurled themselves into hand-to-hand combat with the bluecoats.

Hawkes noticed a dozen or so warriors to his left, a group that had split off from the rest as the cavalry line advanced. Fleeing at first, these Indians realized that the bluecoat line was advancing in close order, and none of the troopers were in pursuit. Perhaps shamed by their initial reaction to the cavalry's advance, a half-dozen of them turned and came in from the rear. This was what the mountain man had been worried about, and why he had told the two troopers at the end of the line with him to pay close attention to his actions. Veering off from the line, he brought down one of the warriors with his long gun—no mean feat from the back of a moving horse. He was gratified to see that, true to their word, Riley and

Billy were coming with him. Closing with the Indians, he launched himself at the nearest one, carrying the Sioux off his war pony and to the ground. Hawkes freed himself from the warrior's grasp and got to his feet, discarding his empty rifle and drawing the pistol from his belt, shooting the Sioux as the brave rose, war club in hand. The mountain man turned just in time to see Riley fall, a lance driven through his chest. Then his attention was drawn to a pair of warriors coming straight at him. The pony of the Sioux he had just slain went down almost at his feet, killed instantly by a stray bullet, and Hawkes didn't hesitate—he hurdled the dead animal and leaped back aboard his own horse, standing calmly in the middle of this storm of violence. Still mounted, Billy was putting his Spencer carbine to good use, dropping one and then a second warrior. The two surviving Indians changed their minds about rejoining the fray and headed for the hills.

Hawkes checked his horse alongside Billy's and glanced at the young man's stricken expression as he gazed at the fallen Riley.

"He's dead," said the mountain man bluntly. "You can mourn him later. Let's go."

He led the way, returning to the end of the line, but as quickly as it had begun the fight was over. The Sioux were in full retreat, leaving the field in all directions, and Furness was smart enough to forgo pursuit. Hawkes anxiously looked for Bridger, and was relieved to see that Old Gabe was still among the living, standing with reins in hand over the body of a Sioux war chief, distinguishable from the other braves by the buffalo-horn headdress that lay near the body.

"This here's Spotted Calf," Bridger told Hawkes as the latter drew near. "One of Red Cloud's chief lieutenants. I reckon he was in charge of this bunch. And when he went down the others lost heart."

Hawkes grimly surveyed the field of battle. He estimated that nearly a hundred Sioux had fallen. Amazingly, the cavalry losses were light—a dozen killed, as many again wounded.

Major Furness joined them. "Think they'll be back?" he asked his scouts.

Bridger shook his head. "Not right away. They'll either go back to their village, or regroup somewhere and try to figure out who will lead them now that Spotted Calf here is dead. But that could take them a while."

Furness nodded. "Good. Then we should waste no time in getting to Fort Phil Kearney."

Hawkes couldn't argue with that.

Chapter Twenty

Brand Gunnison woke up alone. Of late he had come to expect that to happen. In the past he'd been the one who was the first to rise, and he'd always been careful not to wake his still-sleeping wife. But in recent weeks the roles were reversed. Now it was Grace who arose before the crack of dawn, and who went to great pains to make sure she did not disturb him as he lay sleeping. Gunnison had always before been afforded the comfort of feeling her warm, lithe body against his, of indulging in a moment of awe as he gazed at her face, sometimes partially obscured behind a veil of that pale yellow hair Grace had inherited from her mother. But these days he had to do without that moment.

What really bothered him was the way Grace was acting. He was worried about her, more worried than he had ever been. Not just about her safety—he'd worried about that every waking moment ever since they'd arrived in the Powder River country. No, it was her frame of mind that concerned him just as much now. So, instead of waking to the pleasing circumstance of having his wife sleeping snugly and soundly at his side, Gunnison now got up with a persistent uneasiness in the pit of his stomach, and he hastened to get dressed so that he could go out and find her.

As he emerged from their quarters and scanned the parade ground, he noted that the first gray shreds of morning were lightening the eastern sky. It would be a clear day, but cold and windy, as was usually the case this time of year. Snow lay heavy on the trees that blanketed the surrounding heights; here in the fort it had been turned to brown mush by the tread of many feet. The garrison was just now stirring—apart from the night guard on the walls, a few soldiers were moving about between the structures that encircled the parade ground. Grace was nowhere to be seen, however, and Gunnison tried, without much success, to keep that unease in the pit of his stomach from escalating into something approaching panic.

The sergeant appeared, as he always did, with a cup of steaming hot coffee in hand. The noncom was familiar with his captain's routine, and seldom failed to be there when Gunnison first emerged from his billet.

"Have you seen my wife?" Gunnison asked him.

"No, sir. Not today I haven't. Here's some java for you."

Buttoning up his longcoat and turning up the collar against the morning's bitter cold, Gunnison ignored the proffered cup. "I have to find her," he muttered, almost to himself, and turned away.

As he prowled the fort, Gunnison's thoughts were consumed by his wife's recent behavior. Gone was that cheerful smile that had always warmed his heart. Gone was that girlish delight in being with him that she had always before exhibited. What was troubling Grace? He wasn't quite sure. A combination of things, he supposed. Worry about her father, who had been gone for three weeks now, and no word as to whether he was alive or dead. Concern for her friend Laura, as well. And of course she hadn't had the time to come to terms with her mother's passing, either. Gunnison realized that there was precious little he could do to assuage her concerns and fears with regard to all those matters.

But there was more to it. It struck him that, more and more these days, Grace had been acting like Laura Denning following the death of her husband at the hands of the Sioux. It was as though Grace was in mourning. As though she had some dreadful premonition that she, too, would lose her husband, in the same way that Laura had lost hers. So perhaps it was understandable that instead of being happy in his presence, Grace seemed immeasurably saddened. Gunnison couldn't imagine what it was like for her—to look at the man she loved and know that he was a dead man, that soon—perhaps today—she would lose him forever.

He finally found her near the stables, standing at one of the corrals where the teamsters kept their mule teams. Several of the knobheads had come near her, looking for food. She just stood there, watching them, her dress and shawl and yellow hair whipped by the gusty wind. Gunnison's first impulse was to go to her, to give her his longcoat to ward off the cold, perhaps to put his arms around her. But he didn't know what he could say to her. There was really only one thing that he could say that might do any good. And he wasn't sure he could stand to see that look in her eyes when she glanced up at him, that look of profound sorrow that tore at his heart and left his emotions hemorrhaging.

Instead, he turned on his heel and walked with long strides full of purpose back to the parade ground and his quarters. Once there, he did not even bother removing his coat before sitting at a small table, turning up the oil lamp for illumination, and taking out a pen, inkwell and a sheet of paper from a hinged box that contained his writing materials. He sat there for a long while, pen poised over paper, stunned by the enormity of the decision he had just made, more than a little rattled by the uncertain prospects that loomed in his future once he did what he had decided to do. But all that was required to motivate him to go ahead with it was the forlorn image of his wife, standing there in the mud by the corral, battered by the bitter winds.

He put pen to paper—and was interrupted by a hammering on the door.

"Come in," he rasped.

The sergeant stuck his head around the door. "Captain, the relief column!"

Gunnison shot to his feet, and followed the sergeant outside. Suddenly the parade ground—virtually empty only moments before—was swarming with soldiers. Across the way, General Carrington, accompanied by Powell and Ten Eyck and several aides, came boiling out of the headquarters building. The sergeant began running in an ungainly, horse-warped gait, toward the main gate. Gunnison felt the urge to follow, but decided that he could see everything he needed—*wanted*—to see from the porch of weather-warped boards fronting his quarters. Orders

were given and the heavy-timbered portals of the
gate swung open. A few minutes later the men from
Fort Laramie began to file through—and Gunnison
smiled as he recognized first the Second Cavalry col-
ors and then Major Furness at the head of the column. The smile broadened as he saw Gordon
Hawkes, riding alongside Jim Bridger not far behind
the major. It seemed as though the entire garrison
had congregated on the parade ground now, and a
lusty cheer rose up to greet the reinforcements. Not
even the bodies of a dozen troopers lashed down
over their horses at the end of the column could do
much to subdue the enthusiasm of the soldiers in
Carrington's command.

Gunnison's attention was drawn from this spectacle by the arrival of his wife. Grace came around the
corner of the building and joined him on the porch.
He shrugged out of his longcoat and draped it over
her shoulders; she barely noticed, intent on searching
the scene before her for sign of her father.

"He's alive," he said. "Right there." And he
pointed to Hawkes, who at that moment spotted
them and steered his horse through the crowd to
approach their quarters. Grace couldn't wait for
him to reach them—she rushed out across the parade ground, and Hawkes leaped to the ground to
embrace her. Gunnison hesitated, not wanting to
intrude on their reunion, and feeling somewhat
awkward standing there, watching them. Feeling
vastly relieved that Grace hadn't lost her father,
too. In fact, he was far more relieved about that
than he was that the reinforcements had finally
come. He wasn't sure what a hundred more men

could accomplish, but at least now the Army knew the situation on the Powder River. Surely by spring there would be more relief columns on their way. The government had too much riding on keeping the Bozeman Trail open to do otherwise. Or so he wanted to believe.

After a long embrace, Hawkes gently pulled away, smiling at his daughter.

"I was so afraid . . ." she began, but faltered, struggling to maintain her composure.

"I told you I'd come back, didn't I?"

"Yes." She smiled back at him. "And you've always kept your word."

Hawkes took her arm and walked over to where Gunnison was standing. "Morning, Captain."

"Glad to see you, sir," said Gunnison.

"What of Laura?" asked Grace.

"She's on her way home, safe and sound," said Hawkes. He saw no point in telling Grace about the feelings Laura had developed for him. "She's a strong girl, that one, and brave. We ran into a Cheyenne war party on the way to Laramie. She saved my life by killing one of them."

"Well, she was an Army wife, wasn't she?" murmured Grace, and gave Gunnison a look that he could not fathom.

"I had better go see Major Furness," said Gunnison. "He'll want to know the condition of the company." He grimaced. "What's left of it."

As he walked away, Grace pulled her father toward the door to her quarters. "Come in and warm yourself. I'll put some coffee on the stove."

That sounded good to Hawkes. It occurred to him

that he hadn't been warm for about three weeks. In his younger years he had been inured to the cold. But those days were gone. Now that his ordeal was over, he felt tired—and old.

Later that day, General Carrington called a staff meeting. Furness was in attendance, as was Gunnison, along with Ten Eyck and Powell and a couple of junior officers who had been breveted to take the place of those who had fallen. The presence of Hawkes and Bridger was also requested.

"Thanks to the prowess of Major Furness and his Second Cavalry," said Carrington, "and of course that of our scouts, Red Cloud has suffered a great setback. I believe it's possible that if we can demonstrate to the Sioux and their Northern Cheyenne allies that we have every intention of remaining here, and doing what we came here to do, that support for Red Cloud will erode. Possibly, a good many of his warriors will desert him."

The general paused, surveying the faces around the table, trying to judge the reaction of the men to what he had said so far. For his part, Gunnison tried desperately to keep the mounting apprehension he was experiencing from being revealed by his expression. He wasn't sure what Carrington was on the verge of proposing, but he was damned certain that he wasn't going to like it—and that it would probably cost many lives.

"Therefore," continued Carrington, "I have decided that we should act boldly. Red Cloud expects us to cower behind these walls. Well, gentlemen, the United States Army does not cower. It is my intention to press on with our plans to construct an outpost on the Tongue River."

The officers looked at one another. Gunnison was hoping that someone else would have the gumption to speak up, but as the seconds ticked by he realized, with a sinking feeling in his stomach, that such was not the case. So it was up to him.

"In the middle of winter, General?" he asked.

"I intend to proceed immediately, yes," said Carrington a little stiffly. Gunnison knew then that he had failed to keep his tone of voice from betraying his skepticism.

"That'll be mighty hard on the soldier boys you send out, General," drawled Bridger. "Food supplies are low. Forage for the horses and mules is scarce. And we could get hit by another blue norther or two before Old Man Winter is done with us for the year."

"The advantage of it will be that the Sioux will not expect us to act now," said Carrington. "If they understand that we are determined to proceed with our plans, regardless of everything they have done these past months, I am confident then they will grow discouraged. And that is when Red Cloud will find his forces dwindling daily."

"It's true that normally the various Sioux bands might begin to doubt Red Cloud, and they're under no obligation to follow him if they've lost faith in his ability to bring them victory," said Hawkes. "But these times are not normal. They won't ride away in order to fight some other day. Because they know there won't be another day if they don't stop you here and now, General."

Bridger nodded. "That's right," he said. "They won't back down this time."

Carrington frowned. He didn't appreciate the fact that both his scouts were counseling against his plan. "Captain Powell will be in charge of the detachment. He will take two companies of infantry. Major Furness, you will be so kind as to supply him with a company of your Second Cavalry. I want preparations to being immediately. And I expect you to march within the week, Captain Powell."

"Yes, sir," said Powell flatly. Gunnison couldn't tell what Powell's feelings about Carrington's foolhardy scheme really were, since Powell seemed much more competent than he in keeping those feelings hidden.

"Then, if there is nothing else, you gentlemen are dismissed," said Carrington.

As they filed out of the headquarters building, Gunnison lingered just outside the door watching the others scatter, and when he was sure that Major Furness was going to be walking alone, he hurried to catch up with his superior.

"Major Furness!"

Furness stopped and turned. "Yes, Captain?"

Gunnison didn't know any other way to go about what he had to do other than to be straightforward. So he took the folded piece of paper from beneath his longcoat and handed it to the major.

"What is this?" asked Furness.

"My resignation, sir."

Furness looked from the paper to Gunnison and then back to the paper, as though having a hard time comprehending what had just been conveyed to him. Finally, almost reluctantly, he unfolded the paper and read what Gunnison had written.

"Well," he said, at last, seeking the right words, "you could not have picked a more inappropriate time, Captain." He peered at Gunnison. "We've known each other for a couple of years now. You're a fine officer, one of the best in the regiment. And I'm certain that you're no coward. So what is this all about? And why now?"

Gunnison had hoped that Furness would not pry into his motives. It was a subject he desperately wanted to avoid. But then, he'd known all along that hoping along those lines was unrealistic.

"It's just . . . something that has to be done," he said lamely. "A personal matter."

"Does this have something to do with your wife, perhaps?"

Gunnison grimaced. There was no help for it. Furness would not simply accept his resignation and leave it at that. "Yes, sir. She's the reason I'm leaving the Army."

"But I always understood that the cavalry was your life, Captain. And surely she realized that when she married you."

Gunnison nodded. "Yes, sir, she did. But she had no idea, I suppose, how hard it would be on her. And I certainly never realized that."

"Did she ask you to do this? Is she forcing you to make a choice?"

Gunnison shook his head. "Absolutely not. She would never do that. But it's still a choice I have to make."

With a grimace, Furness folded the piece of paper and slipped it into a pocket. "You know what it will look like—your resigning under these circumstances. Some will say that you lost your nerve. That you're a coward. Of course, I know better. I know you've been in at least a dozen scrapes with Indians during your time out here."

"I don't care what people think," replied Gunnison a little defensively. "And I don't expect to be relieved of my duties immediately. I know that there is a shortage of officers in this garrison. And I never thought I could just walk away from the men in my company and leave them in this situation. But I wanted to tender that to you right now. So that you know. So that . . . at the first opportunity you can act upon it."

"I see." Furness nodded. "That's fair enough. And maybe you'll change your mind between now and then."

Gunnison shook his head emphatically. "Not a chance, Major."

"So . . . what will you do once you take off that uniform for the last time?"

Gunnison hesitated. It was a question he'd posed to himself, and always put the answer off until later. The fact was that he had no idea what he would do.

"Maybe there's a compromise here somewhere," murmured Furness.

"Compromise, sir? What kind of compromise?"

"What if you were assigned to ride a desk back East? Do you think that might solve the problem?"

"I had never even considered it," replied Gunnison. "I have no connections—and you have to have connections to get that kind of assignment, sir."

Furness smiled. "That's true. But you're forgetting something. My father is a senator from the great state of Ohio. And remember, he is also a war hero. Mustered the first volunteer regiment of Ohioans when the war broke out. Saw action at Fredericksburg, Chancellorsville, Gettysburg, the Wilderness. I would venture to say he knows just about everyone at the War Department."

"That would be too great an imposition—"

"Let me be the judge of that. Fact is, the Army can't afford to lose good officers, and you're one of the best I've seen."

"I haven't done very well here," said Gunnison. "There isn't much left of my company."

"Under these circumstances, I think it's remarkable that there's still a company at all. No, I know what I'm talking about. And I would go to great lengths to keep a man like you in the Army—where you belong."

A posting back East! Gunnison was stunned. When he'd first joined the cavalry he had scorned those staff officers who sat behind desks in the War Department. There was no glory to be had in such a job. But that was back when he'd been young and foolish—and, most importantly, single. And if it meant being able to wear the uniform of which he was so proud, then who was he to turn down such an offer? There was but one question in his mind: How would Grace react to the idea of moving east? She had been born in the mountains. All she knew was the wild country. The only civilization to which she had been exposed was that provided by the rough-and-tumble frontier metropolis of Denver. The cities back East were quite different. It was an entirely different world back there. Would she go along? And what about her father? To follow him east would mean she might never see her father again. Gunnison wasn't sure about much of anything anymore, but the one thing he *was* sure of was that Gordon Hawkes would never leave this country.

"Thank you, Major," he said, his gratitude heartfelt. "I would owe you a great debt."

"Until then, we'll just have to try to keep you alive," said Furness, smiling. "Your company will not be joining this little excursion the general has planned."

Though the major had not asked for his opinion, Gunnison took the chance of offering it anyway. "It's too risky, sir. Red Cloud is not going to attack this fort. If that had been an option for him he would have done it already—before you arrived. All we have to do is sit tight until spring, wait for more reinforcements. By then Carrington would be right— Red Cloud's warriors would be restless, discouraged. They'd start to drift away. But sending an expedition to the Tongue River is like throwing Red Cloud a bone."

The major's gaze was bleak. "That may all be true. But so is something else. Carrington is commanding officer here. If he ordered me to ride straight into hell, then I would have to do it, wouldn't I?"

"Yes, sir," said Gunnison, with a sigh. "Yes, sir, I guess you would have to."

He didn't think it was appropriate to add that if,

as he suspected, Furness intended to be the one accompanying Powell and his infantry to the Tongue, then that was exactly what he was going to be doing—riding straight into hell.

Chapter Twenty-one

Hawkes awoke abruptly, and realized that somebody was shaking him vigorously. He squinted into the darkness—he had no idea what time it was, but it sure looked like it was the middle of the night.

"You better come see this, hoss."

It was Bridger. Hawkes groaned. He was loath to give up his nice warm nest in the straw in the corner of the stables. Grace had offered—insisted—that he stay in their quarters, but there was very little room to spare in that cabin, and Hawkes didn't fancy the notion of being underfoot all the time. He much preferred the stables, especially since that would surround him with cavalry mounts—horses that were conditioned to act up if an Indian was in the vicinity. This conditioning was accomplished by hiring an Indian to beat the horse with a long switch. After just a few of these treatments, the animal would raise a ruckus if an Indian got close. As far as Hawkes knew, no hostile had ever penetrated Fort Phil Kearney, but it had become fairly common for one, or perhaps a handful, to be seen lurking around the outpost, and hardly a night passed that a sentry on the wall didn't shoot off his gun—often at a shadow, but sometimes at an Indian. Still, Hawkes figured there was a first time for everything, and he knew the Sioux well enough to know that getting inside the walls of the fort and wreaking a little havoc was something on the minds of more than a few of Red Cloud's warriors.

"Go away," said Hawkes. "I'm tired. If we're not under attack, then just leave me be."

Bridger would not cease and desist, but kept shaking Hawkes. "Come on, get up. This is important. You'll be sorry if you don't come on."

"You'll be sorry if it isn't important," groused Hawkes. He threw aside his blankets and got to his feet. As was his custom, he had been sleeping fully clothed, rifle beside him. Cradling the Hawken in his left arm, he looked about him. It was very dark in the stable, and he could see precious little. A horse in a nearby stall whickered softly. He followed Bridger outside. The sky was filled with stars. Even at this hour there was wind, coming in from the north, and cutting to the bone with its chill. The wind always seemed to be blowing on the Plains, regardless of the season or the hour. In fact, it was so constant that Hawkes had heard of it driving people crazy.

Bridger led him toward the water gates, and as they drew near Hawkes was surprised to see about forty soldiers congregated there. Even more surprisingly, the gates were open. He stayed on Old Gabe's heels as the latter elbowed his way through the crowd. Several of the men were holding lanterns aloft, and by the light they gave Hawkes could tell that something was hanging on the outside of one of the portals. In the next instant he realized that it wasn't something, but rather someone. A body had been pinned to the timbers of the gate with three lances. By the symbols on the shafts of those lances, Hawkes recognized them as being of Sioux manufacture. The body had been mutilated, but upon closer inspection Hawkes was sure it was someone he did not know. He glanced at Old Gabe.

"You know him?"

Bridger nodded. "This here is Bob North. Or was."

North—the man who had betrayed the expedition to the Sioux, at the cost of many lives. Hawkes had heard two versions of that betrayal, one from Old Gabe and the other from Gunnison. Both versions had made it plain that North was a man heartily despised. This then, was the man Hawkes had seen emerge from the timber and then turn to flee only a couple of days ago—right before the Sioux sprang their ambush.

"Looks like the Sioux did your job for you, Gabe," said Hawkes.

"Yep. I had about decided that when all this was over I would track North down and make him pay, no matter how long it took. Guess I can strike that off my list of things to do. But what I don't get is why? Why did the Sioux kill him?"

"Maybe they didn't have any more use for him," suggested Hawkes.

Bridger shrugged. "Guess we'll never know."

"Some of you men get him down," said Lieutenant Ten Eyck as he pushed his way through the crowd of soldiers.

"I hope you don't aim to bury him," said Bridger.

"Every white man deserves a Christian burial," said Ten Eyck. "No matter what he's done while alive."

"You can't bury him inside the fort. And if you

bury him beyond the walls, the coyotes will just dig him up anyway."

Ten Eyck didn't challenge Bridger's blunt statement that Bob North should not be interred within the confines of Fort Phil Kearney. He could tell that Old Gabe felt strongly about this, and he wasn't about to buck the famous scout.

"Then what do you suggest we do with the body?" asked the captain, as a handful of soldiers managed to get the corpse off the gate.

Bridger nodded in the direction of the darkness beyond the gate. "Just leave him out there. The scavengers will take care of the rest."

Ten Eyck hesitated. The treatment of Bob North's mortal remains that Bridger was suggesting ran counter to his feelings on the subject. He didn't care for North any more than the next man, but what Bridger wanted done with the corpse was downright uncivilized.

"All right," he said, at last. "You men carry him out about a hundred yards and leave him."

As the soldiers carried the carcass into the darkness, Bridger nodded with grim satisfaction etched on his deeply creased face and turned away. Watching him go as he stood alongside Hawkes, Ten Eyck shook his head and murmured, "You know, if you didn't know any better you might mistake him for a kindly old man."

Hawkes smiled. "He's a good man. But not one you'd ever want to cross."

Captain Powell moved quickly to finish preparations for his expedition to the Tongue River. Under

the present winter conditions, best estimates were
that it would take him at least a week to reach his
destination, and then there was the matter of erecting
an outpost. Scouts assured him that there was plenty
of good timber in that vicinity. As to game, well, that
was another matter altogether. All the fighting that
had taken place in the vicinity of Fort Phil Kearney
had made game scarce. It could only be hoped that
Powell would find enough to sustain his command
in the weeks that it took him to build the outpost,
because Carrington's stores at this point were not
sufficient to supply the expedition for any length of
time and at the same time sustain the garrison at the
fort. Still, the supplies that were provided to Powell,
along with tools, tents, blankets, ammunition and the
innumerable other items that an Army unit was
doomed to transport regardless of its size were
packed into a half-dozen wagons.

Watching the preparations being carried out,
Hawkes couldn't help but compare the way the bluecoat infantry campaigned to the manner in which the
Plains Indian conducted war. Plains warriors traveled light and lived off the land—which was one reason the Indians did not like to engage in winter
warfare. But their first priority was always to move
swiftly. And it was abundantly clear that Powell
would be unable to do that. In the mountain man's
opinion, the goal of reaching the Tongue River in a
week's time was optimistic. Not that he expected
Powell to get anywhere close to the Tongue, really.

He and Bridger talked about it, and Old Gabe
agreed with him; Carrington had provided Red
Cloud with a golden opportunity by insisting that

Powell undertake this expedition. And that the Oglala chief would take full advantage of that opportunity was as certain as the rising of tomorrow's sun in the east. For that reason, Old Gabe refused Carrington's request that he act as Powell's chief scout. Hawkes was with Bridger when the latter was called to Carrington's office, and in spite of the look of extreme disapproval on the general's face when Old Gabe declined to serve, he jumped in and added that he, too, would refuse to go, if asked. This was preemptive, as he fully expected that Carrington would make that same request of him next.

"This is not what I expected from two courageous men who risked their lives to take my message to Fort Laramie," lamented Carrington.

"That was something that had to be done," replied Bridger. "This expedition is unnecessary, to say the least. And I won't be a party to something so . . . so wrongheaded."

Hawkes thought Old Gabe was exercising remarkable restraint; Bridger had called Carrington's scheme a lot worse than "wrongheaded" in their private conversations.

The general scowled. "I never thought you'd turn against me, Mr. Bridger. I'd heard you were a man who could be relied upon. If you were a soldier I'd have you court-martialed."

"Well, that may be," drawled Bridger with a dangerous smile on his face. "But seein' as how I volunteered for this job, you can't do much."

"I can relieve you of your duties as my chief of scouts," replied Carrington, "and you may consider that done. Of course, you will be permitted to remain here at the fort until such time as it is safe for you to leave. I won't have it said that I threw you out and left you at the mercy of the Sioux."

Bridger chuckled. "You're sending a hundred men to their deaths, General. Why worry about one more?"

"Get out," said Carrington coldly.

The general found other scouts for Powell, and the following day the expedition set out with much fanfare. Hawkes and Bridger joined Grace and her husband on the porch of their quarters to watch the departure. They observed in grim silence, with hardly a word passing between them, as all of them believed that the men in Powell's command were doomed.

"Thank God that you're not going with them," Grace told Gunnison as the end of the column passed through the main gates, which were then swung closed. She took his hand and squeezed it.

Gunnison gave her a look she could not fathom, then pulled his hand free. "There are some things I must attend to," he said thickly, and walked away.

Grace watched him go with a stricken expression on her face. For his part, Bridger felt suddenly very uncomfortable; this was the first time he had witnessed discord between Grace and the captain. Hawkes had informed him of the fact that Gunnison had proffered his resignation to Major Furness and why, and that Furness had promised to use his influence to acquire a safe posting back East, so it didn't take a genius to figure out the source of the tension that existed between the couple. Still, Bridger hated to see it, and since there was nothing he could do to improve matters, he quietly took his leave.

Though he felt as uncomfortable as Bridger, Hawkes didn't leave. Instead, he stood there striving to find words that might make it better for his daughter. The only problem was the fact that any words of encouragement he could think of were ones he could not utter with much sincerity. Finally he settled for telling her not to worry, that all her husband needed was a little time.

"No," she said, disconsolate, "he will always hold this against me. Father, what have I done? I—I just couldn't bear to lose him. Oh, if only I'd been stronger. I knew when I married Brand that the career he had chosen for himself was a dangerous one. At first I thought I could live with that, live with the knowledge that our time together might be fleeting. That any day he might ride away, and never return. What happened? What changed?"

"You saw what happened to Laura Denning," replied Hawkes. "And it scared you."

"Yes, yes it did," she conceded, pulling a shawl tighter around her shoulders.

Hawkes put his arm around her, and she leaned against him, thinking back to all those times in her childhood when she had been afraid, or sad, and how sometimes he had been there to comfort her. Sometimes, but not always. And maybe, she thought, maybe it was asking too much to expect any person to be there always, or forever. Wasn't it more important, after all, to be concerned about the quality more so than quantity in a relationship? Her very own father had often stressed that there were no guarantees in life. Wasn't it about time that she accepted the validity of that? Because surely it was true. Life proved it every day, sometimes in small ways, sometimes in big ways.

When she'd married Brand Gunnison, implicit in her vows had been acceptance of him, and the Army was an integral part of him. Without it he was lost. But instead of accepting that she had tried to change him, and in so doing had done harm to him. She could only pray that the harm was not irreparable. That in time he would forgive her. And she could but hope that the mistake she had made would not permanently alter their relationship. Because that would mean that in trying to guarantee the happiness they had shared, she had actually destroyed it.

That evening, as they ate dinner alone in their cabin, Grace picked at her food without eating a bite, and finally summoned up the courage to say what she felt she needed to say.

"I'm sorry, Brand. So very sorry."

Gunnison kept eating, and continued to studiously avoid looking her in the eye. "For what?" he asked.

Grace sighed. He knew perfectly well for what. "I think you should tell Major Furness that you've reconsidered. That you don't want to resign. And you don't want to be posted back East."

This was something he hadn't expected, and for the first time that evening he looked up at her. "You don't mean that," he said.

"I do mean it. I don't want you to leave the Army."

"That wasn't the impression I got," he said dryly.

"Please try to understand," she said, an edge of desperation in her voice. "I was just afraid to lose you. And I didn't think I could live without you.

But, of course, I could. It would be difficult. I don't know that I would ever be happy again. But I could do it. Other people do it all the time. Laura has done it. My own father. If they can do it, I can."

"Well, that's good," said Gunnison. "I'm glad to know you'd be able to survive without me."

"Brand, please . . ."

"But you won't have to, not any time soon. I should be quite safe within the walls of the War Department."

"I don't want you to go to the War Department. I don't want to live in Washington."

"You can't have everything all your own way, Grace."

"I don't want everything my own way. I just want you to be happy. And I want you to love me always."

Gunnison softened. "I will always love you, Grace," he said gently. "But what's done is done. I can't go ask the major for my resignation letter back."

"Why not?"

"For one thing, because he's on his way to the Tongue River with Powell," replied Gunnison, and he couldn't help it that more than a hint of bitterness lurked in his words.

"And you think you should be there." Grace nodded. "Yes, I suppose you should be. But I've been selfish, and because I have been, you aren't where you should be. And you hate me for it."

"No I don't. I just finished telling you—I love you."

"Oh, you can love someone and hate them at the

same time," she said, with an impatient gesture, and tried to fight back tears of frustration. That he was angry with her was almost unbearable. She just had to keep in mind that he had every right to be.

Gunnison reached across the table and put his hand over hers. "I'd do anything for you, darling. You know that."

"Yes, I know. You've proven that you would. You're willing to give up the Army, and the Army is your whole life."

"Not my whole life," he said, smiling. "It was— until you came along. Now, eat your dinner. You'll come to like Washington, as I will, I'm sure."

"We'd both be miserable and you know it," she shot back. "We're not going. I will get that letter back if I have to hold Major Furness at gunpoint to do it."

Gunnison had to laugh. "And you would, wouldn't you?"

"Yes, I would," she said fiercely.

"I can't have you shooting my superiors," said Gunnison wryly. "So I guess I'll have to do it myself."

"Good, then it's settled. Now I can eat."

And she did.

Chapter Twenty-two

Two days later, a commotion at the main gate drew Grace Gunnison to the door of the cabin. Men were running across the parade ground, carrying their rifles, and there was a great deal of shouting, but she couldn't figure out what was happening—until the gates were thrown open and a trooper rode in on a horse that was so weary that it staggered. The man was haggard, too, or wounded—she was too far away to be able to tell which—because he fell out of the saddle instead of dismounting. A couple of soldiers caught him, and then her view of what happened next was obscured as the entire garrison, or at least it seemed that way to her, gathered around the new arrival. The crowd included General Carrington, as well as her husband and her father. Grace wasn't the least bit interested in getting any closer. Instead, she stepped back inside the cabin and slowly shut the door, her heart racing, a knot forming in the pit of her stomach. She had to assume that the horseman had come from the detachment sent to the Tongue River—and that his return meant that something bad had happened. And if she were right, then in all likelihood either her father or her husband—or both—were about to go into harm's way. She closed her eyes, wishing this was all a dream. Wishing that she would suddenly wake up and discover that no rider had just arrived at the fort.

A few minutes later Gunnison entered. His grim expression validated her worst fears. He didn't need to tell her what was going on. For his part, though, he felt compelled to do so, and Grace sat there listening as calmly as possible.

"Red Cloud has attacked Powell's command," he told her, "about sixty miles northwest of here. Major Furness dispatched three messengers. It may be that the other two will never arrive. This one claims there are at least one thousand warriors in the fight. Captain Powell and Major Furness have secured a defensive position on a wooded hill. But it's not clear how long they can hold out."

"They may all be dead already," she said.

Gunnison nodded. "That's true. But we have to find out."

"When are you leaving?" she asked.

"Immediately. My company will be joined by as many infantry as can be mounted."

"How many men ride with you?"

He grimaced. "About seventy. Carrington will be marching in a matter of hours. But it will take him at least a day and a half to reach Powell. That's why we have to ride now."

As he was speaking, Hawkes entered the cabin. Catching the last portion of Gunnison's reply, the mountain man frowned. "And does your general intend to leave this fort with just a skeleton crew? That might be just what the Sioux are waiting for. You could come back here and find everyone killed and this place reduced to smoking rubble."

"I'm well aware of the risks," he said crisply. "But what would you have me do? Tell the general no, I will not ride to the relief of Captain Powell? That's why you need to stay here with Grace."

"I can't hold off the entire Sioux nation, Captain."

"If you think she would be safer outside the fort, then take her away from here."

"That's just it," snapped Hawkes. "She's not safe inside the fort or out of it. She's not safe anywhere in the Powder River country. You should never have brought her with you."

"I wanted to come," said Grace, coming to her husband's defense. But neither man seemed to be aware that she was even in the room.

"I realize that now," Gunnison told Hawkes. "I made a mistake. And I'm sure you think she made one, too, by marrying me."

"I didn't think so at first—not until I heard she was with you on this damned expedition."

"Stop it!" shouted Grace angrily. This time they looked at her, startled by the vehemence in her voice. "Stop it this instant, both of you!" She turned to her father. "You mustn't blame Brand for my being here. That was my decision."

"He could have said no," insisted Hawkes.

"He did. But my place is at my husband's side. I will not be like my mother, waiting for weeks, months, and on two occasions for more than a year, while you were away, and never knowing when she awoke every morning whether you were alive or dead. I suppose she was stronger than I, but that is something I simply could not bear. I'm sorry, Father. You only wanted to protect her. But it was living hell for her, and I was not going to be subjected to that."

Hawkes nodded. His daughter's words opened old wounds, those old feelings of guilt that he figured he would never be able to overcome. Grace was right, of course. Elzia had suffered a great deal for love. So many times he had left her behind, promising her that he would return, even while he knew, as did she, that this was a guarantee he had no power to make.

"I think you're wrong this time, Father," continued Grace. "I don't believe Red Cloud will attack this fort and slaughter everyone within these walls—even if he could. The entire nation would rise up in outrage against the Sioux. The people would insist that the entire United States Army march against them and crush them. That's something Red Cloud wants to avoid."

Hawkes realized that, logically, she was right. It was an argument he had himself made. But logic had nothing to do with the fear for his daughter's safety that churned in his gut.

"So," she said, "I don't want you to stay here and nursemaid me. I want you to go with Brand."

"No," said Gunnison. He looked at Hawkes, a plea in his eyes. How could he voice his own fears in his wife's presence—the fear that if both he and Hawkes went there was a good chance Grace would lose them both? It would be the same as admitting that, in his opinion, this rescue attempt was tantamount to suicide. And that *was* his opinion. The irony of it all did not escape him. He had finally proffered a resignation, with the result that he was on the verge of putting the dangers of field service on the frontier

behind him—something she had desired ever since
their wedding. And now this. What chance did he
have against a thousand Sioux warriors? What
chance did Powell and Furness have? Slim to none.
Still, he had to go. He had his orders, and he was
bound to obey them. Besides that, it would be impossible to live with the knowledge that he had not done
everything in his power to safe the lives of Furness
and Powell and their men. His fellow soldiers. They
would do no less for him. None of this could he air
in her presence; he could only hope that Hawkes was
smart enough to figure it out for himself.

Hawkes suddenly found himself between a rock
and a hard place. His daughter wanted him to join
the relief column so that he could, perhaps, keep her
husband alive. He'd done the same thing before—
back when Gunnison and the Second Cavalry had
been embroiled in the war Governor Evans and the
Colorado Volunteers had tried to make on the Southern Cheyenne. On the other hand, he understood perfectly well why Gunnison was adamantly opposed
to his going along. If both he and the captain fell,
what would happen to Grace? She would have no
family, no place to go. How could he do that to her?

Still, he hesitated, reluctant to deny her request—
something he had seldom done. He was given a momentary reprieve by the arrival of Jim Bridger, who,
as Hawkes had done moments before, entered the
cabin unbidden. This was hardly the time to stand
on protocol.

"I hear you're setting out real quick-like, Captain,"
said Bridger. "I reckon I'll ride with you, if that's
okay."

"I thought you were washing your hands of all this," said Gunnison. "In fact, I heard you were planning to head for points south in the next day or two."

"I was. But you're gonna need all the help you can get. And since my friend here"—he gestured at Hawkes—"can't go along, that means I need to." He grinned at Grace. "Now don't you fret, honey. I'll make sure he comes back to you safe and sound."

"Thank you, Gabe," she said gratefully. She knew she could depend on Bridger—and could only hope that now her father would not feel obliged to honor her recent request.

For his part, Hawkes could only stare at Old Gabe in amazement. Somehow Bridger had anticipated the quandary he'd found himself in. And, true friend that he was, here he came with a solution.

"Come on, hoss," Bridger told him. "These two should have a few minutes alone together."

They stepped outside. The parade ground was buzzing with activity. Bridger brandished a twist of tobacco and offered it to Hawkes, who declined, before biting off a chew for himself.

"You know," he drawled, "it's mighty embarrassing."

"What is?"

"Being right all the time." He pointed with his chin at the soldiers rushing to and fro, making hasty preparations to embark on their rescue mission. "We both tried to warn Carrington, but he wouldn't listen. Generals always think they know better."

Hawkes laughed. "Isn't that why they're generals?"

Bridger looked askance at him. "Now you know better than that."

Hawkes couldn't hold onto his smile for long. "You be careful, Old Gabe. You and the captain are going to need a small miracle to get out of this mess alive."

"I've seen a miracle or two in my time. I believe in 'em. Don't you?"

"I will," said Hawkes, "if you and Gunnison make it back."

Hawkes was amazed—and immensely proud—of the way Grace handled her husband's departure less than two hours later. She remained stalwart throughout, almost serenely calm while some of the other women in the fort, whose men were also riding off into great danger, wept openly. That was the way Eliza had always been. She had seldom given voice to her darkest fears, and never had she burdened him at the moment of his departure with an emotional scene. No, she had waited until later for that, he supposed—when she was alone, so that their children weren't burdened, either. Hawkes could tell Brand Gunnison was grateful for the way Grace comported herself. He had taken her in his arms on the porch of their cabin, kissed her, touched her silken yellow hair—and hesitated, searching for words. She smiled—a smile that let him know that she knew how he felt, that there was no need for words. Turning away from her, he climbed into the saddle and rode to the head of the mounted column and led his band of brave men through the main gates, Jim Bridger at his side. Hawkes felt a twinge of guilt for not riding with them. Bridger had been as stout a friend to him over the years as any man could hope to have. And he suddenly discovered that he cared about what happened to the captain, too, much more than he had ever realized—and certainly more than the angry words they had hurled at one another earlier in the day would indicate.

When the column was gone and the gates had been closed, Grace turned to enter the cabin, and when Hawkes made to follow her she asked him for some time alone. He nodded and settled down with his back to the wall beside the door, packing a pipe and indulging in a smoke, trying to come to terms with the fact that there was nothing left to do now but wait. Wait to see if Gunnison and Old Gabe survived. And wait to see if the Sioux attacked Fort Phil Kearney once Carrington and his infantry departed later that day, leaving but a handful of soldiers to man the walls.

Carrington marched—and the sentries kept an eye peeled for any sign of hostile activity beyond the walls. Not a single Indian was seen. Still, it promised to be a long night. The general had left Captain Kinney in charge, and Kinney split his command, less than fifty men, into two groups, each of which would spend four hours on guard duty. Combined with the sick and wounded soldiers and the band of civilians in the fort, Hawkes figured Kinney could muster not more than eighty combatants if the need arose. The fort was a strong defensive position—he had to give Carrington credit for picking a good spot for the outpost—but any sane man would question the ability of eighty men to hold any position against an enemy that could number in the thousands. Hawkes had heard about a place down in Texas, an old mission called the Alamo, where a little over one hundred Texican rebels had held a Mexican army of four or five thousand at bay for almost a fortnight. The legend of the Alamo siege notwithstanding, the mountain man figured that fight wouldn't have lasted thirteen hours, much less thirteen days, if the Mexican commander had launched a serious attack on the rebel fortifications right away. Plains Indians were not much for launching attacks on walled enemy positions, but that didn't mean they wouldn't do it.

Hawkes could do no less than help the soldiers patrol the walls. He could go all night without sleep and remain alert. Meanwhile, the other Army wives joined Grace, at her invitation, talking and taking tea at her cabin, on the theory, he supposed, that misery loved company.

The night passed uneventfully—until just an hour or so before dawn. A shot rang out from the vicinity of the south wall, and then two more. Hawkes had stationed himself on the north wall, and when he heard the gunfire he raced to the other side of the fort. Others were running to the sound of the guns, but the mountain man was one of the first to reach the sentry who had discharged his carbine.

"What did you see?" asked Hawkes.

"There was somebody out there," said the soldier excitedly. "I swear I saw someone."

"Calm down. I believe you." Hawkes peered into the darkness. "Did you hit your mark?"

"I—I don't think so," admitted the soldier, sheepishly. "But whoever it was, they threw something over the wall."

"Where?"

"Right over here," said the soldier, and led Hawkes along the banquette to the spot. Hawkes scanned the ground below, thought he saw something out of the ordinary, and climbed down the nearest ladder. A soldier was coming his way with a lighted lantern, and Hawkes joined him. When they reached the item Hawkes had seen from the wall, the mountain man recognized it as soon as the lantern light fell across it. He dropped to one knee and picked it up just as Captain Kinney and several other soldiers arrived.

"What is that?" asked Kinney.

"It's Absaroke wampum. Sort of a letter of introduction, you might say."

"Crow Indians?" Kinney looked puzzled. "I didn't know they were involved in this war."

"They're not," Hawkes assured him. "This used to belong to me. An Absaroke chief gave it to me, a long time ago, so that I'd have safe passage through Crow lands."

"Used to? What's going on here? What does this mean?"

Cradling the wampum belt in his hands, Hawkes got to his feet. "It means an old friend of mine is here," he said softly.

Question was, what was Pretty Shield doing here?

"Well, if it's an old friend, why didn't he just come to the gate?"

"It's a she, not a he," said Hawkes. "And she didn't because she's an Indian, and she's smart, and she knew better than to trust your men not to shoot first and ask questions later."

Kinney didn't take offense. He realized that his

men were on edge, and that Hawkes was probably correct in his assessment of what would have happened had an Indian, even a woman, ventured too close to the main gate.

"I guess this means you're going out to get her," said the officer. "But I'd advise you to wait until it's light."

Hawkes checked the sky. Kinney was right. Finding Pretty Shield—and avoiding any hostiles that might be lurking in the fort's vicinity—would be easier in the daylight. He didn't have long to wait.

Chapter Twenty-three

Returning to the place where he'd left the woman—in a wooded, rock-strewn draw about a quarter mile from the fort—the Spaniard wasn't the least bit worried that she might not be there. He had bound her securely, hand and foot, and then tied one end of a rope tightly around her neck and the other end around the stout trunk of a tree. The first shreds of daylight were pushing back the night shadows when he arrived. His prisoner lay quite still on her side, her back to him, but the Spaniard wasn't fooled. He knew she wasn't sleeping, and that she was aware of his presence. Grinning, the Comanchero walked up to her and kicked her, hard, in the lower back. Gasping at the pain, she rolled away, then managed to sit up and glower at him through a veil of raven-black hair. Sitting on his heels in front of her, he laughed softly.

"You can sleep later," he said, in English. "I don't want you to miss what's about to happen. I just sent a message to your friend. He should be along soon. I left a pretty clear trail."

"He'll know by the trail you left that it wasn't me."

"Don't you think I know that? But he'll be curious enough to come anyway."

"He will kill you."

The Spaniard chuckled. "You better hope he does."

In spite of her best efforts, Pretty Shield could not entirely conceal the fear she experienced. She had never in her life been so afraid of anyone or anything as she was of this Comanchero. The way he had butchered Red Renshaw was still vivid in her mind; she doubted the awful memory would ever fade. And she couldn't bear the thought of him doing the same thing to Gordon Hawkes. Hawkes was a fighter. He had survived many attempts on his life. He had prevailed over many men who had meant to do him harm. But there was something about the Spaniard that gave Pretty Shield cause to wonder if perhaps he wasn't more than a match for Hawkes.

"You kill me, too," she said flatly. It wasn't a question. She knew what her fate would be.

"Of course," he said. "But not right away. You and me, we've had some fun the last few nights. I'm not ready to stop, not just yet."

Pretty Shield could not bear to look at the lecherous grin on the Spaniard's face. The memory of what he had done to her ever since she had fallen into his hands made her sick to her stomach. Three times now he had had his way with her, and done so roughly. Her body was covered with bruises and scratches. Her left eye was nearly swollen shut. Her lip had been cut and was swollen as well. But the physical pain was nothing compared to the emotional pain she suffered. The physical injuries might fade. The others never would.

For the thousandth time she cursed herself for a fool. She had been so careless! For two days following her surreptitious departure from the Absaroke village, she had searched for the Spaniard's trail. He was, after all, bound for the Powder River country in his search for Hawkes, and she had decided that the quickest way to locate the man she loved and warn him about the Spaniard was to follow that trail. She was no stranger to the Powder River country, but she figured the Comanchero knew exactly where Fort Phil Kearney was located. And it had seemed safe enough to follow him; that way she would know where he was—a day ahead of her. She knew there was a risk—that the Spaniard might be worried enough about his back trail to circle around and check to see if anyone was following. But it was just as likely, she thought, that he wouldn't bother, since he had eluded the Crow warriors that He Smiles Twice had dispatched to track him down. After a week she had grown careless—and he *had* circled around. The Spaniard claimed he had a sixth sense about such things, said that he felt her presence. And so, only a couple of days away from her destination, Pretty Shield had fallen prey to the Comanchero. He had slipped into her camp while she slept one night. He had raped her. And she had felt sure he would kill her when he was done using her. But he hadn't. Now she knew why. The Spaniard was using her in another way: as bait to lure Gordon Hawkes out of the fort.

Somehow she had to stop him. Even if it cost her her life.

"I will stay with you for as long as you want," she said. "Go anywhere with you. Do anything. Just let him live."

The Spaniard threw back his head and laughed.

"You aren't offering me anything I don't already have. So it's no bargain. Besides, I didn't come all this way just to turn around and go home and leave that bastard alive." He glanced over his shoulder to peer briefly at the morning sun, which was making its appearance low in the eastern sky. "Your friend will be along soon." He rose, began to turn away, and seemed to have a belated thought. "By the way, you can scream and shout all you want. It won't do any good. It won't save him."

He left her then, climbing up through the rocks and timber of the draw, and in a moment was out of sight. Pretty Shield knew he wouldn't go far. She also realized that he was right. Even if she had the opportunity to warn Hawkes that he was walking into a trap, he would not leave her.

As soon as it was light Hawkes left the fort to search for Pretty Shield. It didn't take him long to find the tracks the Spaniard had left. He knew immediately that they did not belong to Pretty Shield. Nor did they belong to a Sioux warrior. The moccasins that Sioux braves wore made distinctive prints because of the way they were made. No, these tracks had been made by a white man. And after a long and careful perusal of the ground outside the south wall of the fort, Hawkes became convinced that the man who had made those tracks was the same one who had hurled the wampum over the wall.

But who was this man—and how had he come into possession of the belt Hawkes had given Pretty Shield several years ago, when she had parted company with him following his campaign of vengeance against the gold seekers at Gilder Gulch? The mountain man was confident that the belt was not something Pretty Shield would part with willingly.

Alarmed by the possibility that some harm had come to Pretty Shield, Hawkes did not hesitate to follow the trail. It took him south, along the western rim of Clear Creek. This was broken country, and the tracks he followed sometimes took him along the base of steep cutbanks, and Hawkes proceeded cautiously, well aware that he might be walking into a trap. The belt he now carried with him had been thrown over the wall of the fort to lure him out into the open. That was obvious.

About a quarter of a mile from the fort, the trail led Hawkes to the base of a rocky, brush-strewn draw. It was a perfect place for an ambush, with countless hiding places for a would-be bushwhacker. But there was nothing Hawkes could do but proceed. He wasn't about to turn back until he found out what had happened to Pretty Shield.

And then he saw her.

She was kneeling, a rope around her neck with the other end tied to a tree, a scant thirty yards away. He couldn't see the bindings because she was facing in his direction, but he assumed she was bound hand and foot, as well. She spotted him an instant later, and shouted a warning.

"Gordon! It's a trap!"

Hawkes crouched behind a pile of rocks and deadwood, scanning the draw above her. He heard the shot, saw the drift of powder and was raising his rifle when he heard another, more chilling sound— Pretty Shield crying out in pain. She had been hit,

and he couldn't tell how badly. She was on the
ground, still moving. Cursing, Hawkes put rifle to
shoulder and fired. He didn't have a target, just a
general idea where the ambusher was, based solely
on the powdersmoke, and he knew that was hardly
reliable—if the man was smart he would have already moved. Hawkes quickly reloaded. Another
gunshot, and he saw the bullet kick up a geyser of
snow just inches from Pretty Shield's head. The ambusher had missed his mark—intentionally? Pretty
Shield was trying to roll toward the tree to which she
was tied. Another gunshot, another geyser of snow.
Hawkes used the powdersmoke in the brush higher
up in the draw as a mark, and fired again. He had
little hope of hitting the man—it would be blind luck
if he did. But the mountain man had already made
up his mind to move, and hoped only to buy a few
precious seconds. As soon as he'd fired, he left cover
and ran across open ground straight for Pretty
Shield. She saw him, and yelled at him to go back,
but he paid no heed. The ambusher was trying to
draw him out by wounding her and then putting
two more bullet within inches of her—he hadn't
missed twice because he was a poor marksman.
Hawkes got the message—if he didn't come out into
the open, Pretty Shield would die.

Well-hidden in the rocks and brush fifty yards
away, the Spaniard drew a bead on the mountain
man, grinned—and squeezed the trigger.

The bullet hit Hawkes high in the left leg and he
fell.

"Nooo!" wailed Pretty Shield.

The mountain man got to his feet and kept coming,

dragging his left leg, trying to ignore the searing pain. Fifteen yards to go. Ten yards. Five. Close enough to see the tears in Pretty Shield's eyes. Another gunshot, and the bullet spun Hawkes around, knocking him down into the blood-splattered snow. He lay still for a moment, and Pretty Shield stifled a sob.

Satisfied that Hawkes was down for good, the Spaniard set aside his long gun and left his place of concealment, heading down the draw toward his prey, and hoping that the mountain man wasn't dead. Not yet. He drew his knife.

Pretty Shield watched in amazement as Hawkes rolled over on his back. She saw the flicker of sunlight on steel as the mountain man hurled his pistol. It landed in the snow just a few feet away from her. She heard the Spaniard coming through the brush, and rolled her body over the weapon, concealing it from his view just as he emerged.

The Spaniard paused a few feet away from her, smiling as he saw the blood on the sleeve of her buckskin dress.

"That won't hurt nearly as much as what comes next," he said.

She gazed at him impassively, groping through the snow with her hands tied behind her back for the pistol that Hawkes had thrown to her.

The Spaniard was disappointed by her failure to react. Shrugging, he moved on to where Hawkes lay on his back. Sitting on his heels, he examined the mountain man, pleased to see that his aim had been true. The second bullet had struck Hawks high in the chest and to one side. Coupled with the first wound,

it had rendered the mountain man completely helpless. Just to be on the safe side, the Spaniard plucked
a knife from Hawkes's belt and tossed it away.

"I think it will take about an hour for you to bleed
to death," said the Spaniard. "But don't worry, you'll
die sooner than that. And more painfully. I'm going
to cut your heart out. If I do it right, you'll live just
long enough to see it still beating in my hands."

Hawkes mumbled something, his voice weak, his
lips barely moving.

"What?" The Spaniard leaned closer.

"You . . . better . . . hurry . . ."

Puzzled, the Spaniard looked at him.

He didn't even hear the gunshot. The bullet entered the back of the Comanchero's skull and killed
him instantly. Its impact hurled his body across
Hawkes. The mountain man saw Pretty Shield then,
standing there with his pistol in both hands, the rawhide strips still bound around her wrists. She
dropped the pistol and ran to him, and he tried very
hard to hang on until she got to him, but just
couldn't manage it. The world seemed to tilt madly,
then blur, and then turned completely black.

He could see her vaguely, as though through a
cottony mist, and all he could really make out was
the yellow hair, and all he wanted to do was run his
fingers through it. How he had missed doing that!
"Eliza," he whispered, and then she started to fade
away, and in desperation he called out to her, beg-
ging her to come back, not to leave him again, but
then the darkness overcame him

He felt her touch on his cheek and opened his eyes,

and as before he saw her, saw that yellow hair, though not clearly. This time she spoke to him, but he could not make out her words for the roaring in his ears. He couldn't figure out where that noise was coming from, or why he could not clear his vision. He wanted to reach out to her, but he couldn't seem to move. That was infuriating, and he struggled against the immobility. But was he really struggling physically? Or was it all in his mind? Exhausted, he let the darkness wash over him again.

When he opened his eyes again Hawkes was startled by the clarity of his vision. The first thing he saw was the yellow hair—it was what he was looking for—but now he could see that it was his daughter's hair, not Eliza's. Grace sat in a chair beside the bed, and she was gazing pensively out of a window, but when he turned his head she jumped to her feet and clutched his hand with both of hers.

"Good morning, Father," she whispered, smiling, but then the smile crumbled, and the tears flowed as she bent down to kiss him. He tried to squeeze her hand, and his weakened condition startled him

"The post surgeon said he doubted you would live," she said, her voice trembling. "But I told him you would. That you were stronger than he thought."

"So I'm alive," he said.

She laughed, almost delirious with joy and relief. "Yes, very much alive. You've been unconscious, but for a time or two, for the past week."

Hawkes nodded. The news triggered mixed emotions. "I . . . I thought I saw your mother. But it was you, I guess."

It was her turn to squeeze his hand. "Maybe not. I think she's right here with us, you know. I think she always is."

"What news of Brand?"

"He's alive. And Gabe, too. I was *so* afraid that I would lose one of you, if not both."

"I know," said Hawkes.

Everything was coming back to him now—he remembered every aspect of the ambush the Spaniard had set for him. Particularly vivid was the intense pain as the bullets had slammed into his body, and of the terror that had filled him as he thought of what would happen to Pretty Shield if he died, and the Spaniard won.

"Pretty Shield," he murmured.

"She's well," said Grace. "Her wound was a minor one. She's been helping me tend to you. She'll want to see you now. I'll go get her."

Again Hawkes nodded. Grace started for the door, then stopped and turned back to smile at him.

"She's so in love with you."

"I know." That old familiar guilt came creeping up on him.

"And I know you care for her." Grace came back to the bedside, her expression a very earnest one. "Father, it's okay. I'm certain of one thing. My mother would not want you to be alone. Don't send Pretty Shield away. You need her, and she needs you—and I need to know that you won't be alone."

She left the room.

A moment later Pretty Shield came in. She stood just inside the door, afraid to come closer until he held out his hand. It was all he had the strength to

do. She came to stand at the bedside, where Grace
had stood, and her hand trembled slightly as she
placed it in his.

"I'm so sorry," she said.

"For what?"

"I almost got you killed. I came to warn you.
You see, I was living with the Absaroke when you
brought your friend there. I was the one who cared
for him. And I was there when the man who called
himself the Spaniard came and killed Renshaw. He
said he was going after you next, and I followed
him here. I thought when we got closer I would
ride through the night and get here before he did,
and warn you. But he captured me. I was so
afraid—for you. He was a terrible man. He did . . ."
She shook her head, remembering what the Spaniard had done to her, but realizing that these were
facts that Hawkes did not need to be acquainted
with.

"You were at the village? Why didn't you let me
know?"

"Even though He Smiles Twice told me that Eliza
had died, I could not allow myself to come between
the two of you. Not again. I knew she would still be
in your heart. And that there was no room for me."

"What do you aim to do?"

"Now that I know you will live, I'll go home."

"Back to the Absaroke?"

She nodded, and gently, reluctantly, pulled her
hand away.

"Pretty," he said, as she began to turn away.

"Yes?"

"Will you wait? Wait until we can go together?"

She stared at him.

"Stay with me," he said.

Eyes shining, Pretty Shield bent down to brush her soft lips against his cheek.

She was still with him, standing by the bed, holding his hand as though she would never let go, when Brand Gunnison and Jim Bridger—having been informed that Hawkes was conscious—entered the room.

"Pretty Shield there told us what happened," said Old Gabe. "That Spaniard was one mean hombre."

"The worst," said Hawkes. "But tell me, how did you two manage to keep your hair?"

Gunnison laughed. "I have Mr. Bridger to thank for that. He talked me into splitting my command up into four groups. I thought it was crazy. But when the Sioux saw soldiers on four hills with flags flying and bugles blowing they thought my seventy men were a much larger force and they broke off the attack on Powell's position. I guess by the time they'd figured out their mistake, General Carrington had arrived with the Twenty-eighth, and they'd lost their advantage."

"Red Cloud ain't stupid," said Bridger. "He wasn't going to send a thousand warriors against five hundred troops armed with carbines."

"The Sioux are still around," added Gunnison. "But I don't think they'll attack the fort. And even better news is that the general seems to have come to his senses. There's been no more talk of an expedition to the Tongue River."

"So," drawled Old Gabe, "all we got to do now is

wait for green-up. Then I reckon they'll send
reinforcements."

"Are you sticking around?" Hawkes asked him.

"Reckon so. Are you?"

They both laughed. "That's a stupid question,"
said Hawkes. "Look at me."

Bridger glanced at Pretty Shield. "And what about
you? Are you sticking around, too?"

She smiled shyly and nodded.

"Well, good," said Old Gabe happily. "We still got
some winter left to go yet. You just make sure my
friend stays warm."

"Shut up, Gabe," said Hawkes.

Bridger just laughed at the mountain man's
embarrassment.

His recovery was slow, but steady. Within a fortnight he was getting out of bed and was able to move
around the cabin, but he tired very quickly. Within
another two weeks, though, as he regained his
strength, he was venturing outside. Either Grace or
Pretty Shield were always right there by his side—
and sometimes both accompanied him. Hawkes was
relieved to see that a rapport had developed between
his daughter and the Sioux woman. Understandably,
Grace had harbored some resentment toward Pretty
Shield during those years when the latter had stayed
with them. But she had put that behind her now, and
on more than one occasion expressed to Pretty Shield
just how happy she was to know that her father would
not spend the rest of his years alone. For her part,
Pretty Shield assured Grace that she would never
again leave the side of the man she loved.

Red Cloud's Sioux, with their Northern Cheyenne allies, remained a menacing presence around Fort Phil Kearney as the winter progressed. But, as Gunnison had reported, Carrington had learned his lesson. He kept his men within the shelter of the fort's walls. Still, he discussed at great length his plans for a spring campaign to establish outposts along the Bozeman Trail, once reinforcements arrived.

Instead of reinforcements, though, the end of winter brought news from Forth Laramie. U.S. commissioners had met with Sioux leaders, including Red Cloud, at Laramie, and, much to everyone's amazement—Red Cloud's most of all—they agreed to Sioux demands that Fort Phil Kearney be evacuated, and guaranteed to the Sioux that no white men would encroach on their lands. That included the Black Hills, an area that was sacred to the Sioux nation. This, in spite of the fact that rumors of gold in the Black Hills were beginning to excite the interest of fortune seekers across the land.

"I can't believe the United States government is gonna back down from the Sioux," said Bridger, as he and Gunnison and Hawkes stood on the porch of the cabin, enjoying the warmth of a sunny spring day.

"There are uprisings among the southern tribes, from what I've been told," said Gunnison. "The Comanches and the Kiowas are making a lot of trouble." He glanced at Hawkes. "Even the Southern Cheyenne are kicking up some dust these days. General Sherman has been ordered to focus the Army's attention on those difficulties."

"I know one thing," said Hawkes. "Red Cloud is

too smart to believe that he's won the war. That the guarantees of those commissioners are worth the paper they're written on."

Bridger nodded. "Yep. Not gonna keep the settlers out of this country for long, that's for sure. But you listen up now, Captain. Next time you all have a war up here, you can count me out. I'm too old to be doing this kind of thing."

"Me, too," said Hawkes.

Gunnison smiled, a little pensively. "Well, gentlemen, I won't be engaged in that war, either. When it comes." He held up an envelope. "I've been reassigned to the War Department."

Hawkes and Bridger exchanged astonished glances. "You're going to live back East?" asked Old Gabe.

"Looks that way."

"How does your wife feel about that?" asked Bridger.

"She's relieved that I will no longer serve in the field. But she's always a little scared. She's not sure how she'll like Washington. As she's never been east of the Mississippi, I can understand her trepidation."

"She'll do fine," said Hawkes, confidently.

"You'll have to come visit us sometime, sir," said Gunnison.

With a faint smile, Hawkes shook his head. "I'm not sure I'd be able to do that, Captain."

"Oh, you mean those murder charges?" Gunnison produced another envelope from his tunic. "Those should no longer concern you. This came in the dispatch case, along with my new orders." He handed the envelope to Hawkes.

Bridger waited as long as he could while his friend perused the envelope's contents. "Well?" he asked, impatiently. "What is it?"

"A full amnesty," murmured Hawkes. "Signed by the President of the United States himself."

"I'll be damned," breathed Bridger. "Looks like General Merritt came through after all."

"Yes," said Hawkes quietly. "Yes, it looks that way."

A few weeks later, General Carrington's command marched through the main gates of Fort Phil Kearney and headed south for Laramie. That same day, bidding his daughter and her husband and his old friend Bridger so long, Gordon Hawkes rode west, aiming for the mountains that had been his home for so many years. His home and—in spite of the amnesty that he carried with him—his refuge, still. Pretty Shield rode at his side, where she belonged, and where she would stay. Their destination was the Absaroke village. Hawkes had decided that living among the Crow was the only logical course of action. They were, after all, his people.

A few miles from the fort, Hawkes checked his horse and looked behind him. As he'd expected, there was a plume of black smoke rising into the warm blue sky. Red Cloud's Sioux had wasted no time in putting Fort Phil Kearney to the torch. Though the Sioux had been his mortal enemies for many years now, Hawkes was content that they had won this battle. Their triumph would be short-lived. But the next time that the warriors painted themselves and their ponies for war, and when the bluecoat columns marched across the Plains with guidons fluttering in the wind, he would not be there to see it.

He glanced at Pretty Shield, and she smiled at him—a smile filled with warmth and love and contentment. And promise.

Turning his horse toward the distant high country, Hawkes realized that there were a *few* guarantees in life after all.